Kid Sherlock

CASE FILE 1:
"The Smell"

THE CREATIVE TEAM

Written
and lettered by
JUSTIN PHILLIPS

Art by
SEAN GREGORY MILLER

Colors by
LESLEY ATLANSKY

Kid
Sherlock

CREATED BY JUSTIN PHILLIPS AND SEAN GREGORY MILLER
BASED ON CHARACTERS BY SIR ARTHUR CONAN DOYAL

THE SMELL

WRITTER/LETTERER –JUSTIN PHILLIPS
PENCILER/INKER – SEAN GREGORY MILLER
COLORIST – LESLEY ATLANSKY

"CLASS, IF I COULD HAVE YOUR ATTENTION, PLEASE. I'D LIKE TO INTRODUCE OUR NEWEST STUDENT."

BAKER ELEMENTARY

JOHN WATSON, WELCOME TO BAKER ELEMENTARY.

WATSON

GULP

Bryan Seaton: Publisher • **Dave Dwonch:** President of Marketing & Development • **Shawn Gabborin:** Editor In Chief • **Jason Martin:** Publisher-Danger Zone
Nicole DAndria: Marketing Director/Editor • **Jim Dietz:** Social Media Manager • **Scott Bradley:** CFO • **Chad Cicconi** - Space Brawler

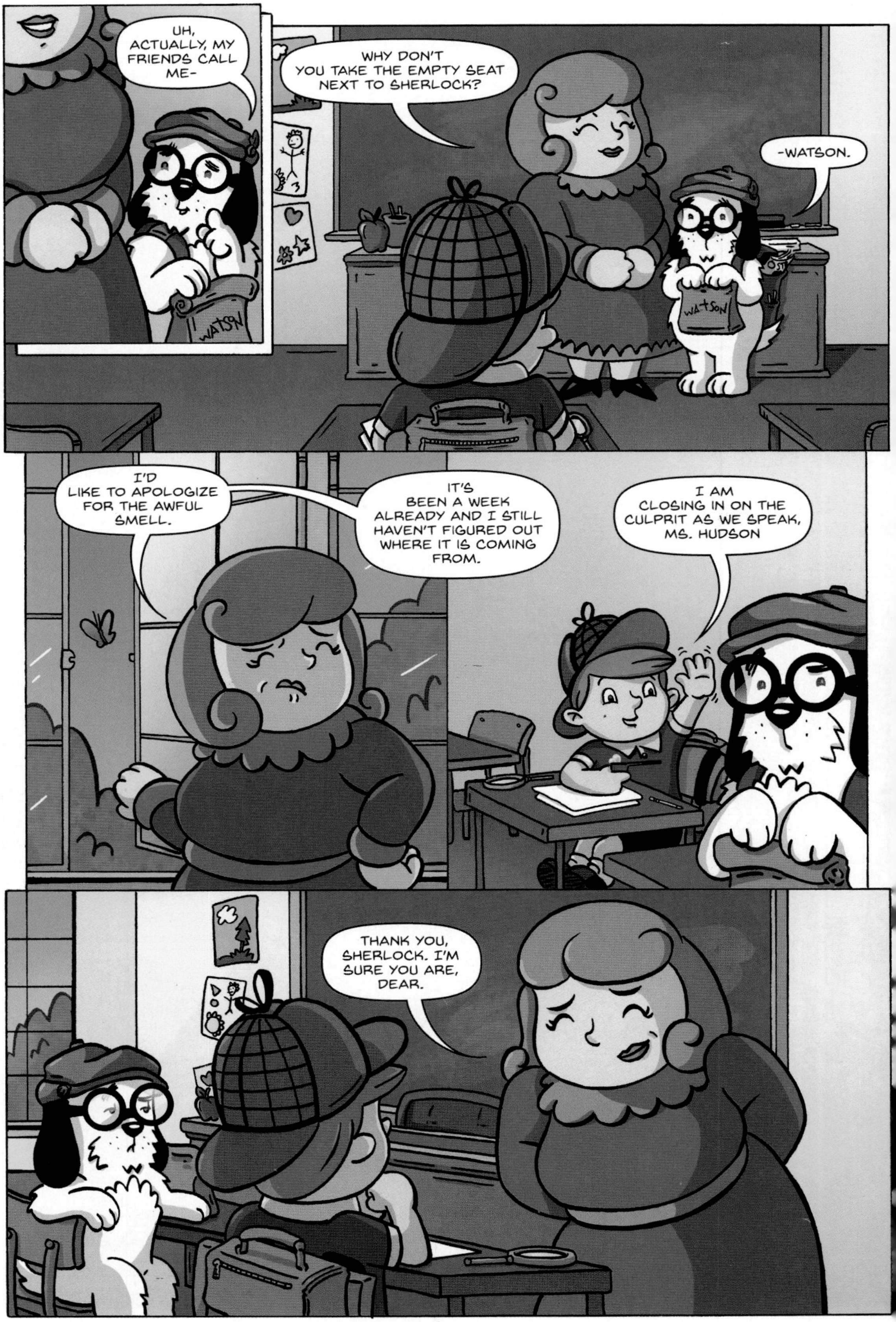
UH, ACTUALLY, MY FRIENDS CALL ME-
WATSON
WHY DON'T YOU TAKE THE EMPTY SEAT NEXT TO SHERLOCK?
-WATSON.
WATSON
I'D LIKE TO APOLOGIZE FOR THE AWFUL SMELL.
IT'S BEEN A WEEK ALREADY AND I STILL HAVEN'T FIGURED OUT WHERE IT IS COMING FROM.
I AM CLOSING IN ON THE CULPRIT AS WE SPEAK, MS. HUDSON
THANK YOU, SHERLOCK. I'M SURE YOU ARE, DEAR.

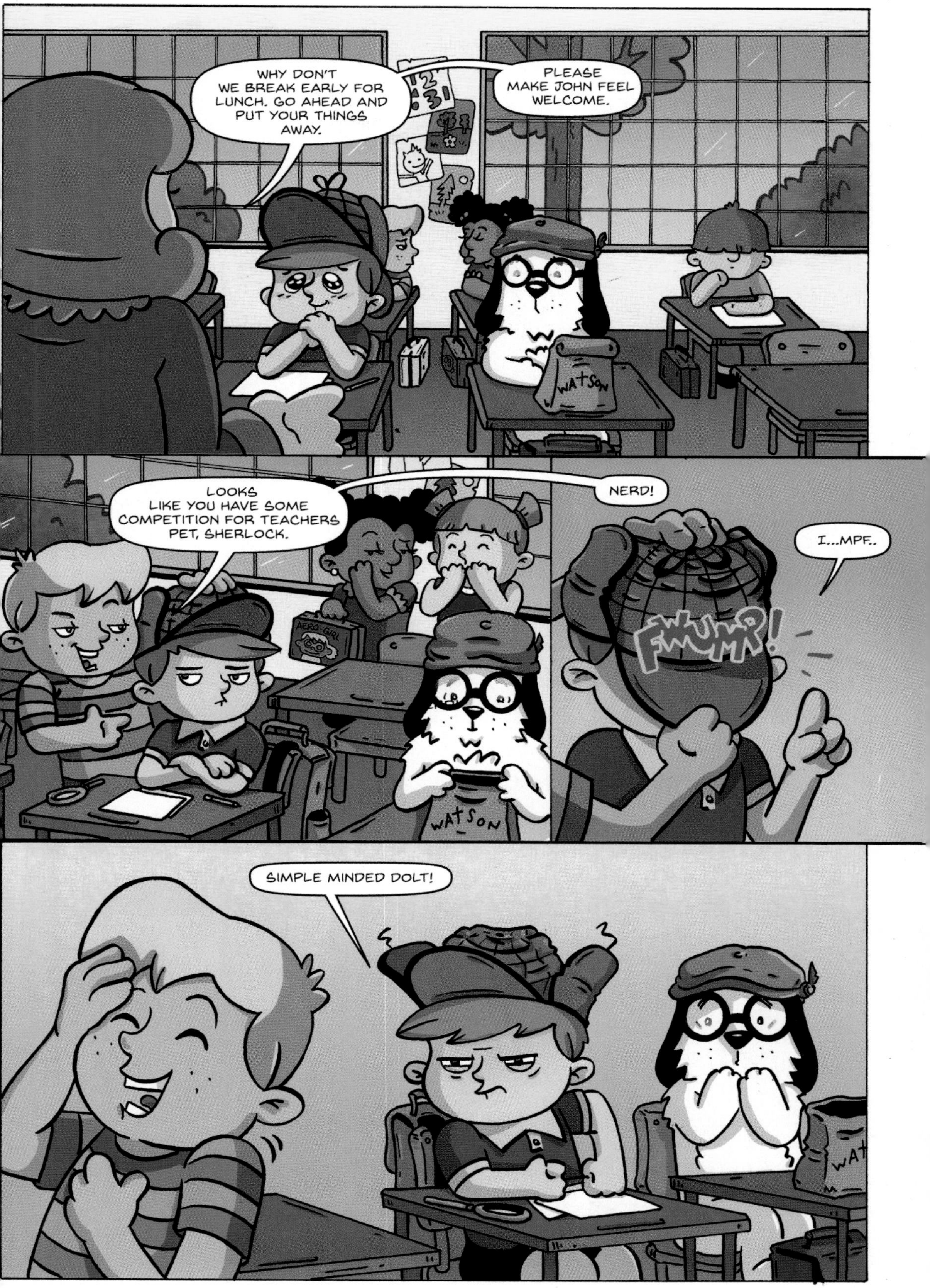
WHY DON'T WE BREAK EARLY FOR LUNCH. GO AHEAD AND PUT YOUR THINGS AWAY.
PLEASE MAKE JOHN FEEL WELCOME.
WATSON
LOOKS LIKE YOU HAVE SOME COMPETITION FOR TEACHERS PET, SHERLOCK.
NERD!
AERO GIRL
WATSON
I...MPF..
FWUMP!
SIMPLE MINDED DOLT!

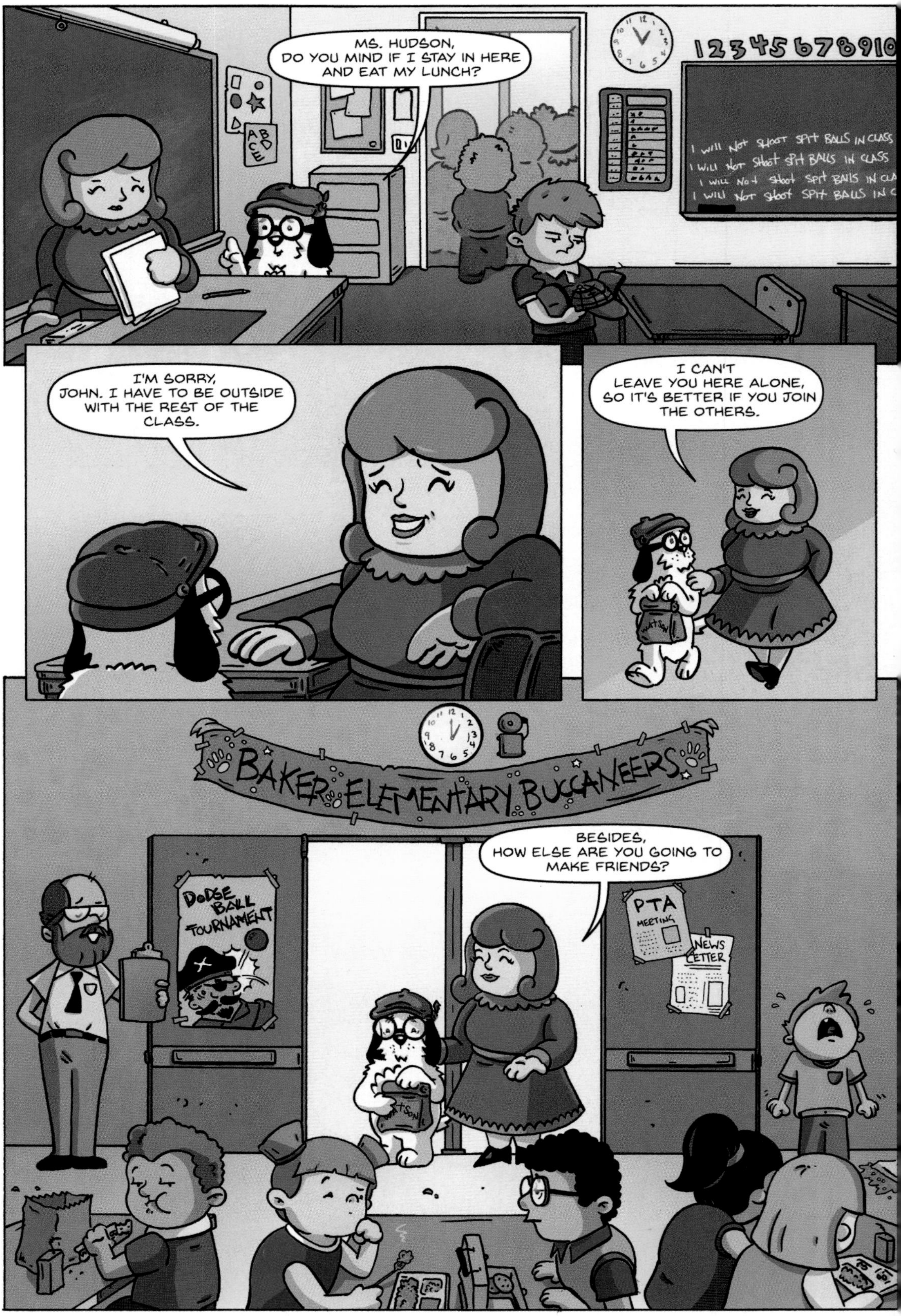
MS. HUDSON, DO YOU MIND IF I STAY IN HERE AND EAT MY LUNCH?
12345678910
I WILL NOT SHOOT SPIT BALLS IN CLASS
I WILL NOT SHOOT SPIT BALLS IN CLASS
I WILL NOT SHOOT SPIT BALLS IN CLA
I WILL NOT SHOOT SPIT BALLS IN C
I'M SORRY, JOHN. I HAVE TO BE OUTSIDE WITH THE REST OF THE CLASS.
I CAN'T LEAVE YOU HERE ALONE, SO IT'S BETTER IF YOU JOIN THE OTHERS.
BAKER ELEMENTARY BUCCANEERS
BESIDES, HOW ELSE ARE YOU GOING TO MAKE FRIENDS?
DODGE BALL TOURNAMENT
PTA MEETING
NEWS LETTER

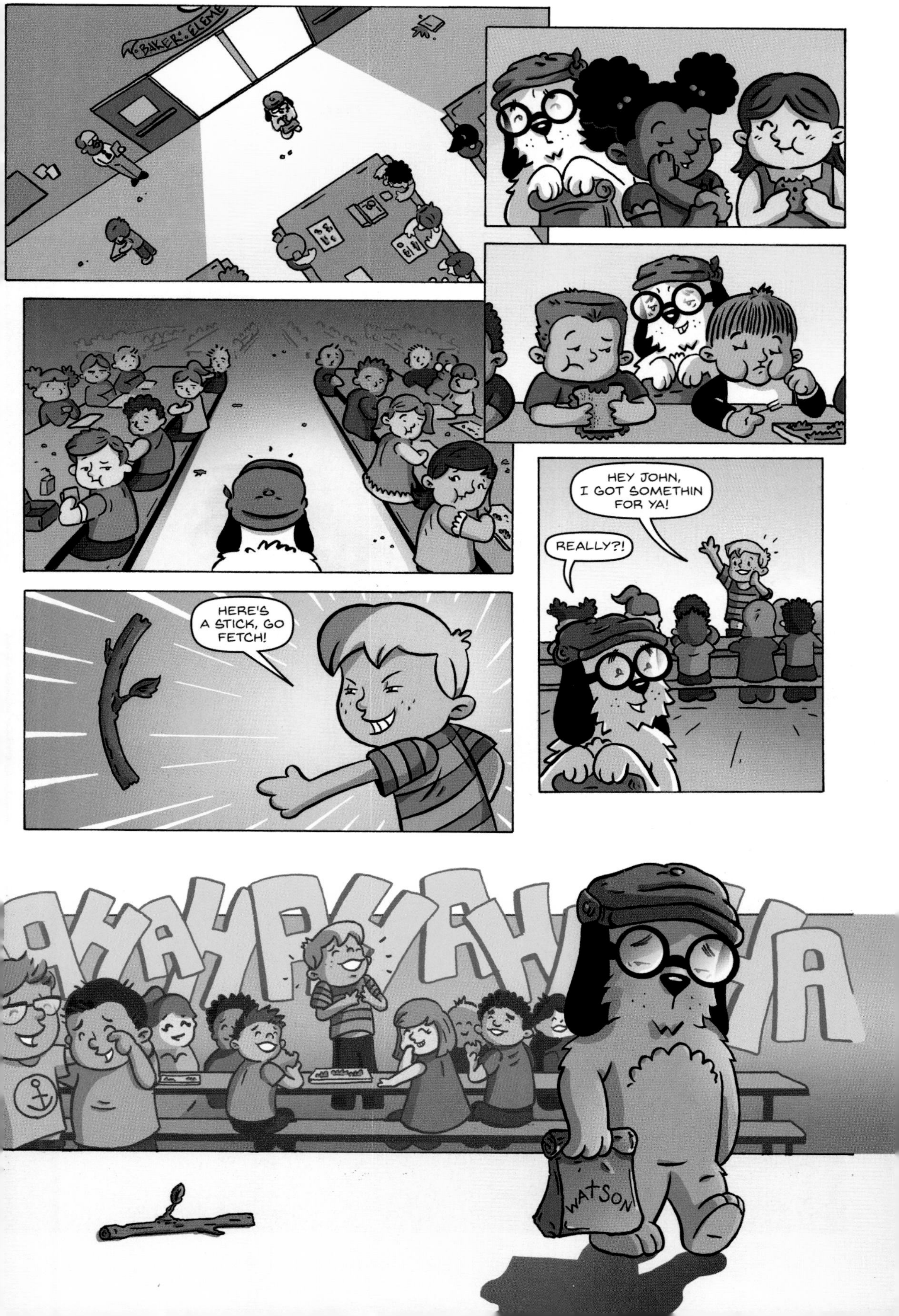
BAKER ELEME
HEY JOHN, I GOT SOMETHIN FOR YA!
REALLY?!
HERE'S A STICK, GO FETCH!
HAHAHAHAHA
WATSON

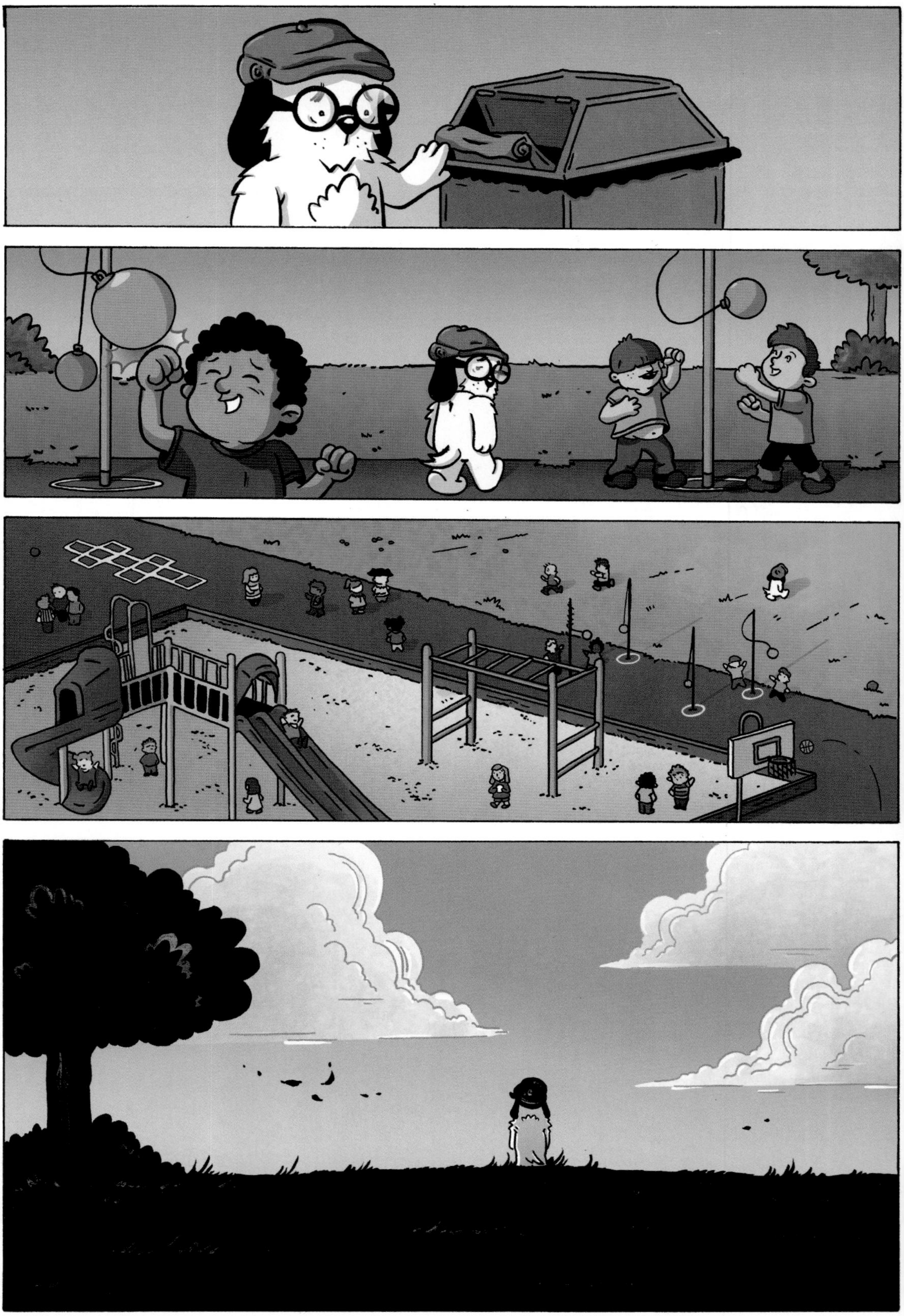

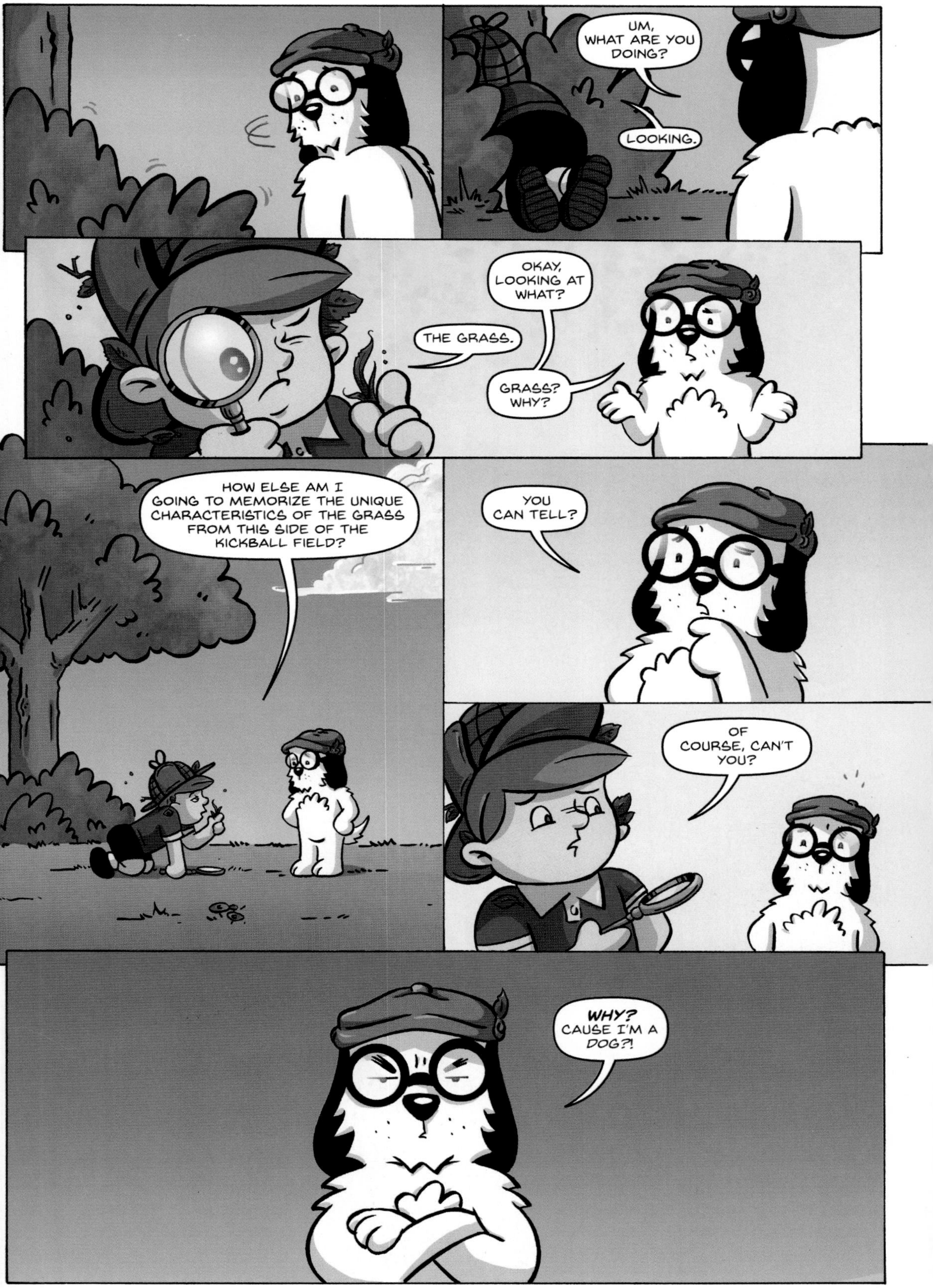
UM, WHAT ARE YOU DOING?
LOOKING.
OKAY, LOOKING AT WHAT?
THE GRASS.
GRASS? WHY?
HOW ELSE AM I GOING TO MEMORIZE THE UNIQUE CHARACTERISTICS OF THE GRASS FROM THIS SIDE OF THE KICKBALL FIELD?
YOU CAN TELL?
OF COURSE, CAN'T YOU?
WHY? CAUSE I'M A *DOG?!*

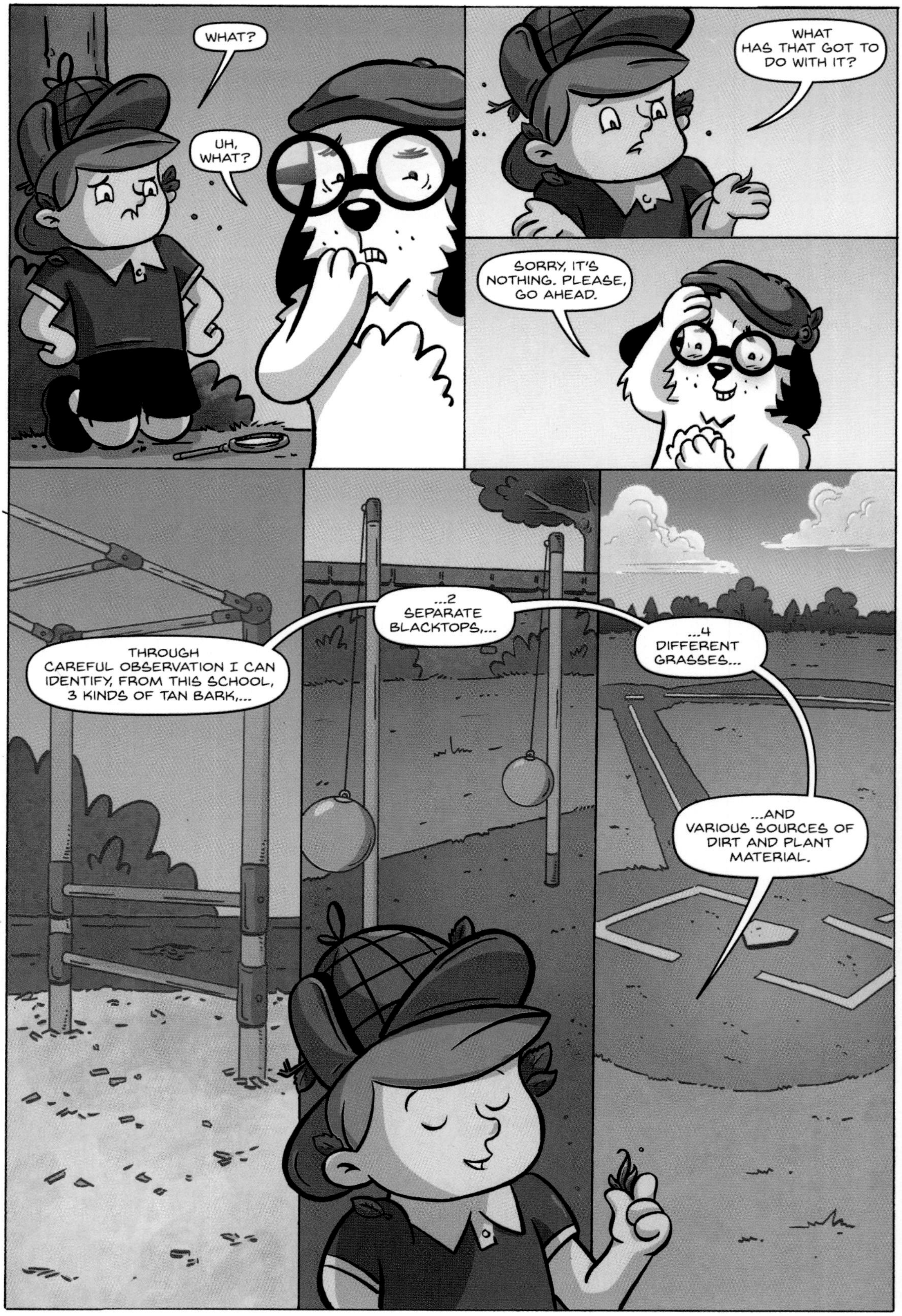
WHAT?
UH, WHAT?
WHAT HAS THAT GOT TO DO WITH IT?
SORRY, IT'S NOTHING. PLEASE, GO AHEAD.
THROUGH CAREFUL OBSERVATION I CAN IDENTIFY, FROM THIS SCHOOL, 3 KINDS OF TAN BARK,...
...2 SEPARATE BLACKTOPS,...
...4 DIFFERENT GRASSES...
...AND VARIOUS SOURCES OF DIRT AND PLANT MATERIAL.

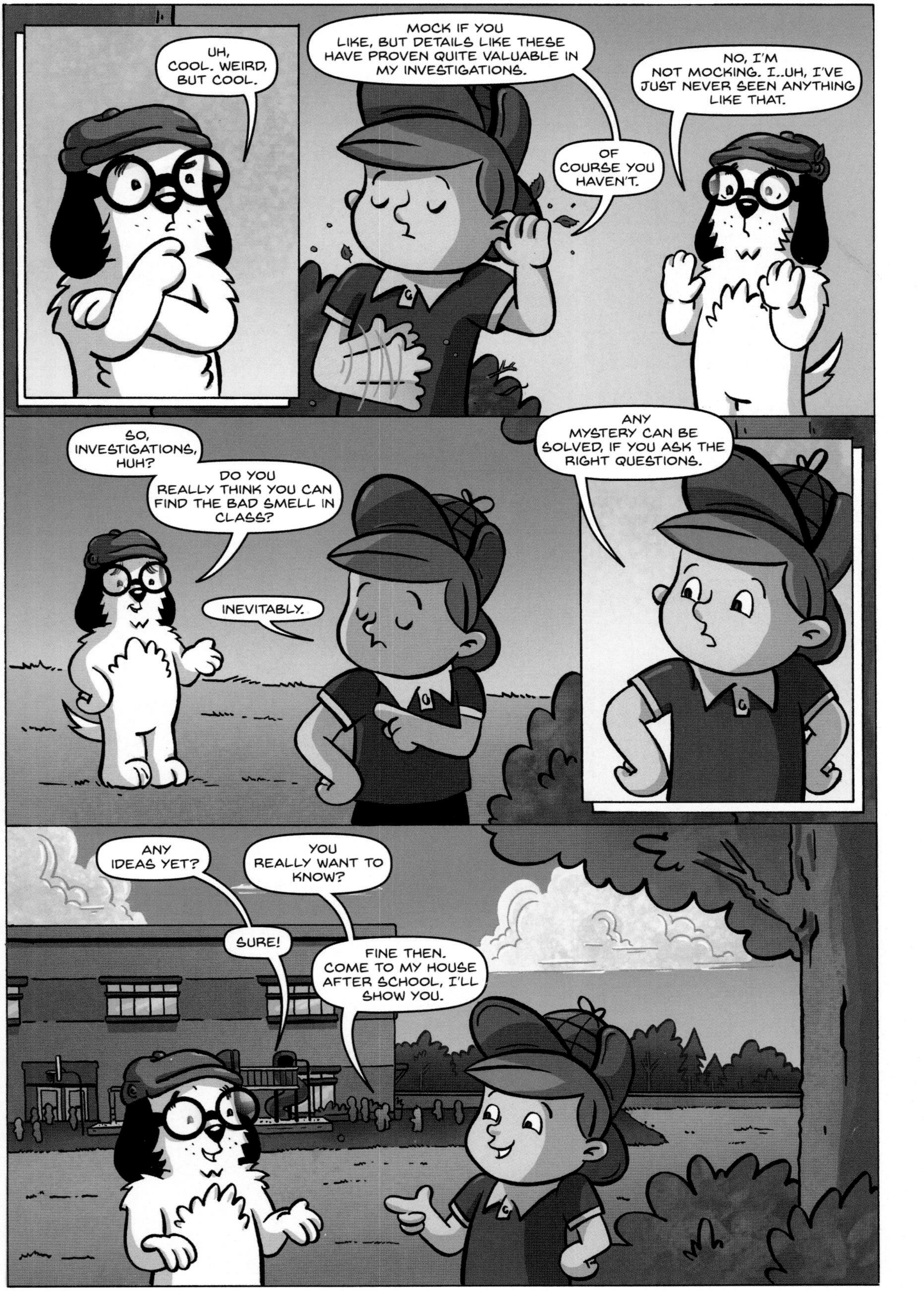
UH, COOL. WEIRD, BUT COOL.
MOCK IF YOU LIKE, BUT DETAILS LIKE THESE HAVE PROVEN QUITE VALUABLE IN MY INVESTIGATIONS.
NO, I'M NOT MOCKING. I..UH, I'VE JUST NEVER SEEN ANYTHING LIKE THAT.
OF COURSE YOU HAVEN'T.
SO, INVESTIGATIONS, HUH?
DO YOU REALLY THINK YOU CAN FIND THE BAD SMELL IN CLASS?
INEVITABLY.
ANY MYSTERY CAN BE SOLVED, IF YOU ASK THE RIGHT QUESTIONS.
ANY IDEAS YET?
YOU REALLY WANT TO KNOW?
SURE!
FINE THEN. COME TO MY HOUSE AFTER SCHOOL, I'LL SHOW YOU.

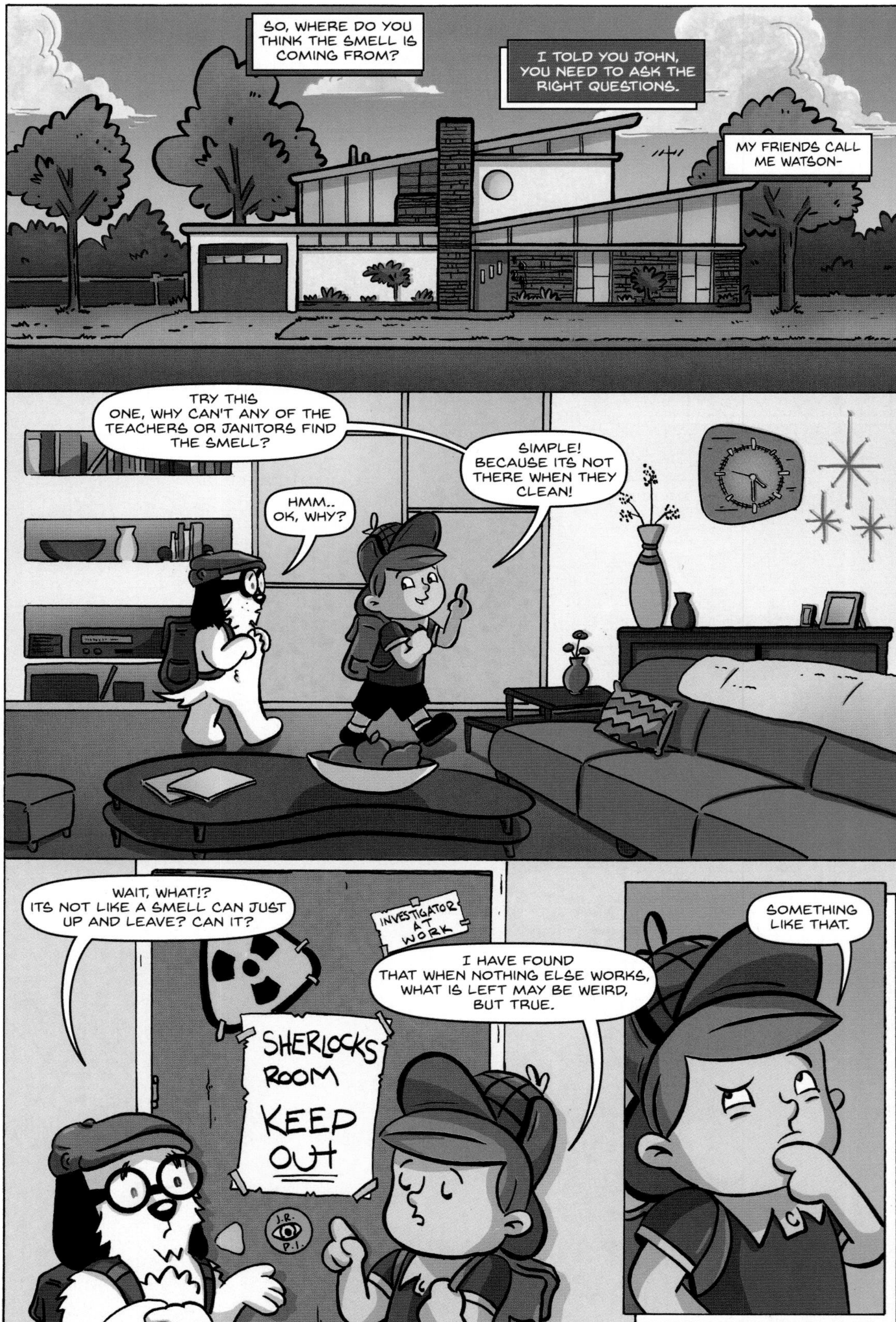
SO, WHERE DO YOU THINK THE SMELL IS COMING FROM?
I TOLD YOU JOHN, YOU NEED TO ASK THE RIGHT QUESTIONS.
MY FRIENDS CALL ME WATSON-
TRY THIS ONE, WHY CAN'T ANY OF THE TEACHERS OR JANITORS FIND THE SMELL?
HMM.. OK, WHY?
SIMPLE! BECAUSE ITS NOT THERE WHEN THEY CLEAN!
WAIT, WHAT!? ITS NOT LIKE A SMELL CAN JUST UP AND LEAVE? CAN IT?
INVESTIGATOR AT WORK
SHERLOCKS ROOM KEEP OUT
J.R. P.I.
I HAVE FOUND THAT WHEN NOTHING ELSE WORKS, WHAT IS LEFT MAY BE WEIRD, BUT TRUE.
SOMETHING LIKE THAT.

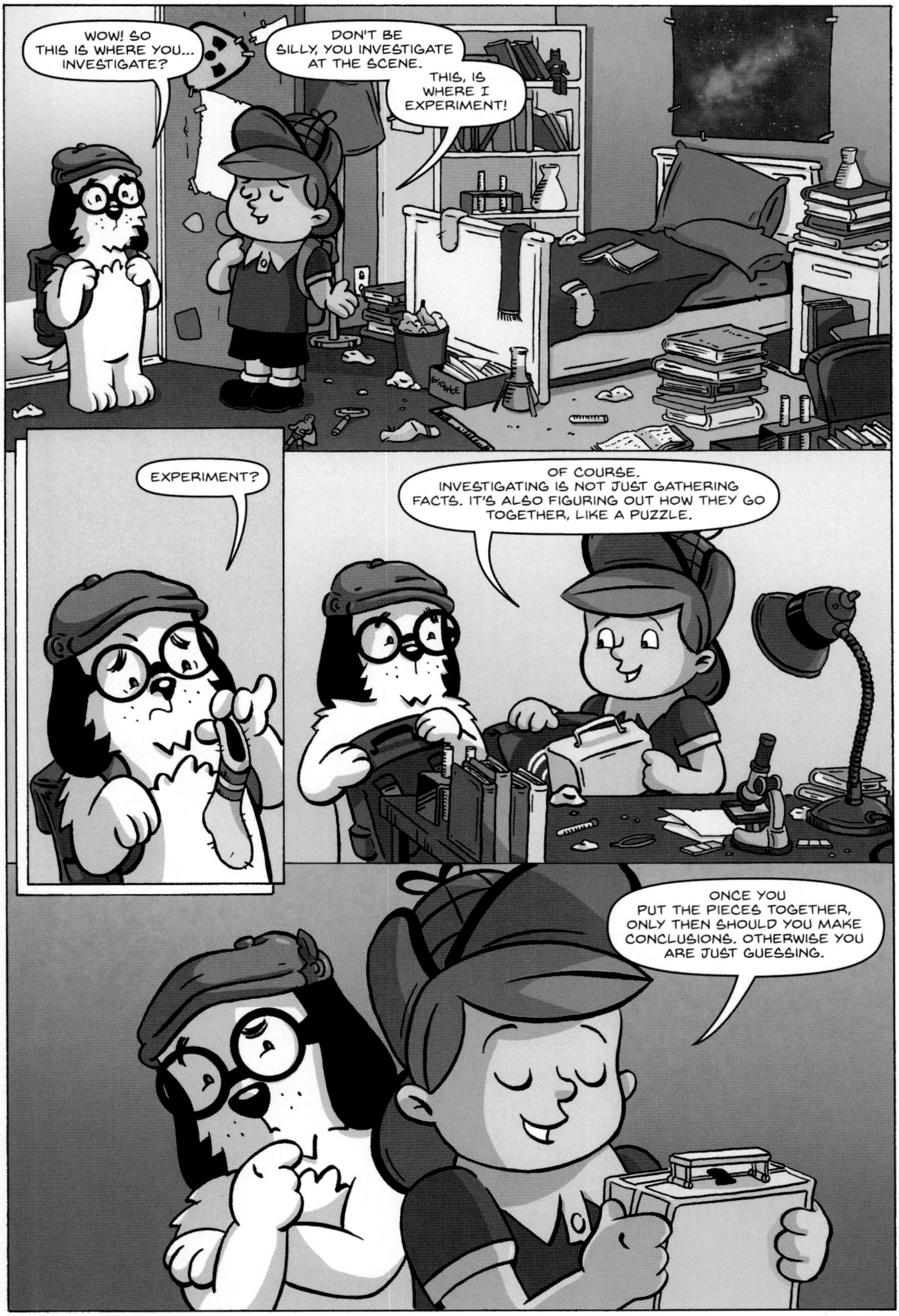
WOW! SO THIS IS WHERE YOU... INVESTIGATE?
DON'T BE SILLY, YOU INVESTIGATE AT THE SCENE.
THIS, IS WHERE I EXPERIMENT!
EXPERIMENT?
OF COURSE. INVESTIGATING IS NOT JUST GATHERING FACTS. IT'S ALSO FIGURING OUT HOW THEY GO TOGETHER, LIKE A PUZZLE.
ONCE YOU PUT THE PIECES TOGETHER, ONLY THEN SHOULD YOU MAKE CONCLUSIONS. OTHERWISE YOU ARE JUST GUESSING.

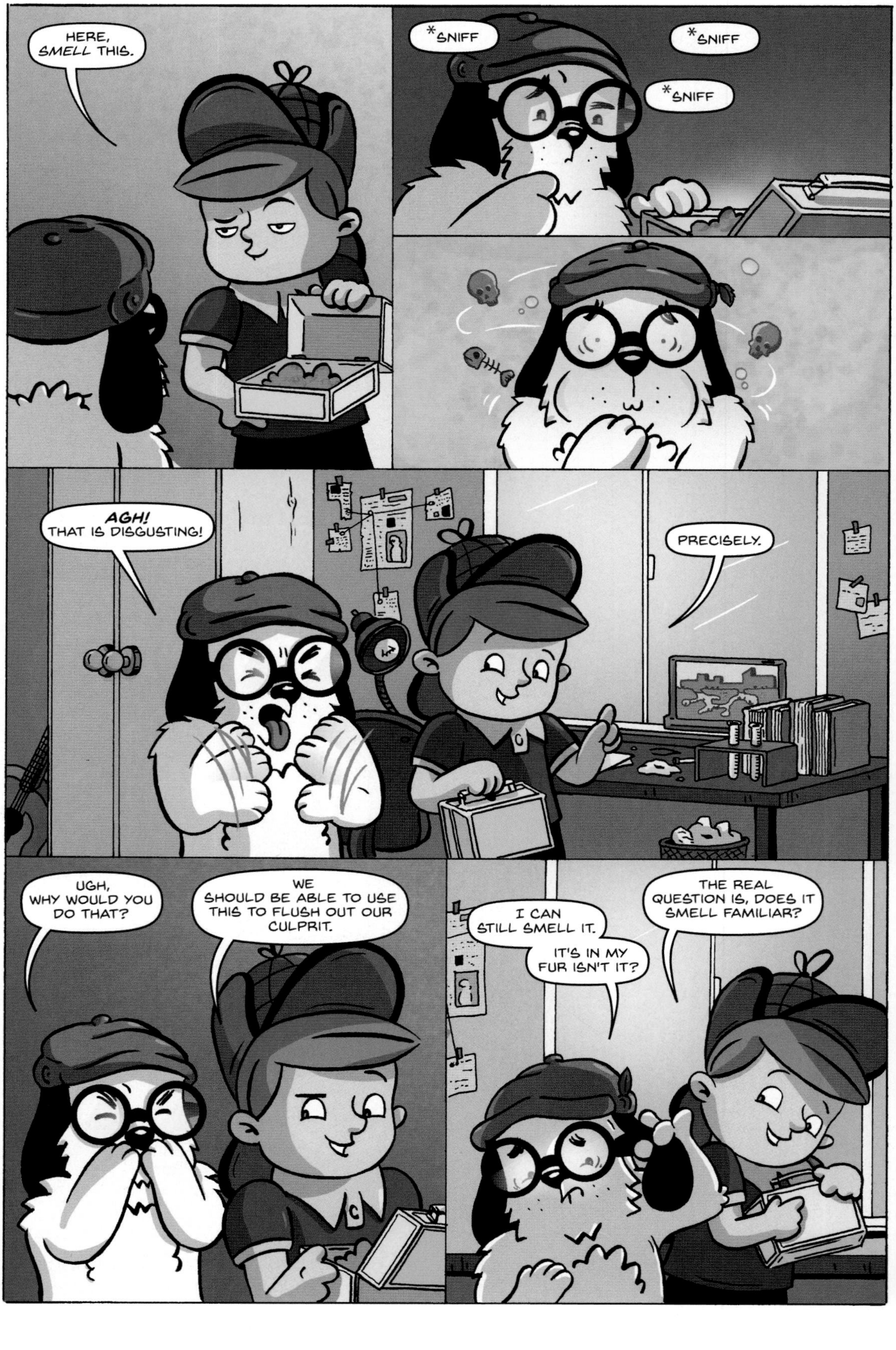
HERE, SMELL THIS.
*SNIFF
*SNIFF
*SNIFF
AGH! THAT IS DISGUSTING!
PRECISELY.
UGH, WHY WOULD YOU DO THAT?
WE SHOULD BE ABLE TO USE THIS TO FLUSH OUT OUR CULPRIT.
I CAN STILL SMELL IT.
IT'S IN MY FUR ISN'T IT?
THE REAL QUESTION IS, DOES IT SMELL FAMILIAR?

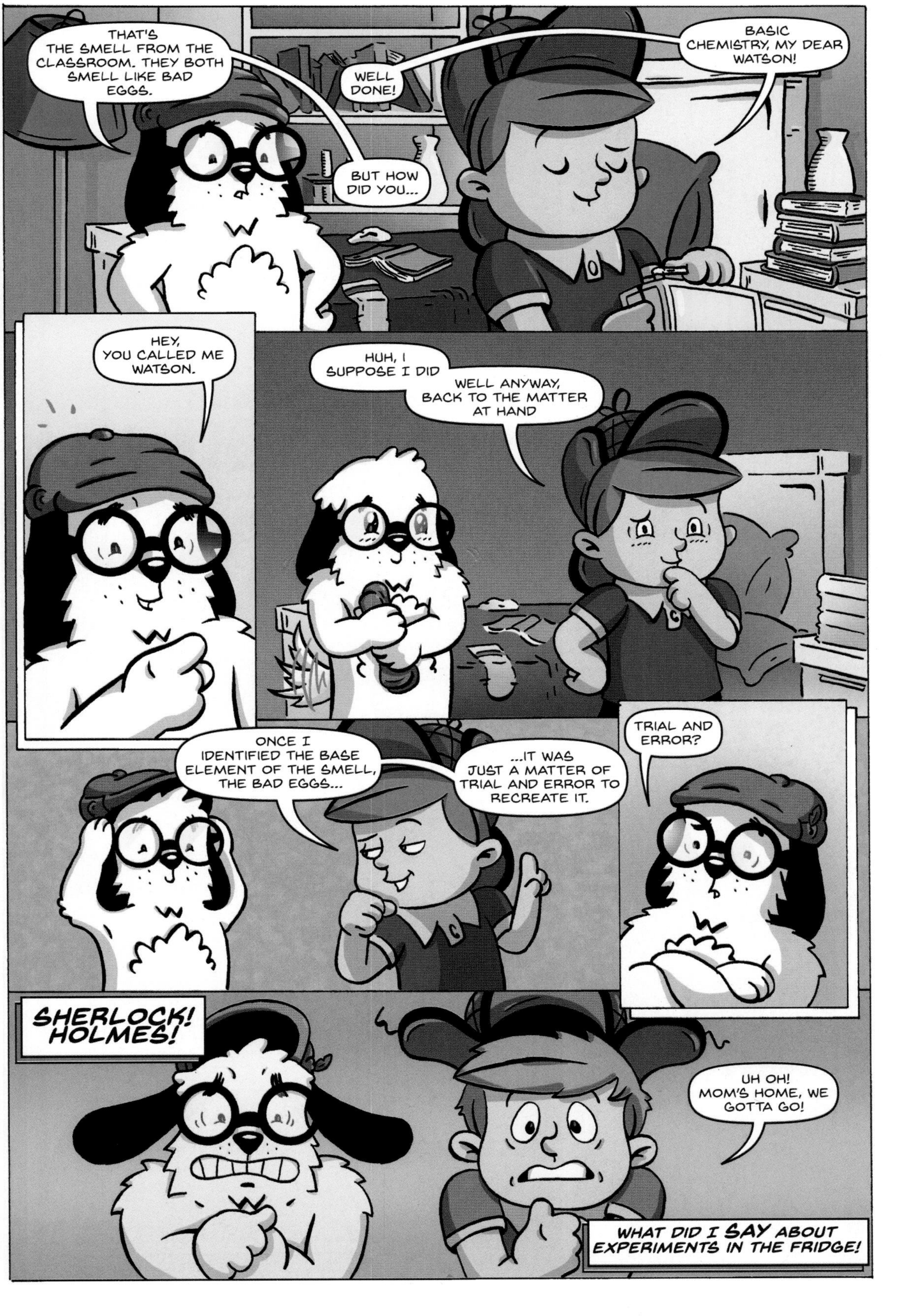
THAT'S THE SMELL FROM THE CLASSROOM. THEY BOTH SMELL LIKE BAD EGGS.
WELL DONE!
BUT HOW DID YOU...
BASIC CHEMISTRY, MY DEAR WATSON!
HEY, YOU CALLED ME WATSON.
HUH, I SUPPOSE I DID
WELL ANYWAY, BACK TO THE MATTER AT HAND
ONCE I IDENTIFIED THE BASE ELEMENT OF THE SMELL, THE BAD EGGS...
...IT WAS JUST A MATTER OF TRIAL AND ERROR TO RECREATE IT.
TRIAL AND ERROR?
SHERLOCK! HOLMES!
UH OH! MOM'S HOME, WE GOTTA GO!
WHAT DID I SAY ABOUT EXPERIMENTS IN THE FRIDGE!

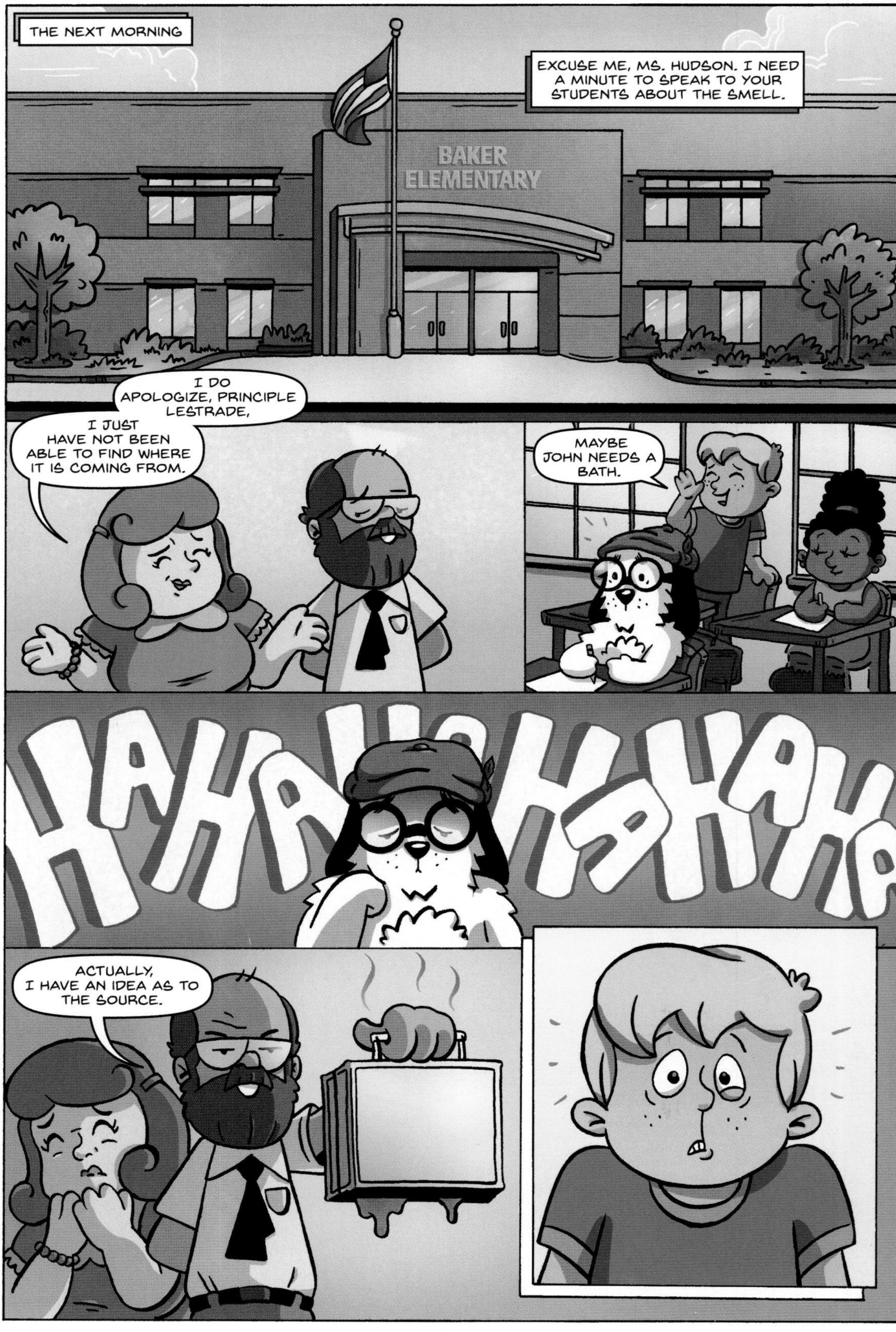
THE NEXT MORNING
EXCUSE ME, MS. HUDSON. I NEED A MINUTE TO SPEAK TO YOUR STUDENTS ABOUT THE SMELL.
BAKER ELEMENTARY
I DO APOLOGIZE, PRINCIPLE LESTRADE,
I JUST HAVE NOT BEEN ABLE TO FIND WHERE IT IS COMING FROM.
MAYBE JOHN NEEDS A BATH.
HAHAHAHAHAHA
ACTUALLY, I HAVE AN IDEA AS TO THE SOURCE.

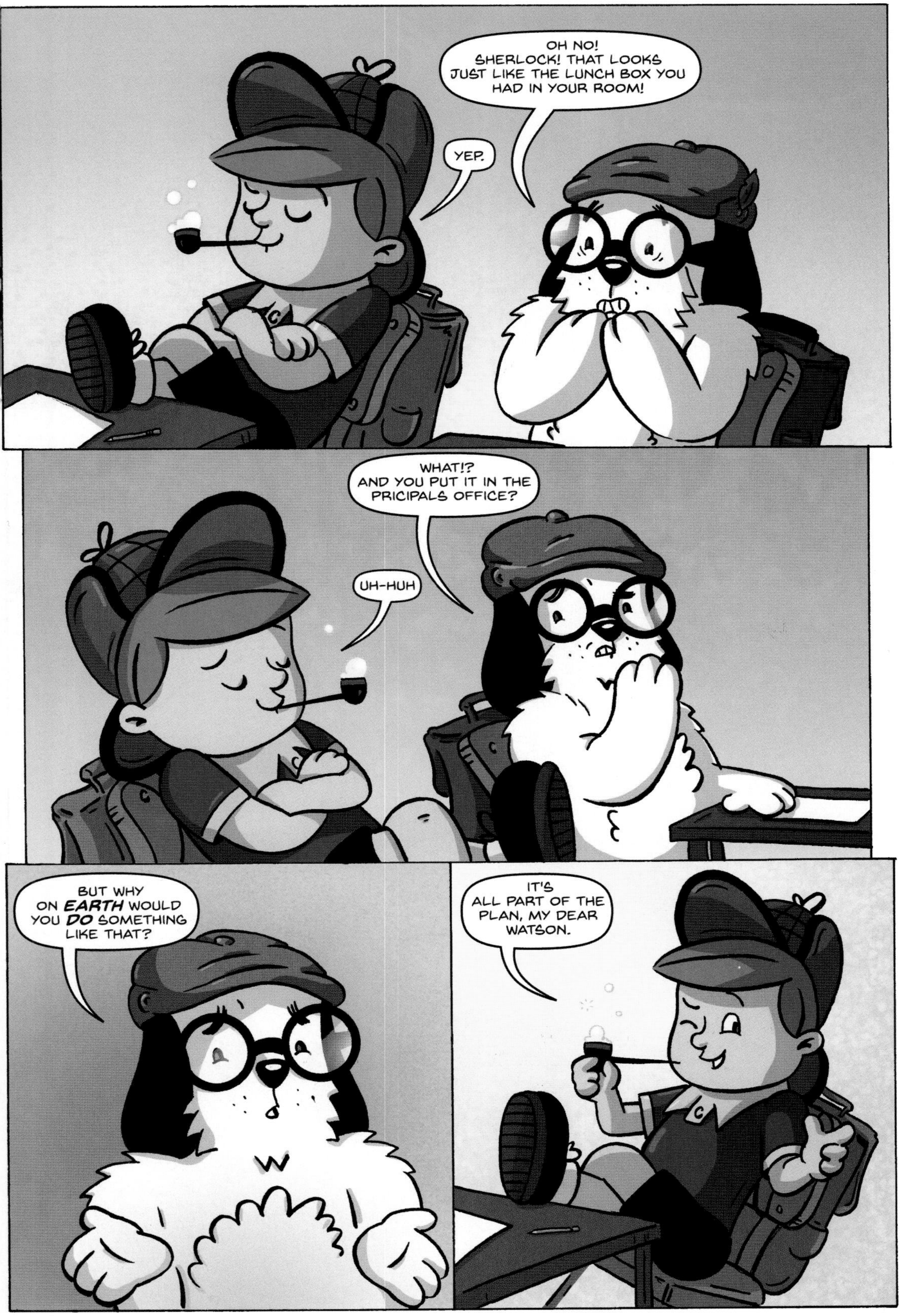
OH NO! SHERLOCK! THAT LOOKS JUST LIKE THE LUNCH BOX YOU HAD IN YOUR ROOM!
YEP.
WHAT!? AND YOU PUT IT IN THE PRICIPALS OFFICE?
UH-HUH
BUT WHY ON **EARTH** WOULD YOU **DO** SOMETHING LIKE THAT?
IT'S ALL PART OF THE PLAN, MY DEAR WATSON.

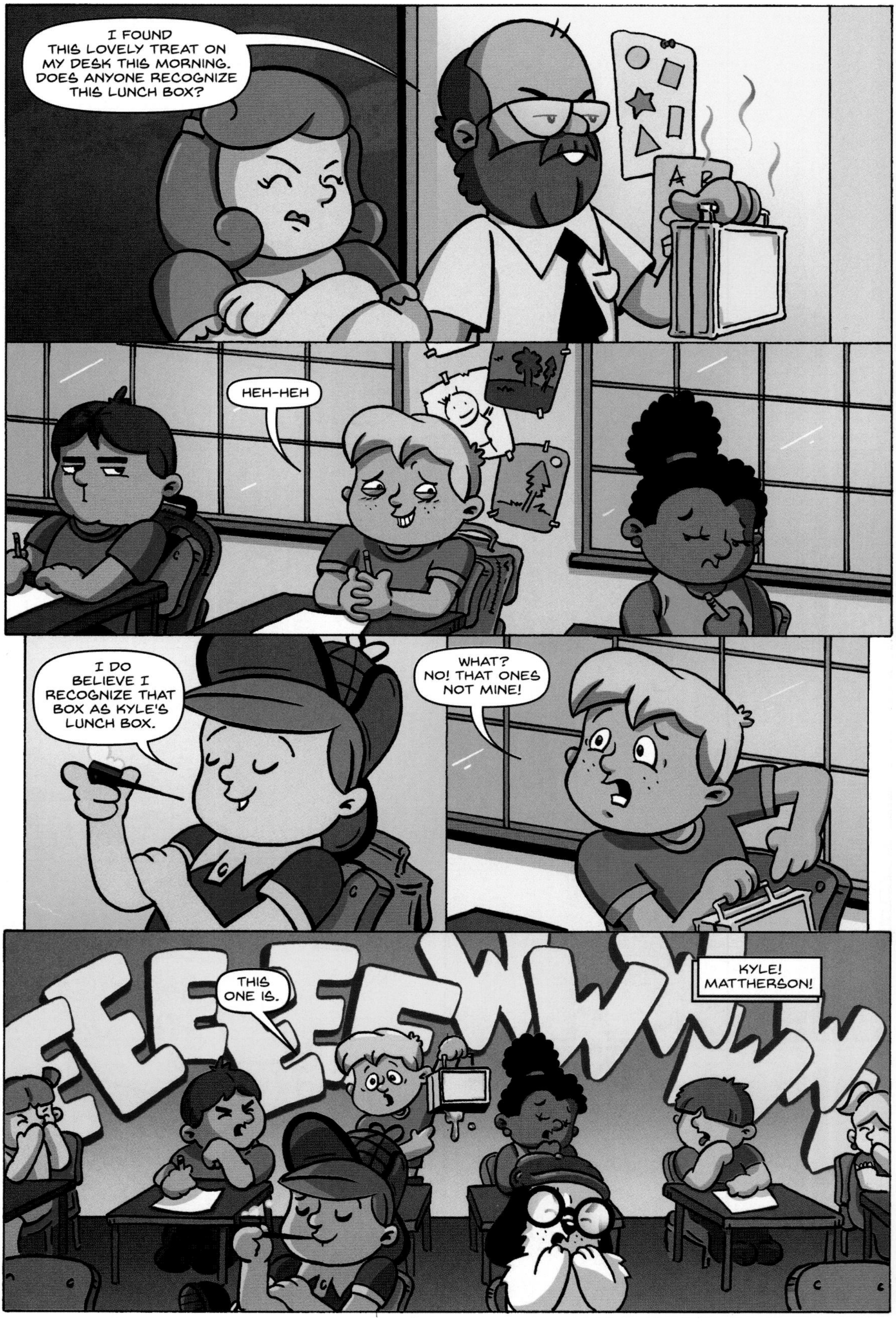

I FOUND THIS LOVELY TREAT ON MY DESK THIS MORNING. DOES ANYONE RECOGNIZE THIS LUNCH BOX?
A B
HEH-HEH
I DO BELIEVE I RECOGNIZE THAT BOX AS KYLE'S LUNCH BOX.
WHAT? NO! THAT ONES NOT MINE!
THIS ONE IS.
EEEEWWWW
KYLE! MATTHERSON!

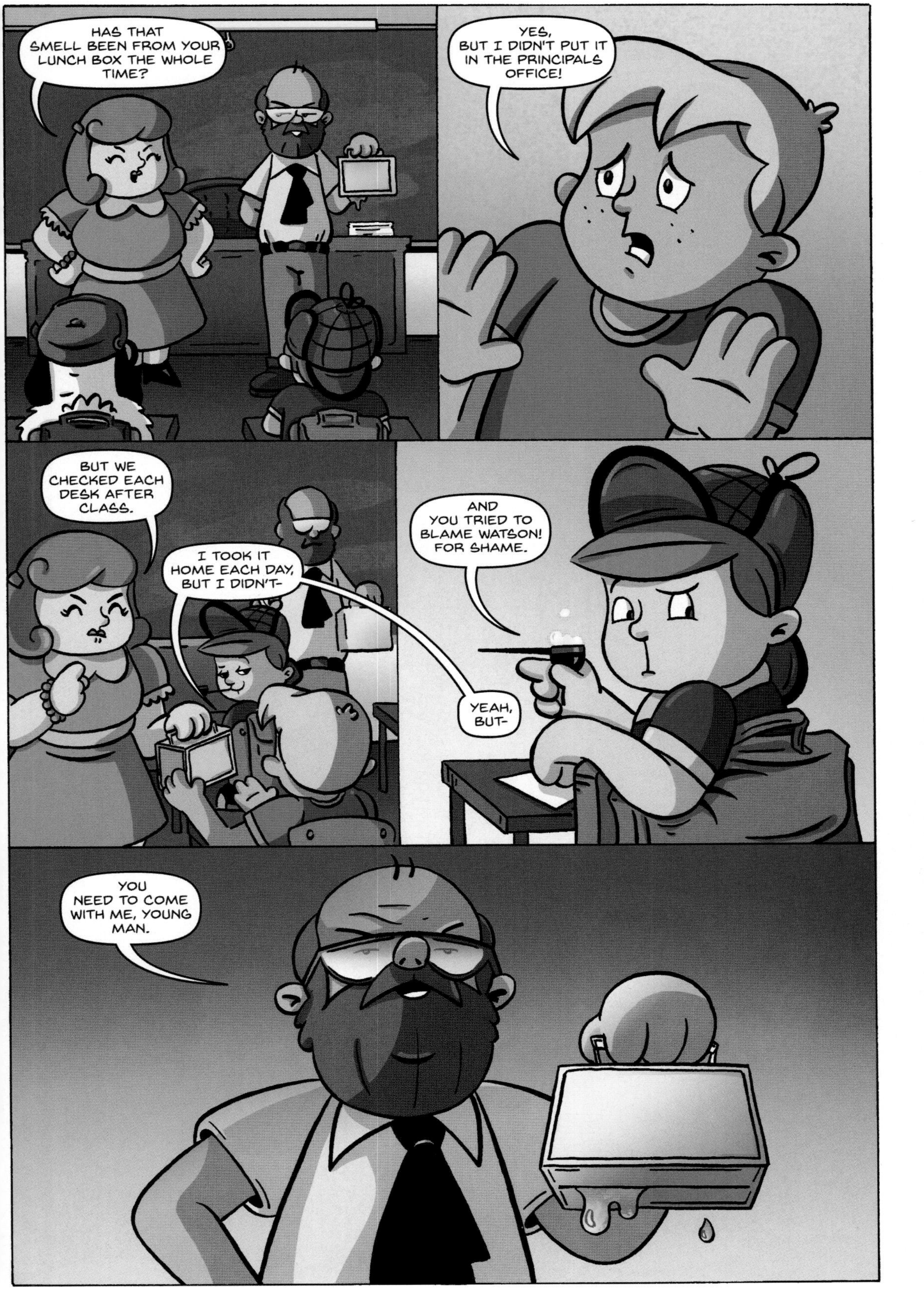
HAS THAT SMELL BEEN FROM YOUR LUNCH BOX THE WHOLE TIME?
YES, BUT I DIDN'T PUT IT IN THE PRINCIPALS OFFICE!
BUT WE CHECKED EACH DESK AFTER CLASS.
I TOOK IT HOME EACH DAY, BUT I DIDN'T-
AND YOU TRIED TO BLAME WATSON! FOR SHAME.
YEAH, BUT-
YOU NEED TO COME WITH ME, YOUNG MAN.

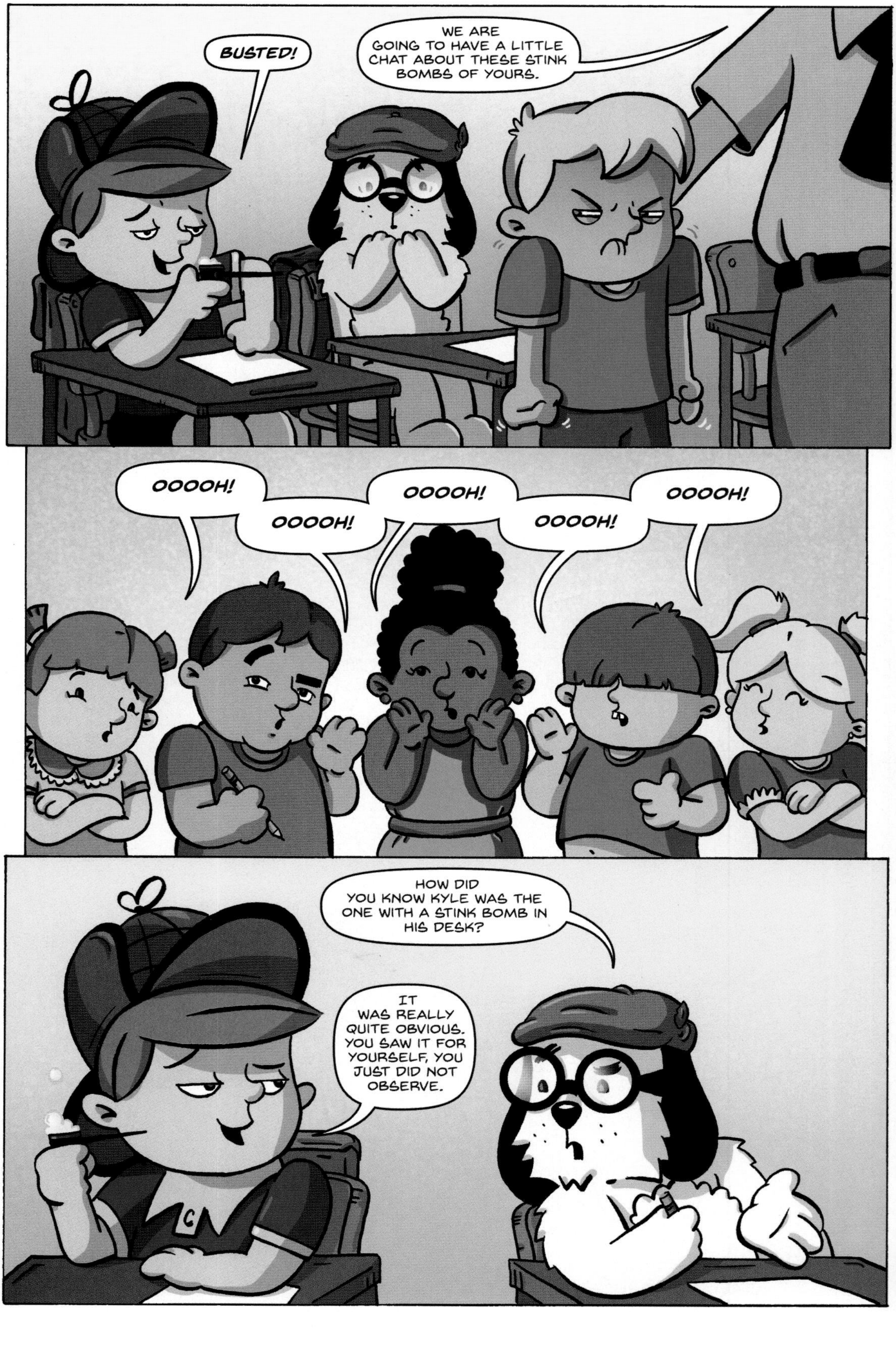
BUSTED!
WE ARE GOING TO HAVE A LITTLE CHAT ABOUT THESE STINK BOMBS OF YOURS.
OOOOH!
OOOOH!
OOOOH!
OOOOH!
OOOOH!
HOW DID YOU KNOW KYLE WAS THE ONE WITH A STINK BOMB IN HIS DESK?
IT WAS REALLY QUITE OBVIOUS. YOU SAW IT FOR YOURSELF, YOU JUST DID NOT OBSERVE.

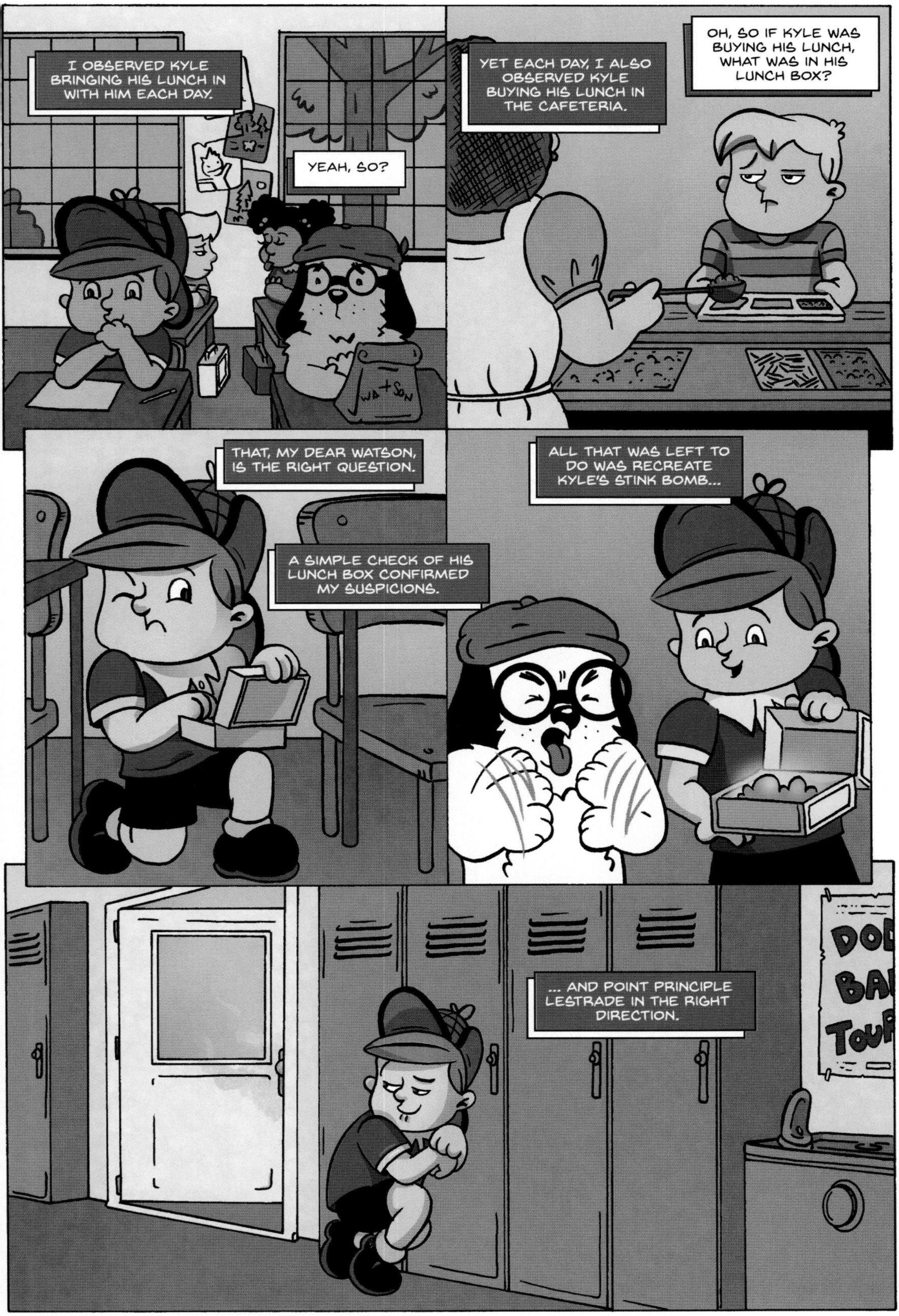
I OBSERVED KYLE BRINGING HIS LUNCH IN WITH HIM EACH DAY.
YEAH, SO?
YET EACH DAY, I ALSO OBSERVED KYLE BUYING HIS LUNCH IN THE CAFETERIA.
OH, SO IF KYLE WAS BUYING HIS LUNCH, WHAT WAS IN HIS LUNCH BOX?
THAT, MY DEAR WATSON, IS THE RIGHT QUESTION.
A SIMPLE CHECK OF HIS LUNCH BOX CONFIRMED MY SUSPICIONS.
ALL THAT WAS LEFT TO DO WAS RECREATE KYLE'S STINK BOMB...
... AND POINT PRINCIPLE LESTRADE IN THE RIGHT DIRECTION.

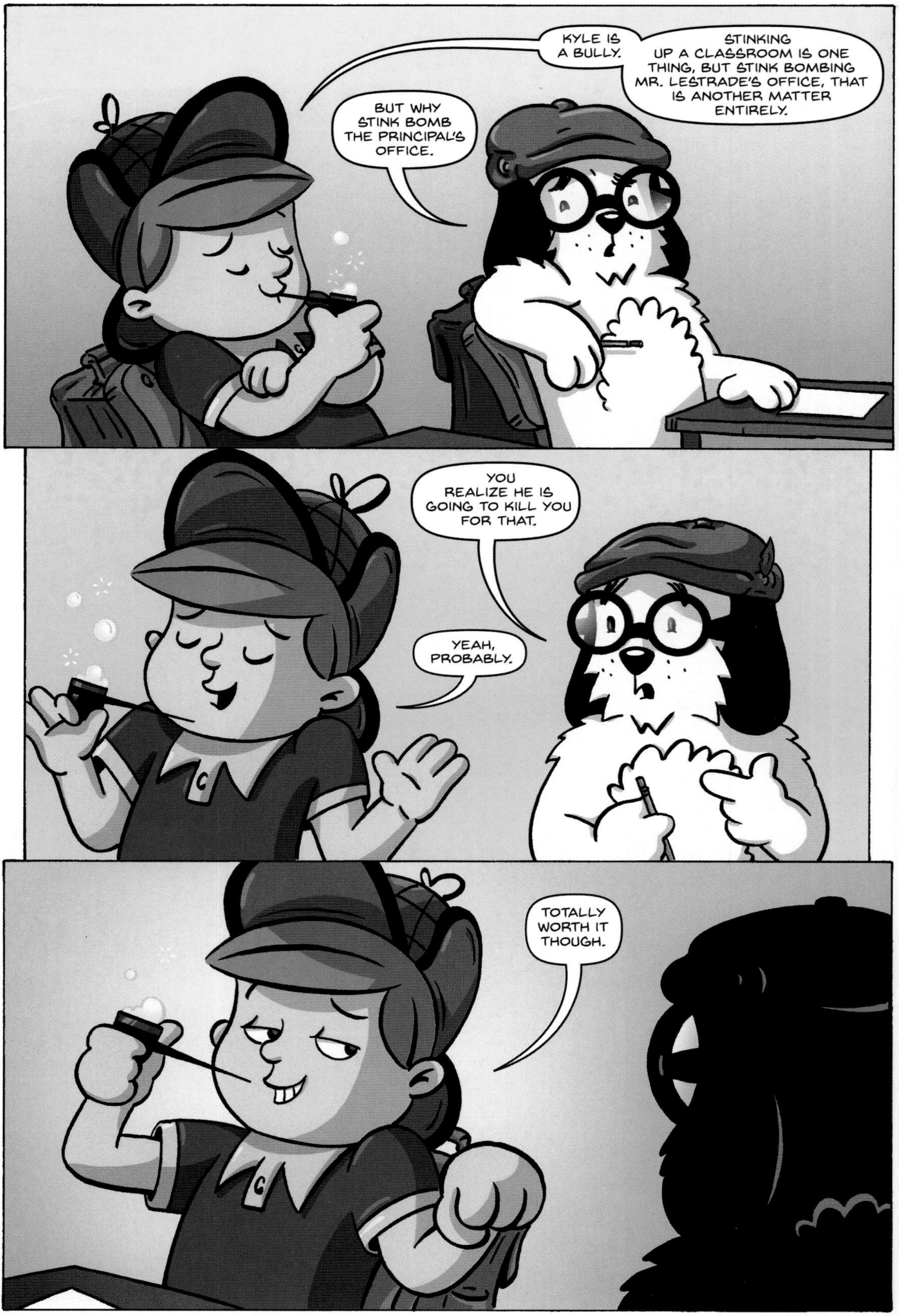

KYLE IS A BULLY.
STINKING UP A CLASSROOM IS ONE THING, BUT STINK BOMBING MR. LESTRADE'S OFFICE, THAT IS ANOTHER MATTER ENTIRELY.
BUT WHY STINK BOMB THE PRINCIPAL'S OFFICE.
YOU REALIZE HE IS GOING TO KILL YOU FOR THAT.
YEAH, PROBABLY.
TOTALLY WORTH IT THOUGH.

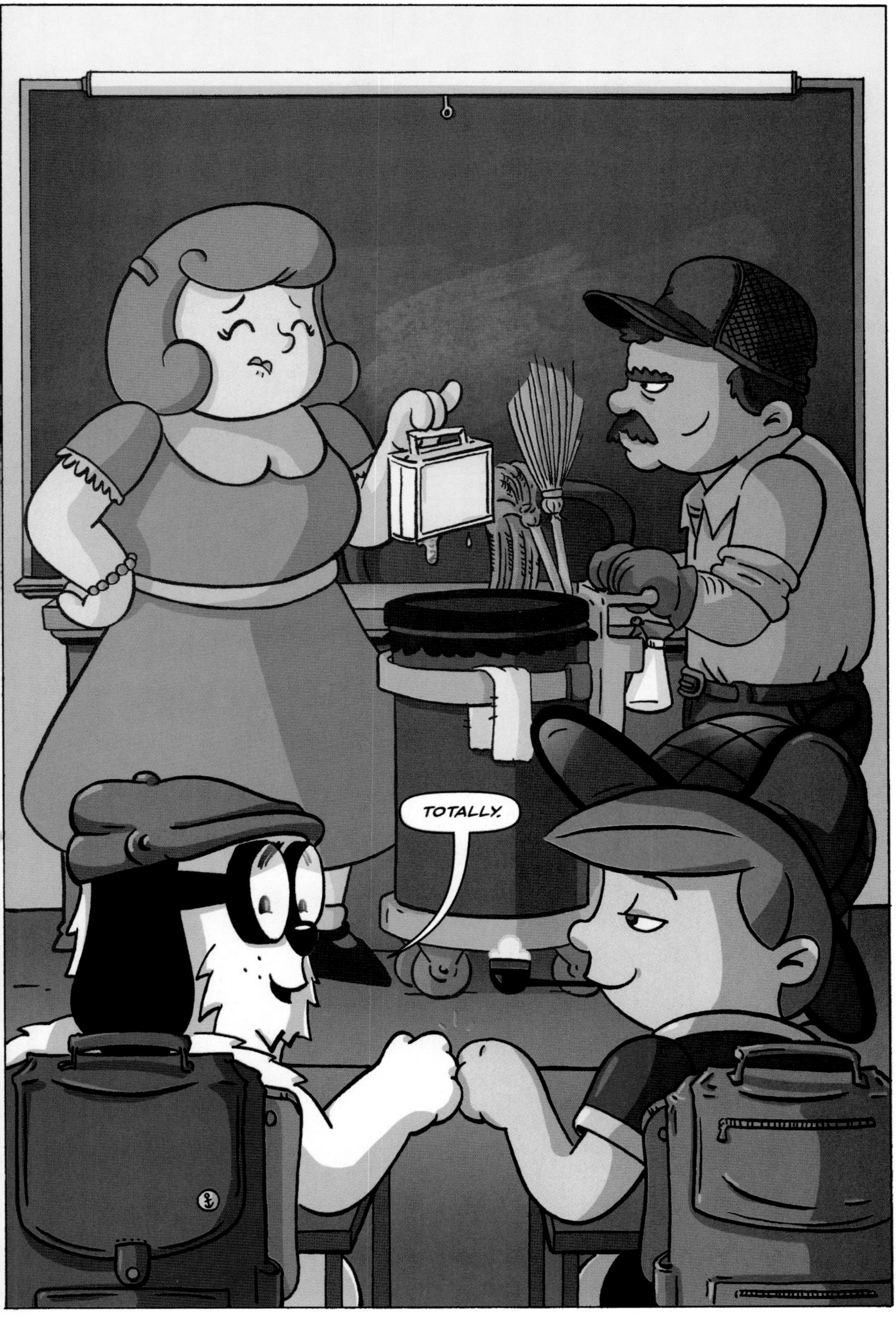
TOTALLY.

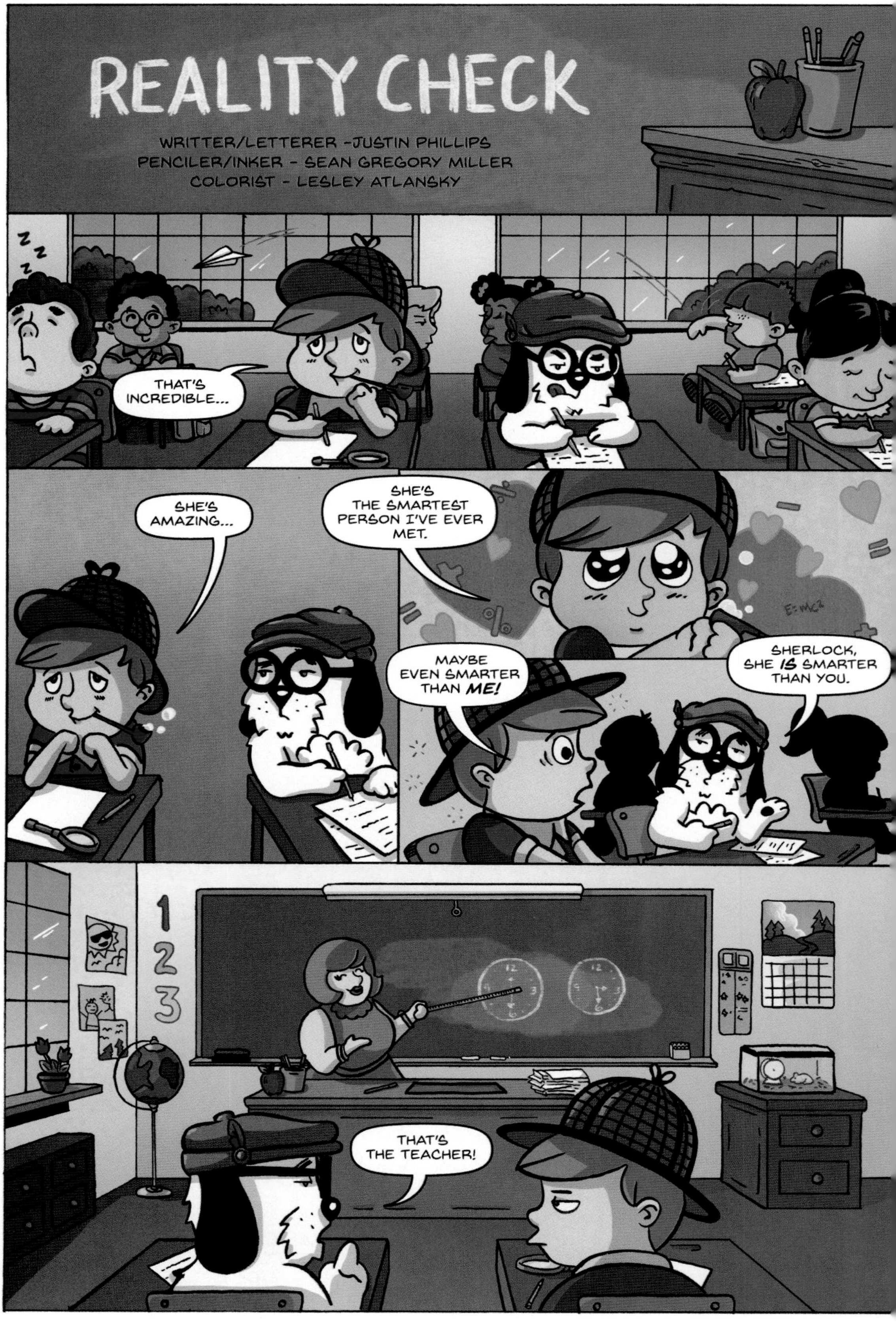
REALITY CHECK
WRITTER/LETTERER -JUSTIN PHILLIPS
PENCILER/INKER - SEAN GREGORY MILLER
COLORIST - LESLEY ATLANSKY
Z Z Z
THAT'S INCREDIBLE...
SHE'S AMAZING...
SHE'S THE SMARTEST PERSON I'VE EVER MET.
MAYBE EVEN SMARTER THAN ME!
SHERLOCK, SHE IS SMARTER THAN YOU.
1
2
3
THAT'S THE TEACHER!

LEARN TO DRAW!

LEARN TO DRAW
IN SIX EASY STEPS!
ALL YOU NEED IS
A PENCIL, PEN, AND
PAPER.

SHERLOCK

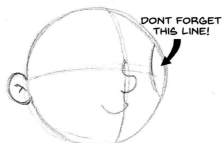

DON'T FORGET
THIS LINE!

START WITH A
SIMPLE CIRCLE!

ADD SHERLOCK'S EAR,
NOSE, AND MOUTH.

KEEP
YOUR LINES
LIGHT AND
LOOSE IN THIS
STAGE!

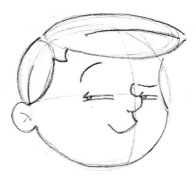

NEXT, ADD HIS EYES
AND TWO OVALS FOR
HIS HAIR.

START TO DEFINE
HIS FEATURES!

TIME
TO INK!

YOU'RE ALMOST THERE!
USE OVALS AND HALF CIRCLES
TO MAKE SHERLOCKS
TRADEMARK HAT!

NOW DRAW OVER YOUR LINES
WITH A PEN. ERASE THE
LEFT OVER PENCIL AND YOU'RE
DONE!

LOOK AT THAT!
ON YOUR WAY TO BECOMING
A COMIC BOOK ARTIST!

LEARN TO DRAW!

LEARN TO DRAW IN SIX EASY STEPS! ALL YOU NEED IS A PENCIL, PEN, AND PAPER.

WATSON

START WITH A SIMPLE CIRCLE!

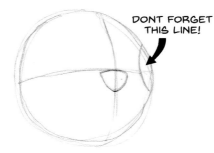

DONT FORGET THIS LINE!

ADD WATSON'S NOSE IN THE MIDDLE.

FUN FACT: WATSON IS THE FIRST CHARACTER SEAN DRAWS IN EVERY SCENE!

NEXT, ADD TWO BIG CIRCLES FOR HIS GLASSES. LETS GIVE HIM A SMIRK TOO!

NOW LETS DRAW SOME FACIAL FEATURES. BE SURE TO GIVE WATSON SOME PERSONALITY!

WE'RE ALMOST DONE! FINISH HIS HAT AND THE REST OF HIS FEATURES.

NOW DRAW OVER YOUR LINES WITH A PEN. ERASE THE LEFT OVER PENCIL AND YOU'RE DONE!

TIME TO INK!

DON'T WORRY IF YOU MAKE A MISTAKE! THAT'S WHAT AN ERASER IS FOR! JUST PRACTICE, PRACTICE, PRACTICE!

COLORING WITH LESLEY!

LEARN ABOUT THE STEP BY STEP PROCESS OF COLORING A COMIC BOOK!

LESLEY HELPS BRING OUT THE CHARACTERS PERSONALITY WITH COLOR!

THE FIRST THING LESLEY DOES IS GET THE BLACK AND WHITE LINE ART FROM SEAN. THEN SHE CHECKS JUSTIN'S SCRIPT FOR COLORING CLUES. SHE MAKES NOTE OF SOME BASIC THINGS - IS IT DAY OR NIGHT? DOES THE SCRIPT SAY ANYTHING SPECIFIC, LIKE WHAT COLOR A SHIRT OR BALL IS?

ONCE SHE HAS GONE THROUGH THE SCRIPT, THE NEXT STEP IS WHAT IS CALLED "FLATTING". BASICALLY, IT IS FILLING IN EACH SHAPE IN THE PAGE WITH A COLOR. SORT OF LIKE COLORING IN BETWEEN THE LINES LIKE A COLORING BOOK. THIS MAKES IT EASY TO DO THE REST OF THE COLORING.

THIS IS ALSO THE TIME WHEN LESLEY DECIDES ON WHAT COLOR TO MAKE THINGS. ITS THE FUN PART! SHE CHANGED TO COLOR OF SHERLOCK'S BEDROOM WALLS A FEW TIMES BEFORE SETTLING ON PURPLE.

COLORING WITH LESLEY!

THE NEXT THING LESLEY DOES IS ADD DETAILS AND TEXTURES TO THE BACK-GROUNDS. EVERY COLORIST WORKS DIFFERENTLY, AND FOR LESLEY, DOING THE BACKGROUNDS FIRST HELPS HER FIGURE OUT WHERE THE LIGHT IS COMING FROM. FOR THIS PAGE, THE WINDOW IS LETTING IN A LOT OF LIGHT, WHICH GIVES HER THE CLUES TO FIGURE OUT THE BEST PLACE FOR SHADOWS.

FUN FACT:
COLORING IS JUST AS IMPORTANT AS THE ART!

AFTER GETTING THE BACKGROUNDS DONE, LESLEY GETS TO WORK ON THE FIGURES. SHE ADDS SHADOWS AND SOME HIGH-LIGHTS TO GIVE EVERYTHING SOME DEPTH.

FUN FACT:
SEAN DRAWS WATSON FIRST, BUT LESLEY COLORS HIM LAST.

THE FINAL STEP IS CHANGING SOME OF THE LINE ART FROM BLACK TO A COLOR. THESE ARE CALLED COLOR HOLDS.

YOU CAN SEE AN EXAMPLE OF THIS ON THE ORNAGE MOVEMENT LINES AROUND WATSON'S PAWS. THIS HELPS EMPHASIZE HIS DISGUST OVER THE SMELL. SHE ALSO ADDS REFLECTIONS TO WATSON'S GLASSES AND WINDOWS. AND THAT'S IT!

COLOR, COLOR, COLOR!

NOW ITS YOUR TURN!
TRY COLORING SHERLOCK, WATSON,
AND THAT SMELLY LUNCH BOX!

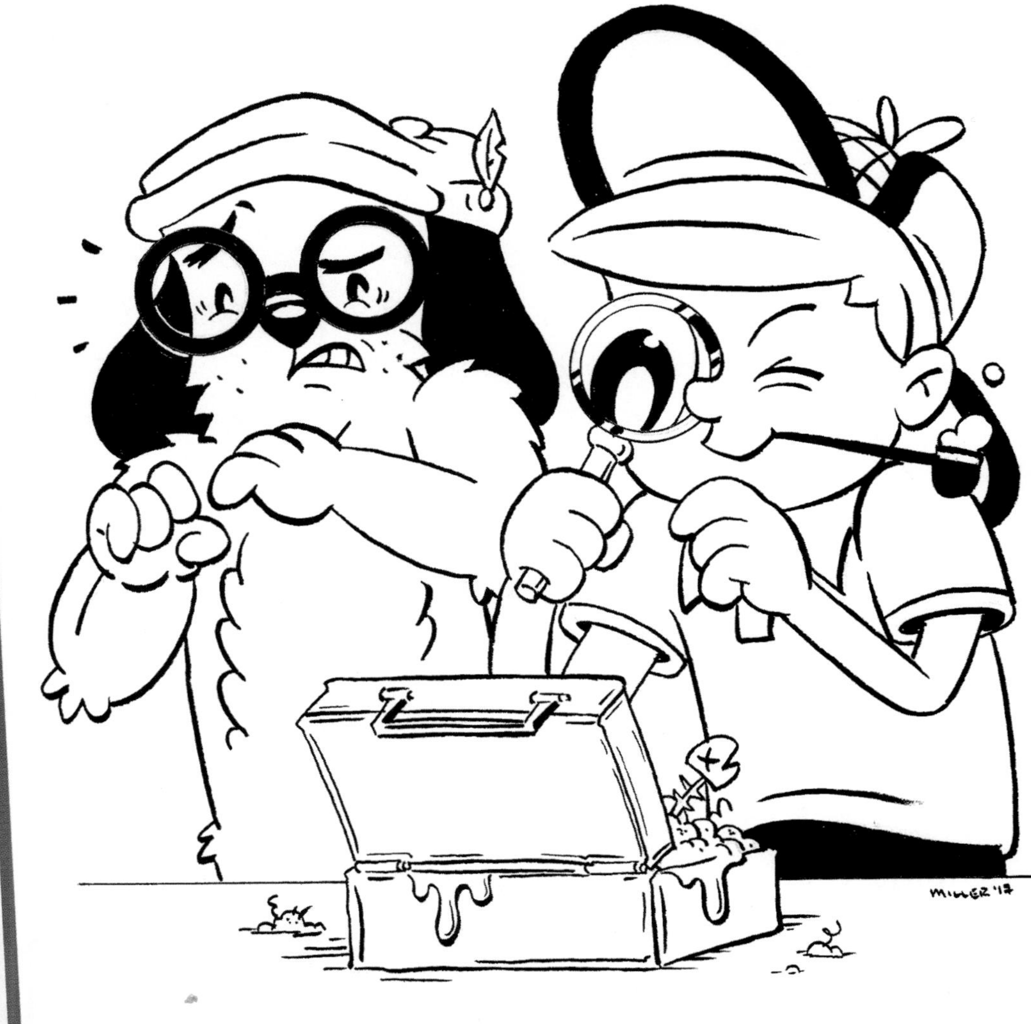
MILLER '17

USE MARKERS OR CRAYONS
TO COLOR THIS PAGE.

YOU CAN EVEN SCAN IT ON YOUR COMPUTER
AND PRINT MULTIPULE COPIES TO
PRACTICE COLORING AGAIN
AND AGAIN!

WORD SEARCH!

SEE IF YOU CAN
FIND ALL THE WORDS
FROM THIS ISSUE
HIDDEN IN THE
WORD SEARCH!

```
Z  B  S  T  I  N  K  Y  U  K  V  M
T  L  A  L  X  D  T  W  M  G  N  P
W  U  E  C  L  A  X  A  B  S  S  A
B  N  F  U  I  B  T  U  H  M  O
J  C  Y  F  F  I  U  S  R  E  E  Q
M  H  K  F  K  O  L  O  X  R  L  B
J  B  C  L  U  E  L  N  B  L  L  A
N  O  Q  P  Q  B  Y  Q  C  O  K  F
O  X  C  Y  D  F  B  N  G  C  Y  A
B  Y  Q  T  K  G  E  M  O  K  L  U
Y  K  S  C  H  O  O  L  X  B  E  A
D  R  E  C  E  S  S  U  X  J  S  T
```

SHERLOCK

WATSON

STINKY

RECESS

KYLE

LUNCHBOX

FUN

BULLY

SCHOOL

SMELL

CLUE

DID YOU FIND THEM ALL?

HINT:
LOOK FOR
WORDS GOING
ACROSS **AND**
UP AND DOWN!

MAZE!

HELP SHERLOCK FIND THE CLUE AT THE END OF THE MAZE!

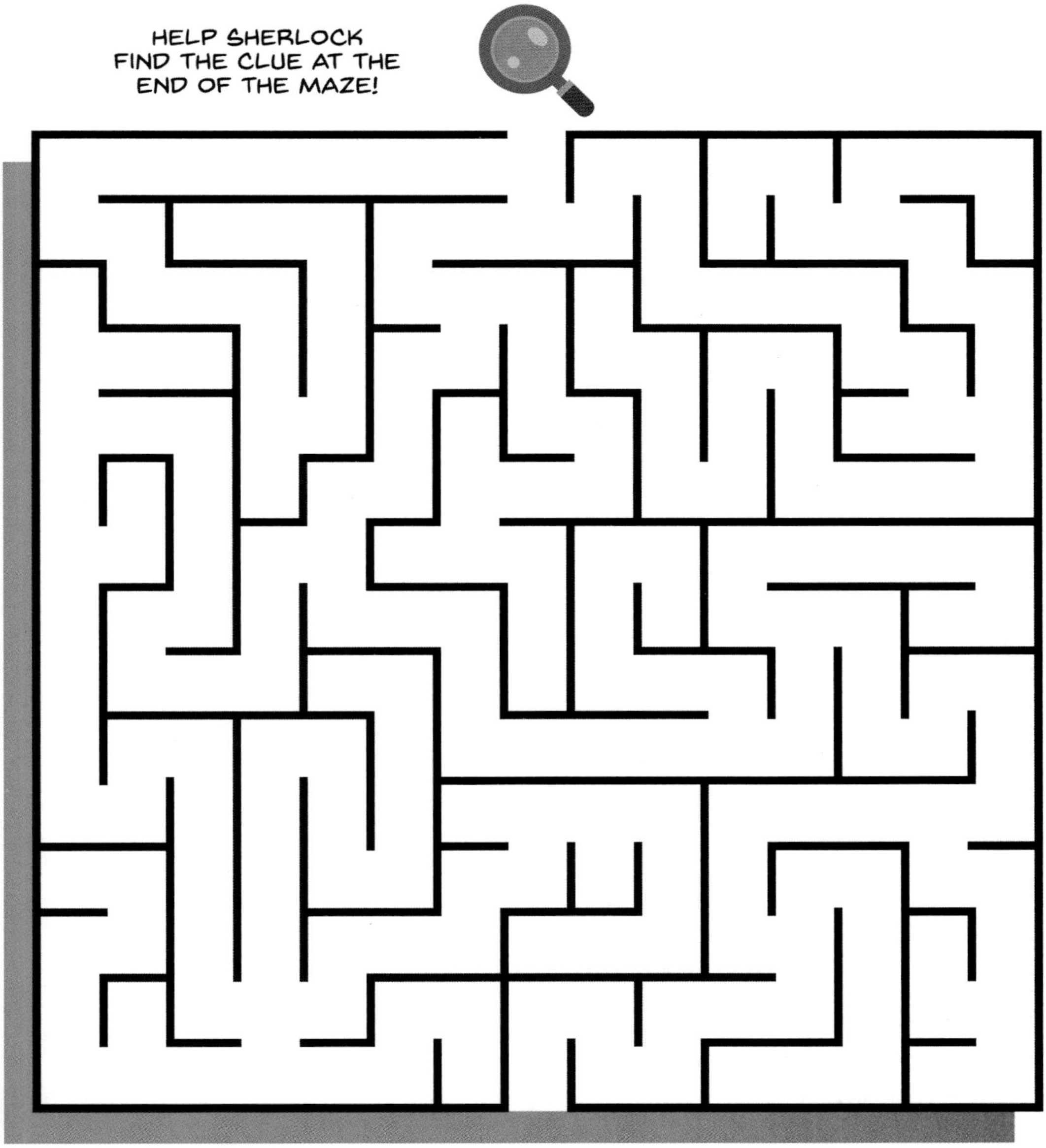

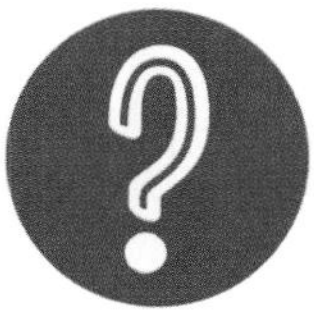

HINT: ACTUALLY, THERE ARE NO HINTS FOR THIS ONE. WHERE'S THE FUN IN THAT?!

FUN FACT: THE FIRST RECORDED MAZE WAS FOUND IN EGYPT!

FAN ART!

CHECK OUT
THESE PICTURES FROM
OUR FANS!
(WE HAVE THOSE)

SHERLOCK & WATSON BY ASHLEY

AGE 7
FROM GALT, CA.

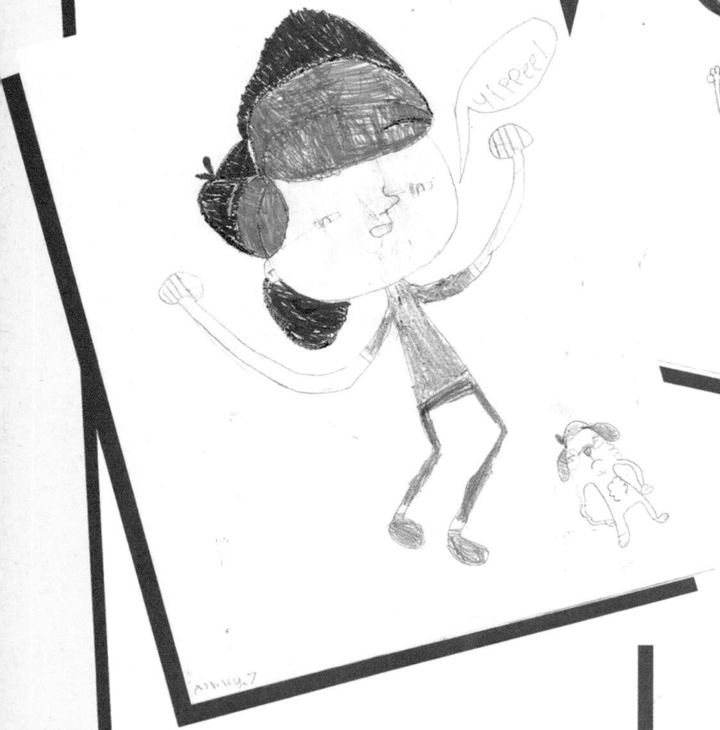
Yippee!
ashley.7

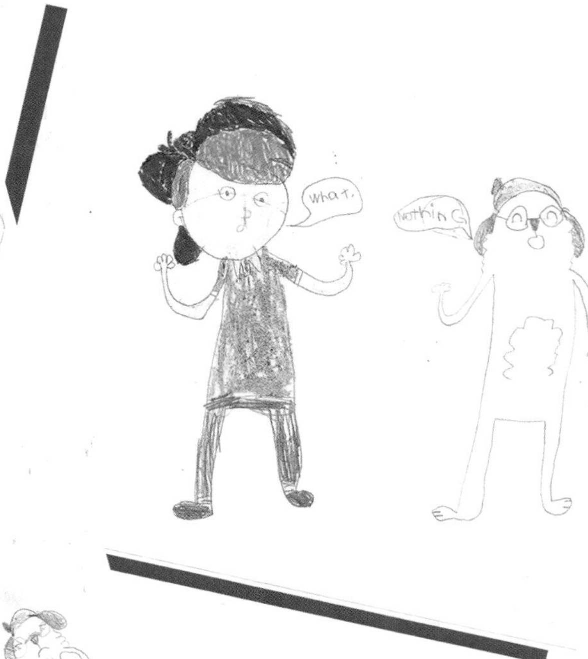
what.
nothing

GREAT JOB,
GIRLS!

SHERLOCK BY MEGAN

AGE 5
FROM GALT, CA.

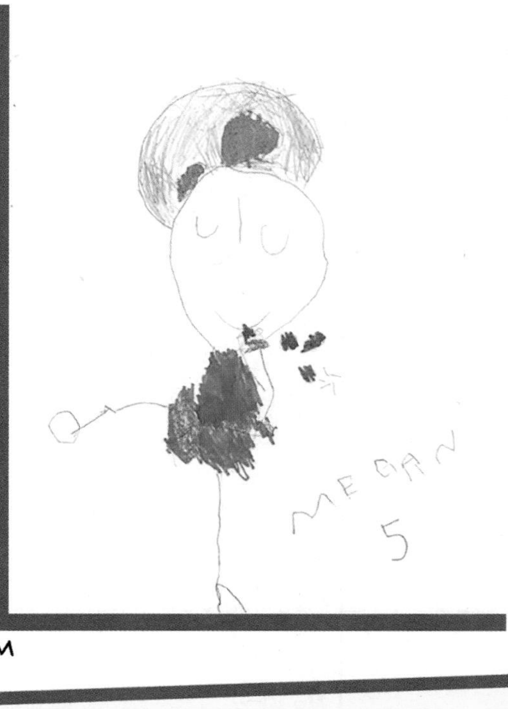
MEGAN
5

IF YOU HAVE
ANY ART THAT YOU
WOULD LIKE TO SHARE
OR WOULD LIKE TO
SEND US A LETTER,
YOU CAN!

WE'D LOVE
TO HEAR FROM YOU!

YOU CAN REACH US AT:
KIDSHERLOCKANDWATSON@GMAIL.COM

Kid Sherlock

CASE FILE 2:
"The Stolen Toy"

THE CREATIVE TEAM

Written
and lettered by
JUSTIN PHILLIPS

Art by
SEAN GREGORY MILLER

Colors by
LESLEY ATLANSKY

CREATED BY JUSTIN PHILLIPS AND SEAN GREGORY MILLER
BASED ON CHARACTERS BY SIR ARTHUR CONAN DOYLE

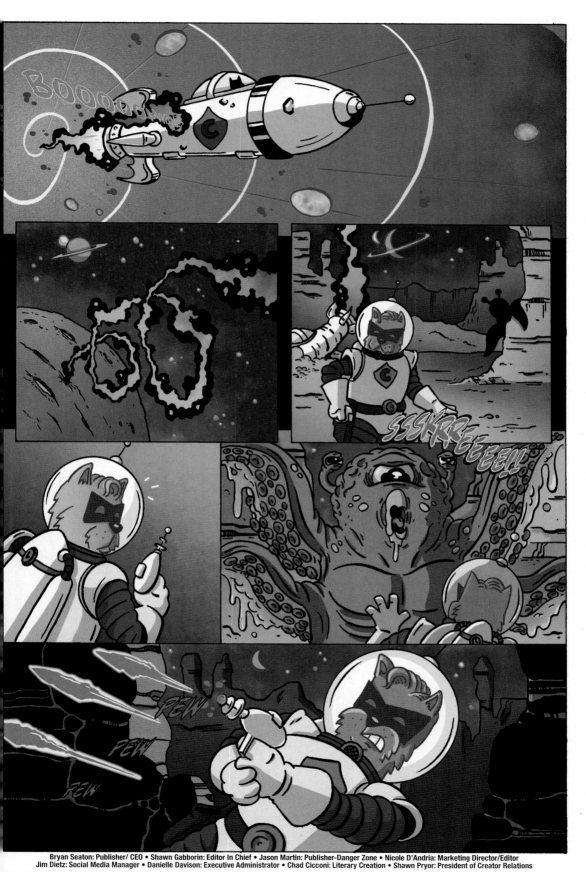

KID SHERLOCK #2, July, 2017. Copyright Justin Phillips, 2017. Published by Action Lab Entertainment. All rights reserved. All characters are fictional. Any likeness to anyone living or dead is purely coincidental. No part of this publication may be reproduced or transmitted without permission, except for review purposes. Printed in Canada. First Printing.

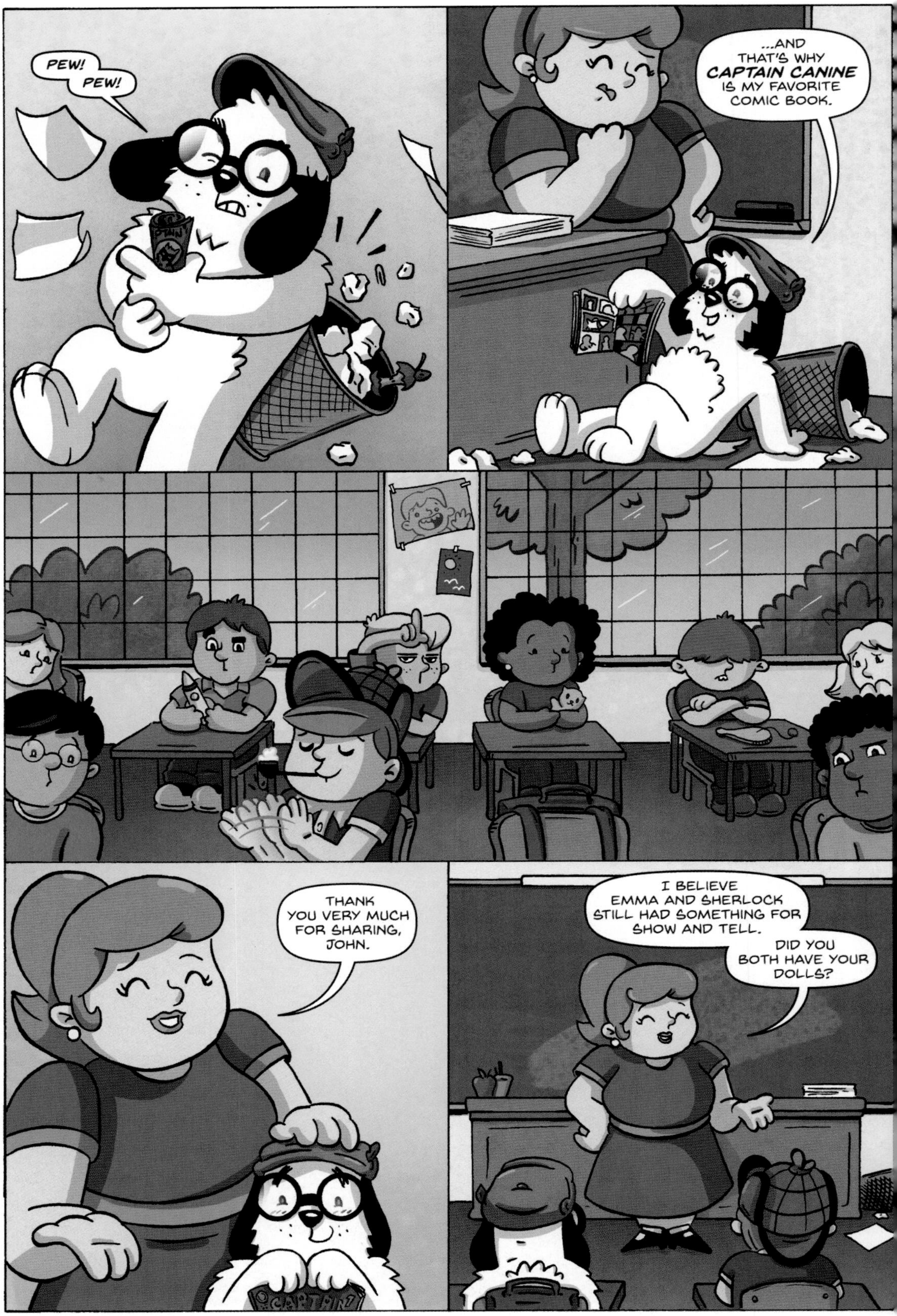
PEW! PEW!
...AND THAT'S WHY CAPTAIN CANINE IS MY FAVORITE COMIC BOOK.
THANK YOU VERY MUCH FOR SHARING, JOHN.
I BELIEVE EMMA AND SHERLOCK STILL HAD SOMETHING FOR SHOW AND TELL.
DID YOU BOTH HAVE YOUR DOLLS?

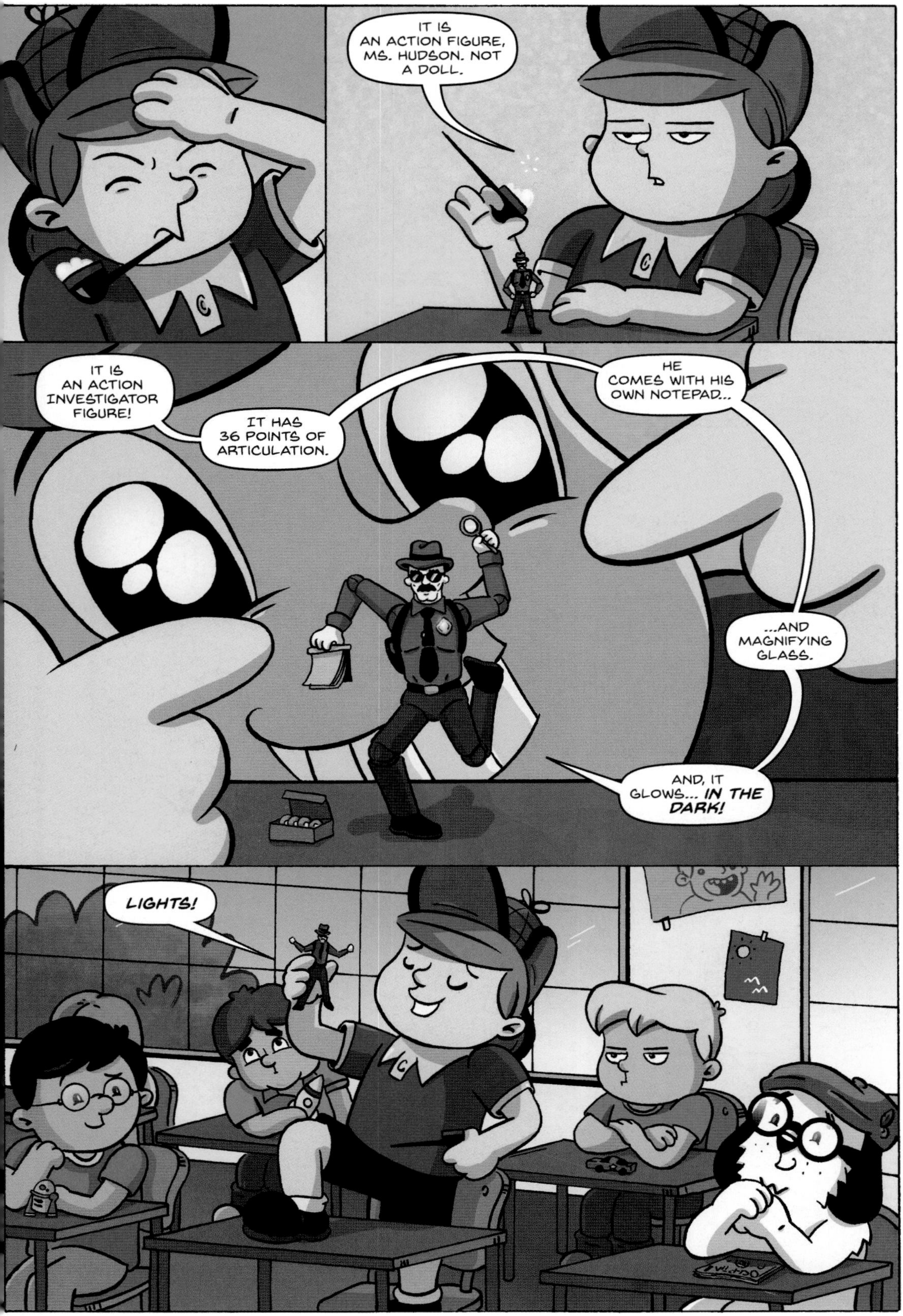
IT IS AN ACTION FIGURE, MS. HUDSON. NOT A DOLL.
IT IS AN ACTION INVESTIGATOR FIGURE!
IT HAS 36 POINTS OF ARTICULATION.
HE COMES WITH HIS OWN NOTEPAD...
...AND MAGNIFYING GLASS.
AND, IT GLOWS... *IN THE DARK!*
LIGHTS!

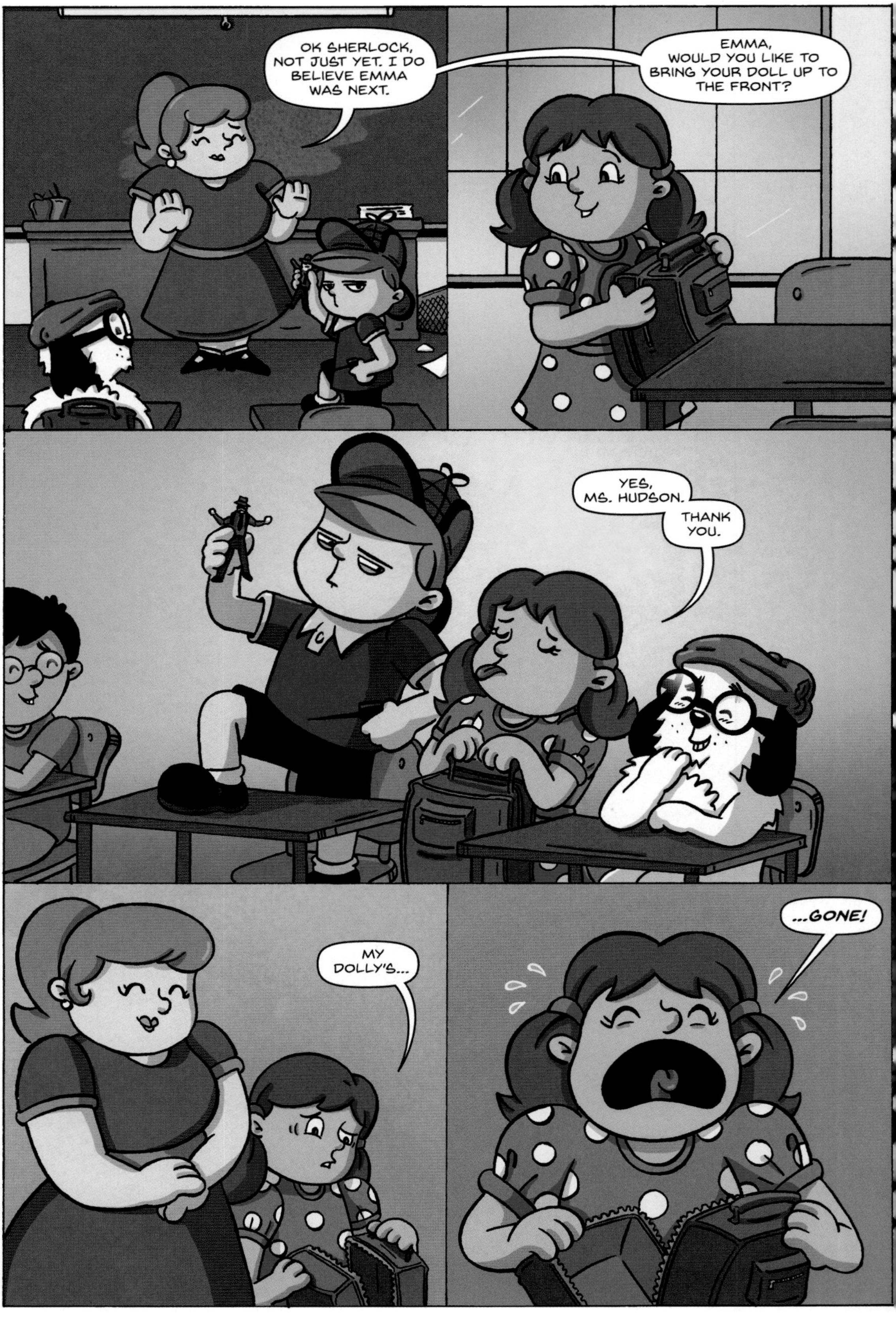
OK SHERLOCK, NOT JUST YET. I DO BELIEVE EMMA WAS NEXT.
EMMA, WOULD YOU LIKE TO BRING YOUR DOLL UP TO THE FRONT?
YES, MS. HUDSON.
THANK YOU.
MY DOLLY'S...
...GONE!

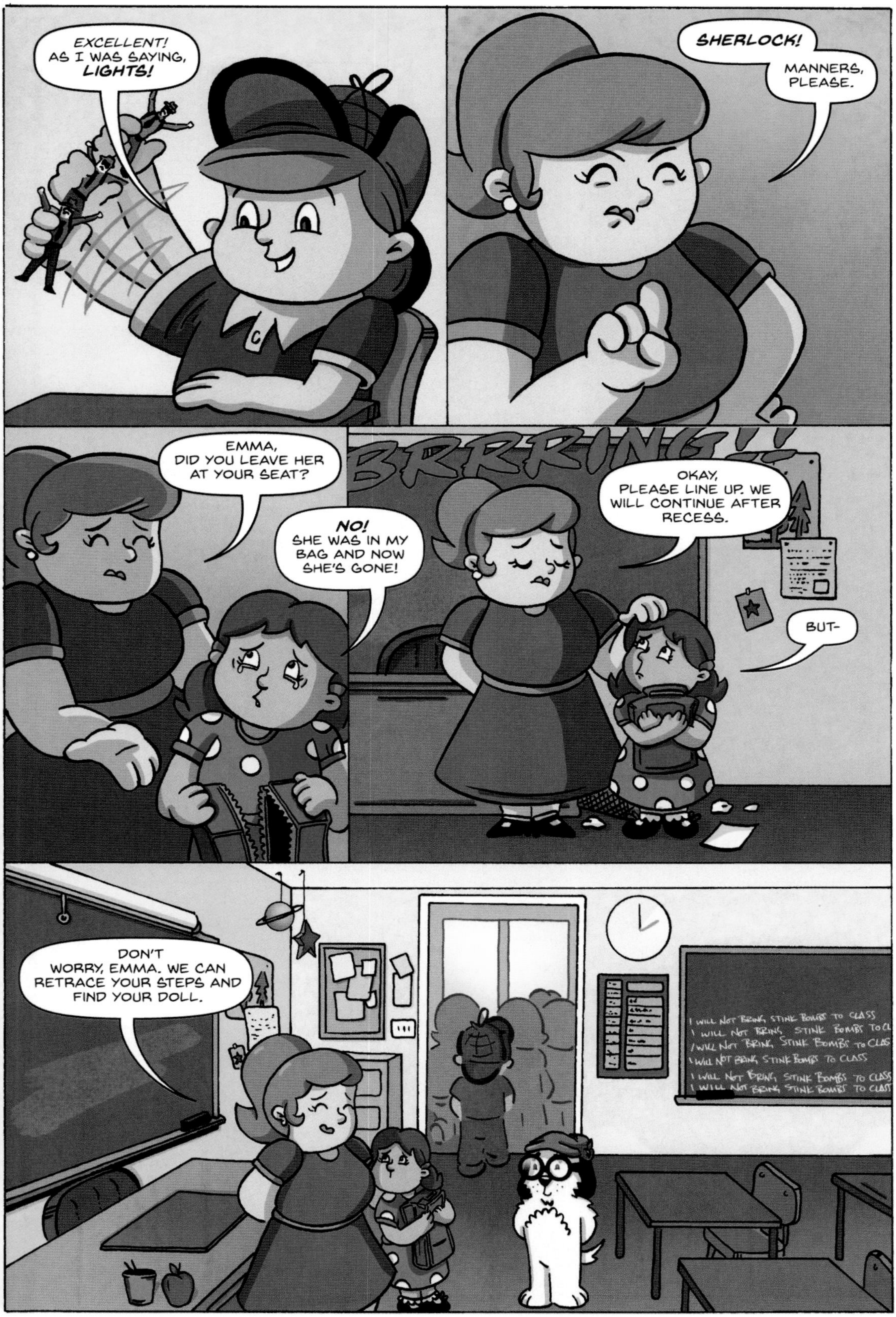
EXCELLENT! AS I WAS SAYING, LIGHTS!
SHERLOCK!
MANNERS, PLEASE.
EMMA, DID YOU LEAVE HER AT YOUR SEAT?
NO! SHE WAS IN MY BAG AND NOW SHE'S GONE!
BRRRING!!
OKAY, PLEASE LINE UP. WE WILL CONTINUE AFTER RECESS.
BUT-
DON'T WORRY, EMMA. WE CAN RETRACE YOUR STEPS AND FIND YOUR DOLL.
I WILL NOT BRING STINK BOMBS TO CLASS
I WILL NOT BRING STINK BOMBS TO CLASS
I WILL NOT BRING STINK BOMBS TO CLASS
I WILL NOT BRING STINK BOMBS TO CLASS
I WILL NOT BRING STINK BOMBS TO CLASS
I WILL NOT BRING STINK BOMBS TO CLASS

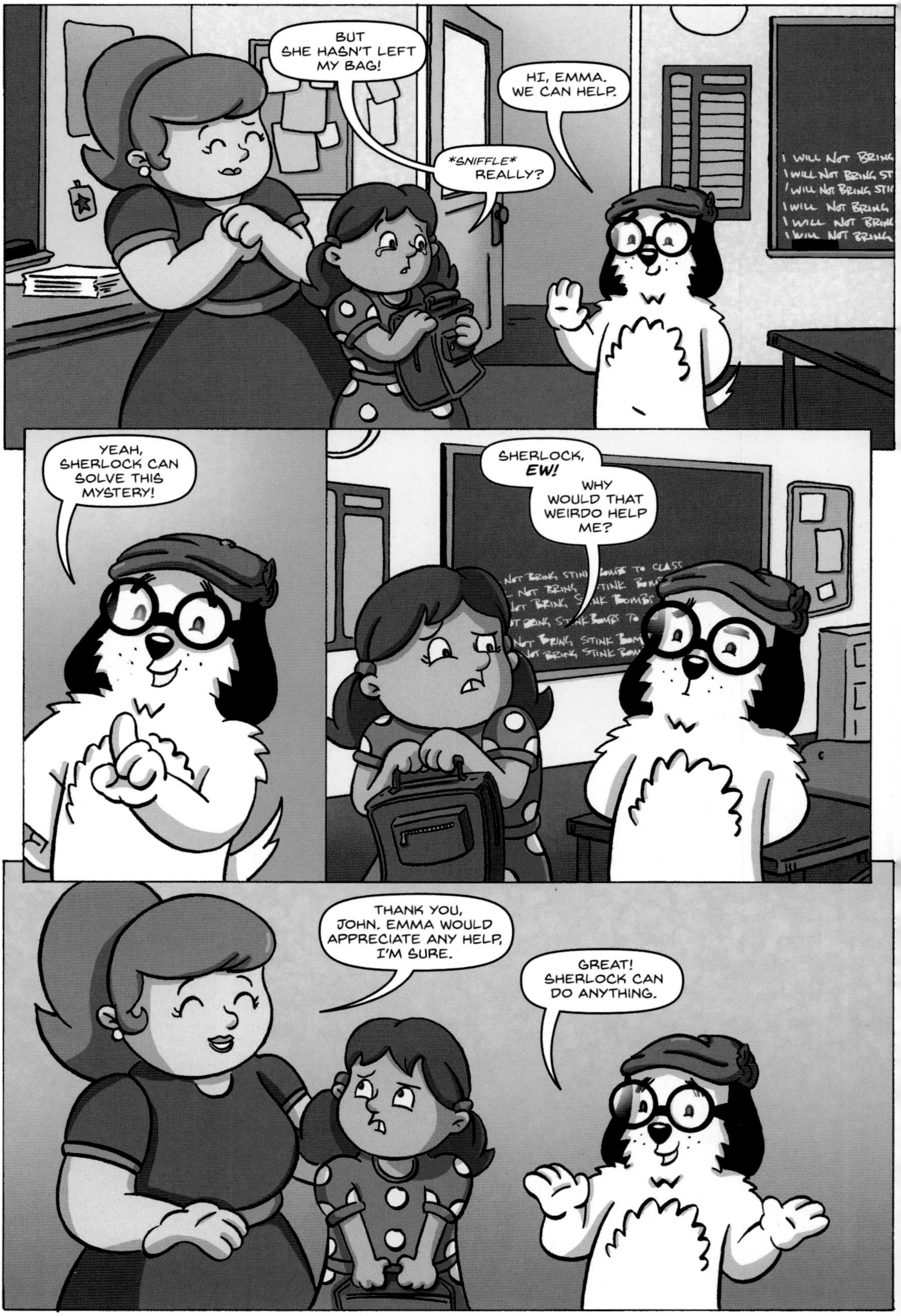

BUT SHE HASN'T LEFT MY BAG!
HI, EMMA. WE CAN HELP.
SNIFFLE REALLY?
I WILL NOT BRING
I WILL NOT BRING
I WILL NOT BRING
I WILL NOT BRING
I WILL NOT BRING
I WILL NOT BRING
YEAH, SHERLOCK CAN SOLVE THIS MYSTERY!
SHERLOCK, EW!
WHY WOULD THAT WEIRDO HELP ME?
NOT BRING STINK BOMBS TO CLASS
THANK YOU, JOHN. EMMA WOULD APPRECIATE ANY HELP, I'M SURE.
GREAT! SHERLOCK CAN DO ANYTHING.

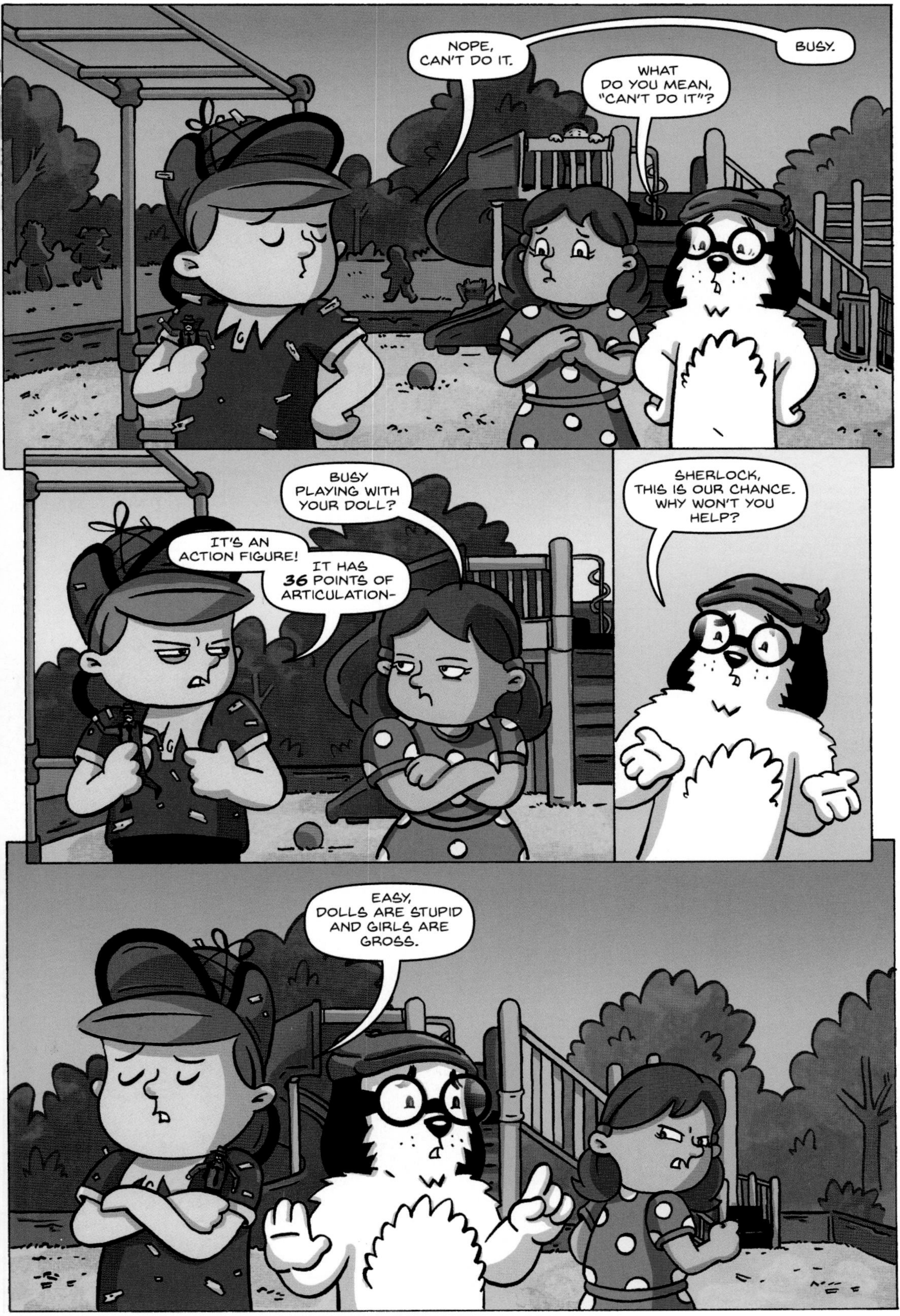
NOPE, CAN'T DO IT.
BUSY.
WHAT DO YOU MEAN, "CAN'T DO IT"?
BUSY PLAYING WITH YOUR DOLL?
IT'S AN ACTION FIGURE!
IT HAS 36 POINTS OF ARTICULATION-
SHERLOCK, THIS IS OUR CHANCE. WHY WON'T YOU HELP?
EASY, DOLLS ARE STUPID AND GIRLS ARE GROSS.

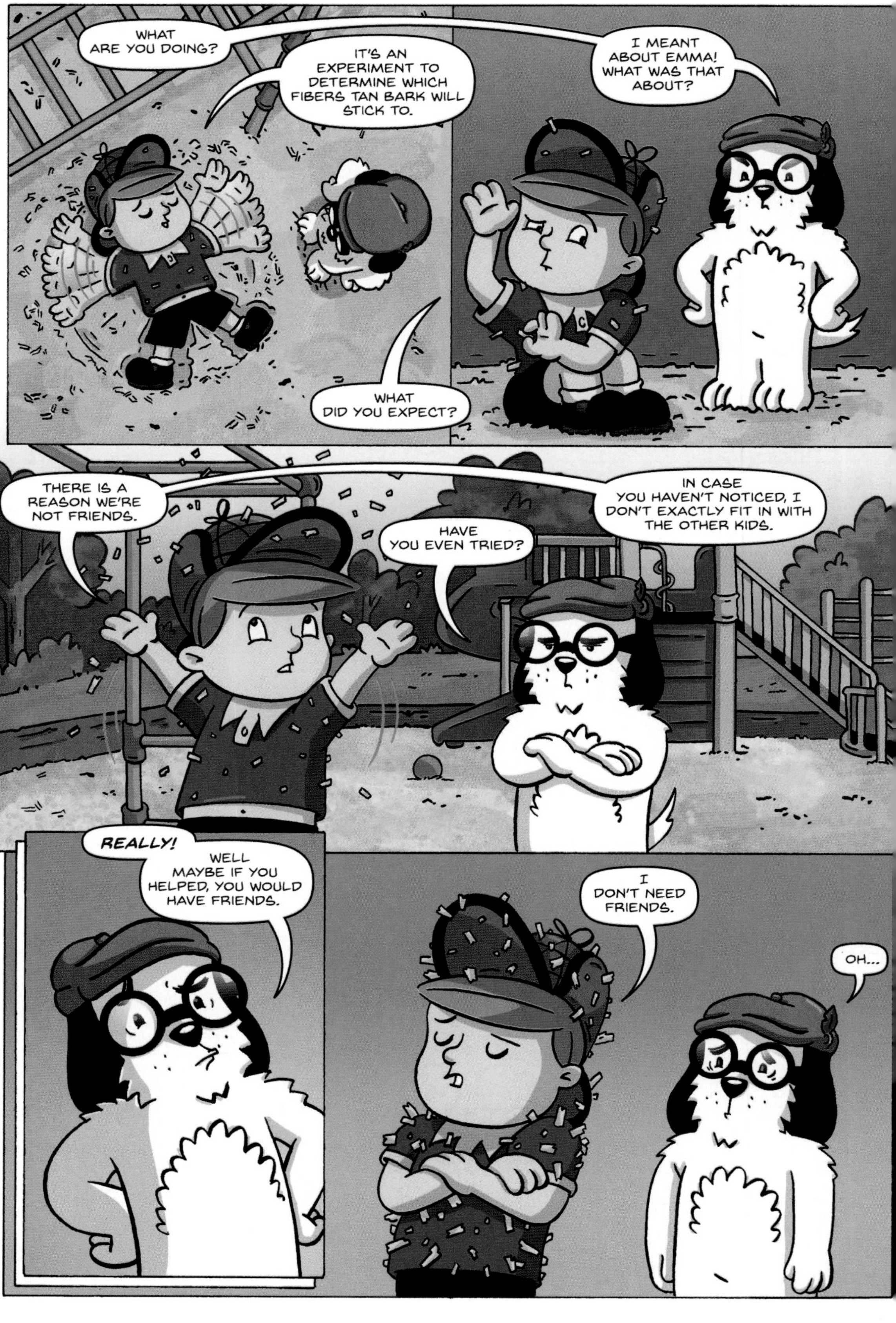
WHAT ARE YOU DOING?
IT'S AN EXPERIMENT TO DETERMINE WHICH FIBERS TAN BARK WILL STICK TO.
I MEANT ABOUT EMMA! WHAT WAS THAT ABOUT?
WHAT DID YOU EXPECT?
THERE IS A REASON WE'RE NOT FRIENDS.
IN CASE YOU HAVEN'T NOTICED, I DON'T EXACTLY FIT IN WITH THE OTHER KIDS.
HAVE YOU EVEN TRIED?
REALLY!
WELL MAYBE IF YOU HELPED, YOU WOULD HAVE FRIENDS.
I DON'T NEED FRIENDS.
OH...

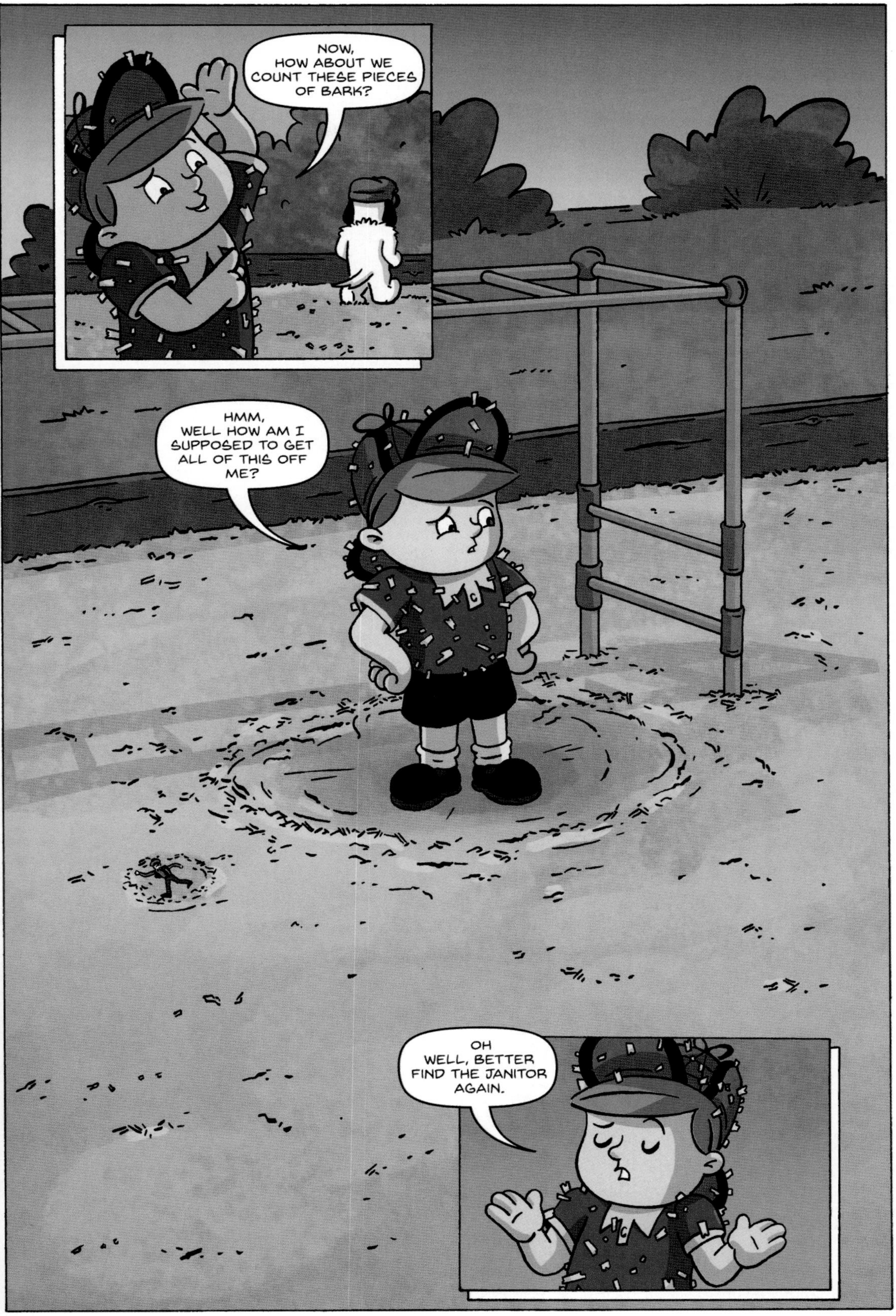
NOW, HOW ABOUT WE COUNT THESE PIECES OF BARK?
HMM, WELL HOW AM I SUPPOSED TO GET ALL OF THIS OFF ME?
OH WELL, BETTER FIND THE JANITOR AGAIN.

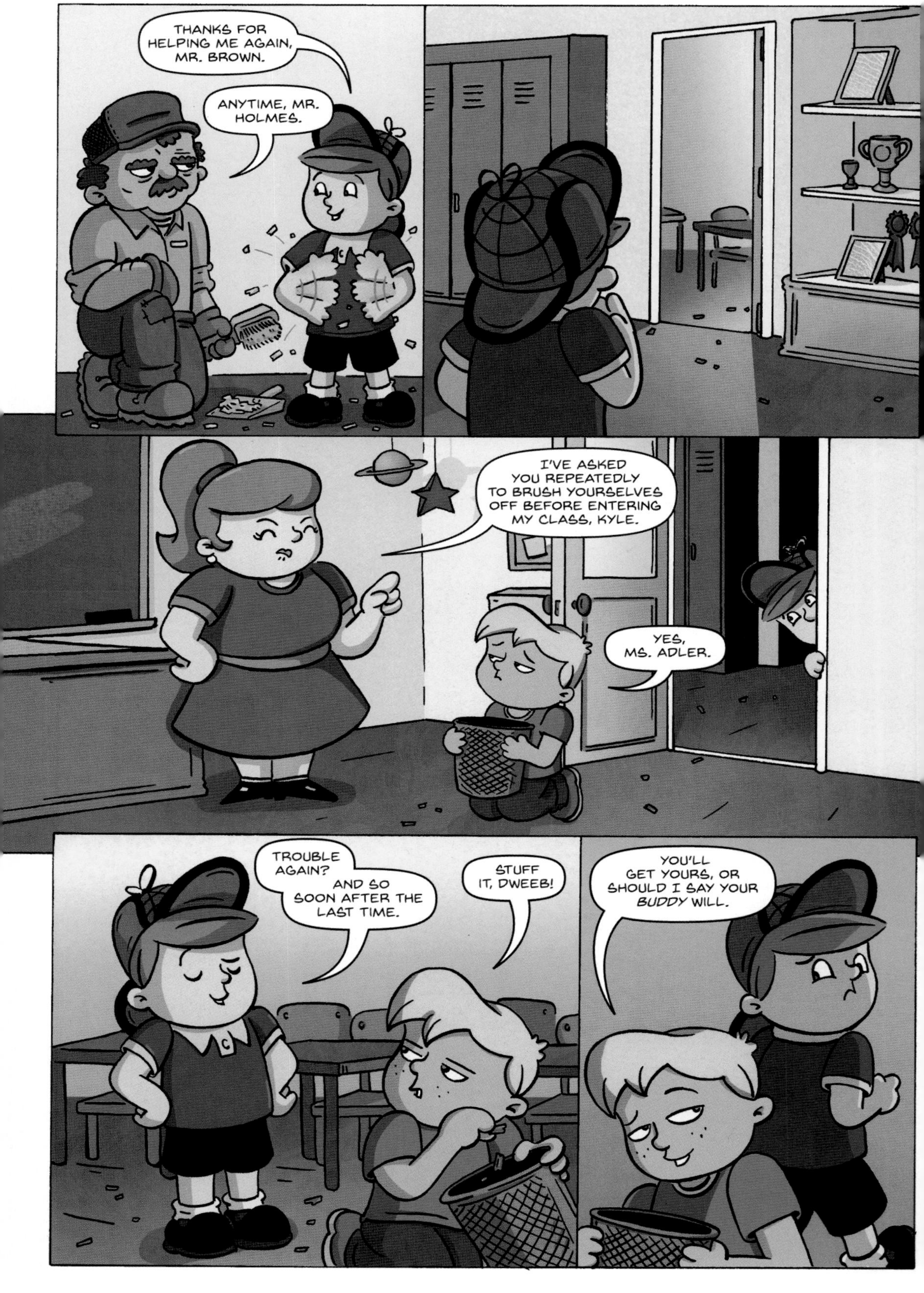

THANKS FOR HELPING ME AGAIN, MR. BROWN.
ANYTIME, MR. HOLMES.
I'VE ASKED YOU REPEATEDLY TO BRUSH YOURSELVES OFF BEFORE ENTERING MY CLASS, KYLE.
YES, MS. ADLER.
TROUBLE AGAIN? AND SO SOON AFTER THE LAST TIME.
STUFF IT, DWEEB!
YOU'LL GET YOURS, OR SHOULD I SAY YOUR *BUDDY* WILL.

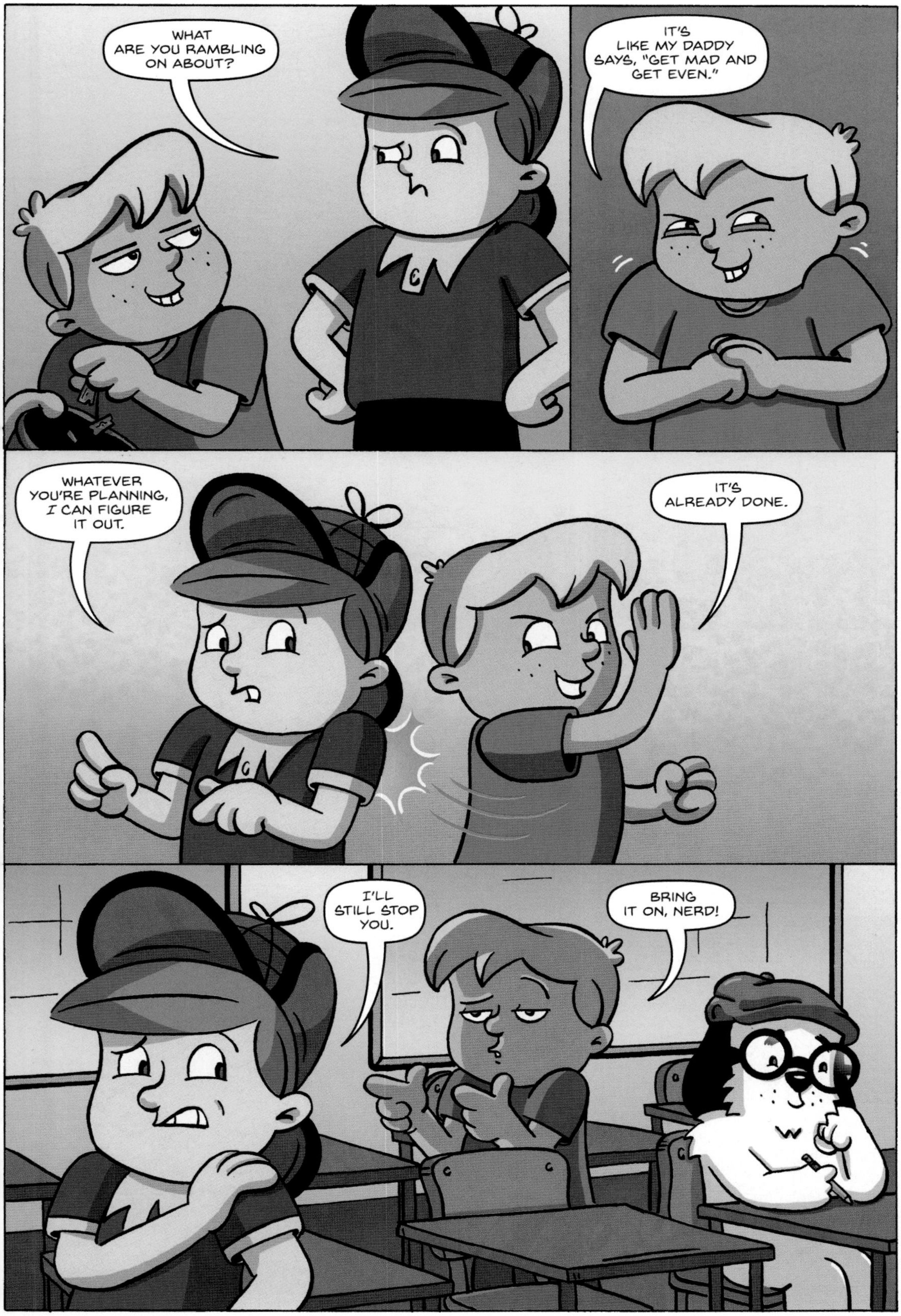
WHAT ARE YOU RAMBLING ON ABOUT?
IT'S LIKE MY DADDY SAYS, "GET MAD AND GET EVEN."
WHATEVER YOU'RE PLANNING, I CAN FIGURE IT OUT.
IT'S ALREADY DONE.
I'LL STILL STOP YOU.
BRING IT ON, NERD!

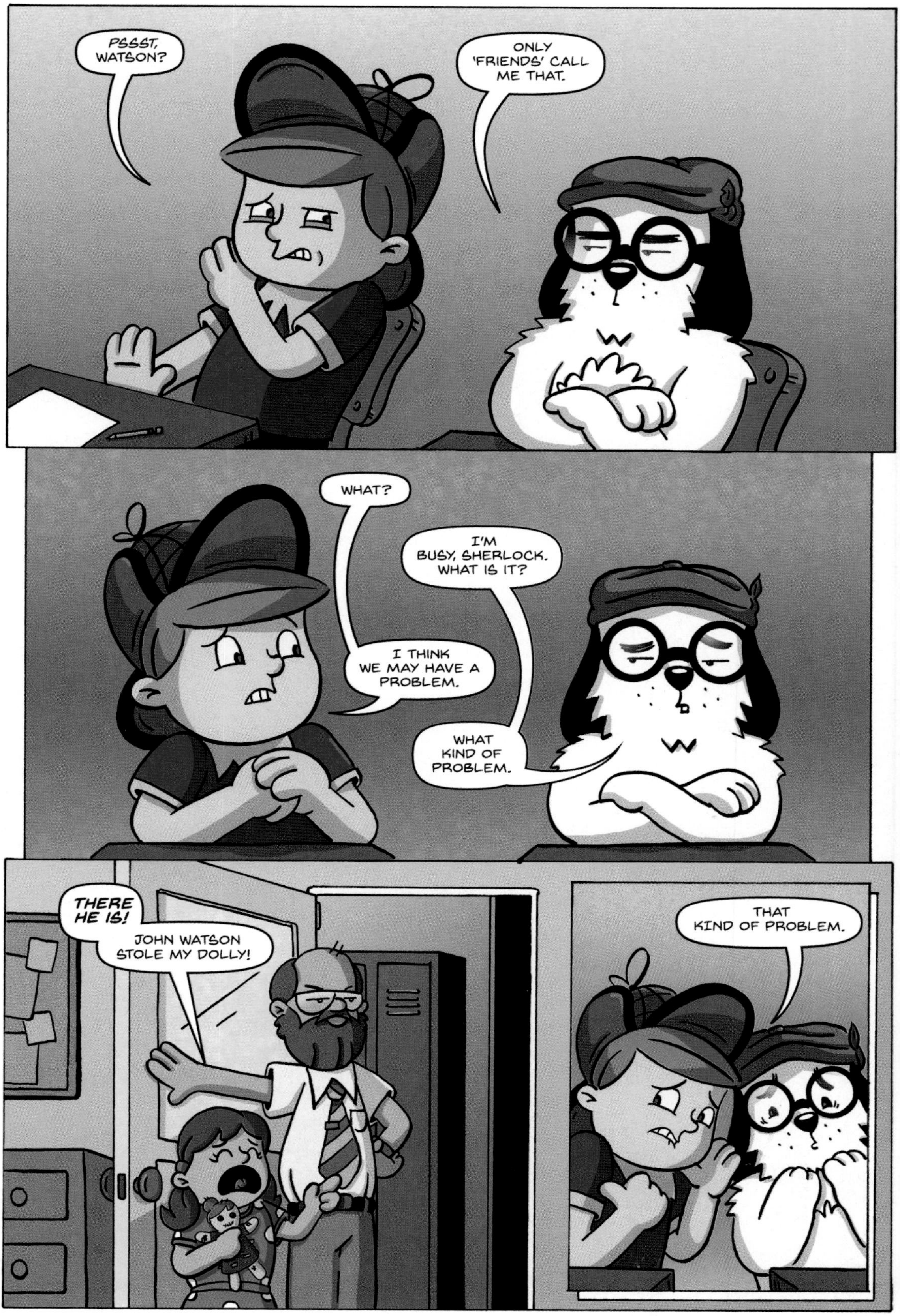
PSSST, WATSON?
ONLY 'FRIENDS' CALL ME THAT.
WHAT?
I'M BUSY, SHERLOCK. WHAT IS IT?
I THINK WE MAY HAVE A PROBLEM.
WHAT KIND OF PROBLEM.
THERE HE IS!
JOHN WATSON STOLE MY DOLLY!
THAT KIND OF PROBLEM.

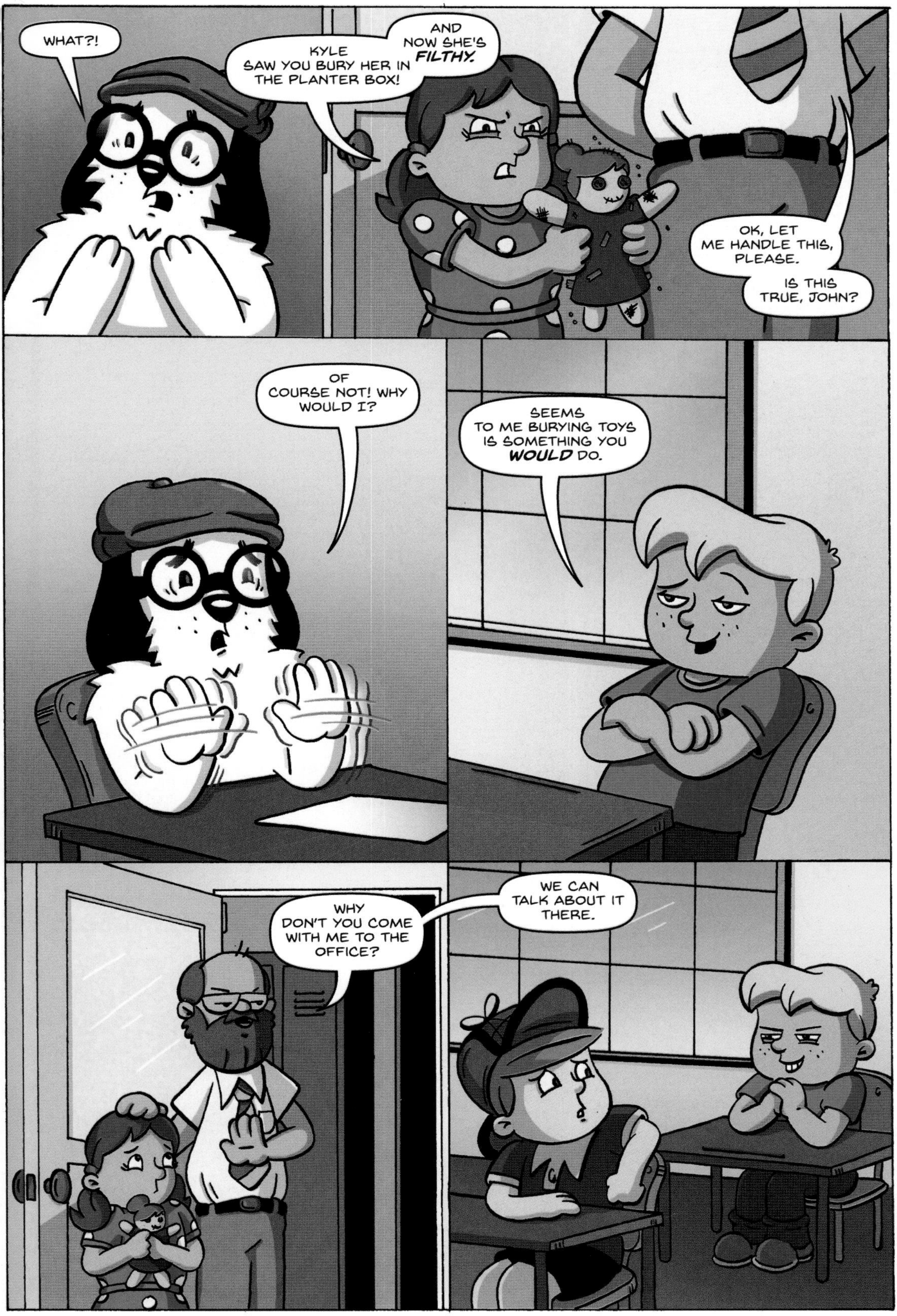
WHAT?!
KYLE SAW YOU BURY HER IN THE PLANTER BOX!
AND NOW SHE'S *FILTHY.*
OK, LET ME HANDLE THIS, PLEASE.
IS THIS TRUE, JOHN?
OF COURSE NOT! WHY WOULD I?
SEEMS TO ME BURYING TOYS IS SOMETHING YOU ***WOULD*** DO.
WHY DON'T YOU COME WITH ME TO THE OFFICE?
WE CAN TALK ABOUT IT THERE.

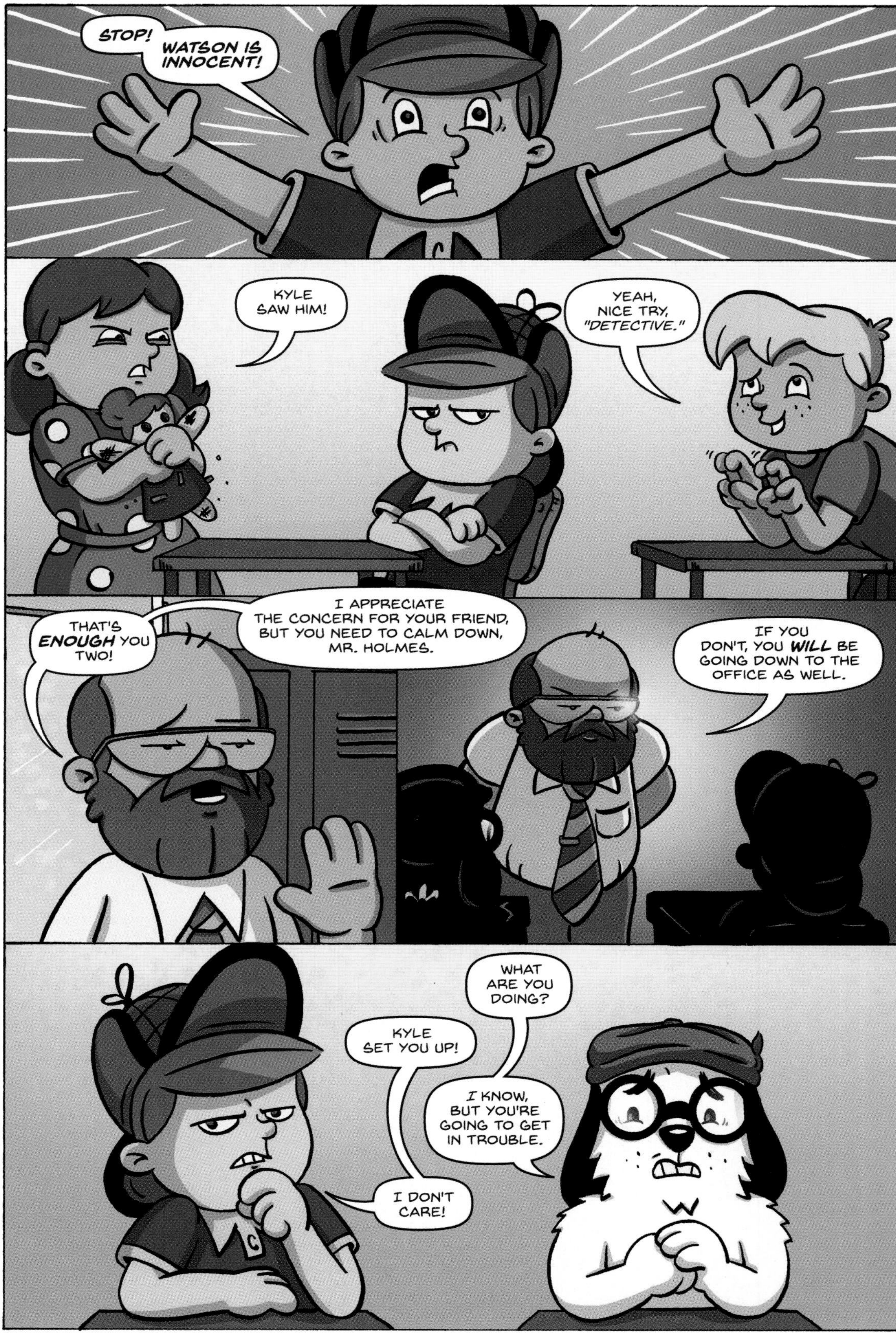
STOP!
WATSON IS INNOCENT!
KYLE SAW HIM!
YEAH, NICE TRY, "DETECTIVE."
THAT'S **ENOUGH** YOU TWO!
I APPRECIATE THE CONCERN FOR YOUR FRIEND, BUT YOU NEED TO CALM DOWN, MR. HOLMES.
IF YOU DON'T, YOU **WILL** BE GOING DOWN TO THE OFFICE AS WELL.
WHAT ARE YOU DOING?
KYLE SET YOU UP!
I KNOW, BUT YOU'RE GOING TO GET IN TROUBLE.
I DON'T CARE!

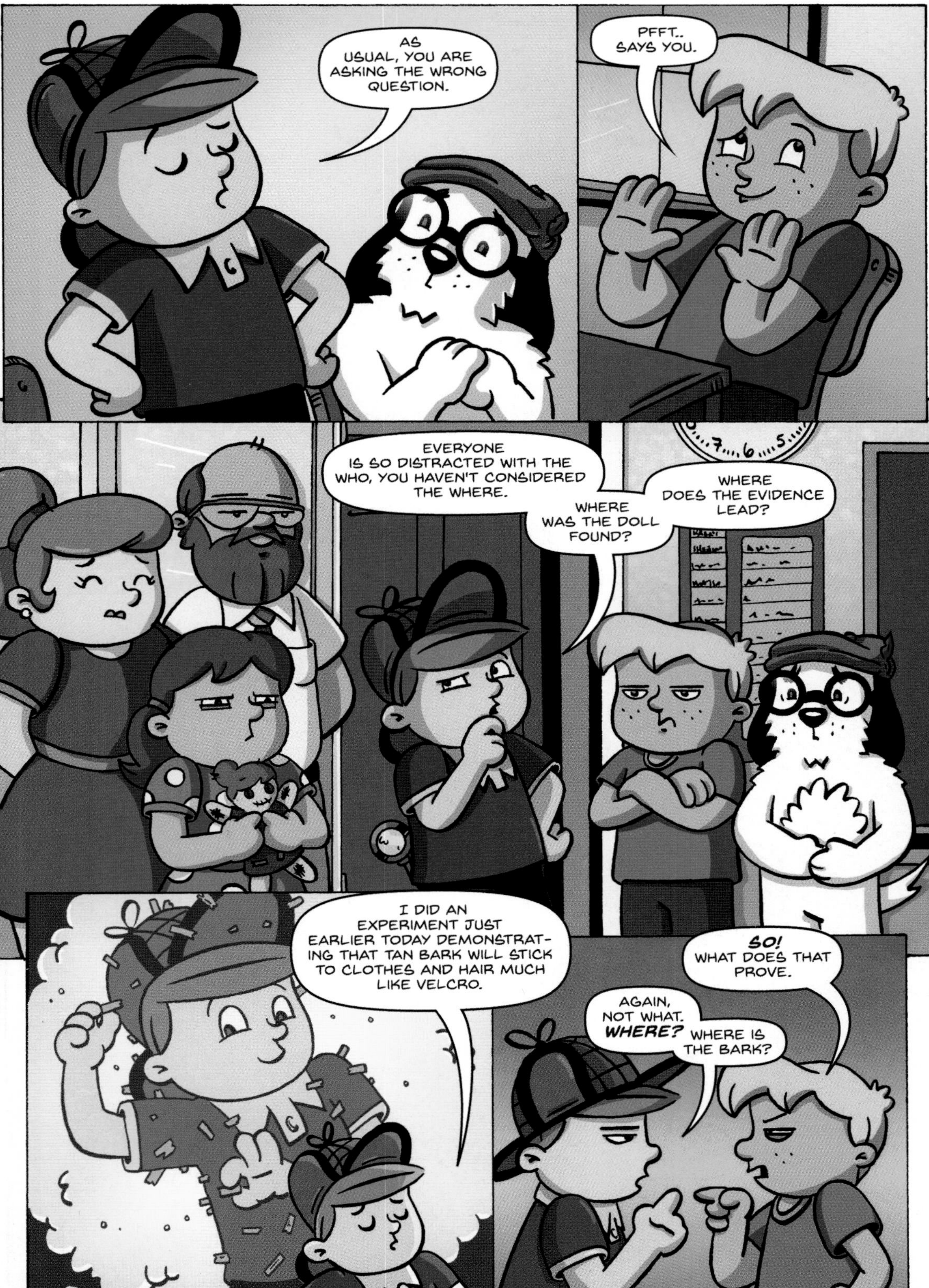
AS USUAL, YOU ARE ASKING THE WRONG QUESTION.
PFFT.. SAYS YOU.
EVERYONE IS SO DISTRACTED WITH THE WHO, YOU HAVEN'T CONSIDERED THE WHERE.
WHERE WAS THE DOLL FOUND?
WHERE DOES THE EVIDENCE LEAD?
I DID AN EXPERIMENT JUST EARLIER TODAY DEMONSTRATING THAT TAN BARK WILL STICK TO CLOTHES AND HAIR MUCH LIKE VELCRO.
SO! WHAT DOES THAT PROVE.
AGAIN, NOT WHAT. WHERE?
WHERE IS THE BARK?

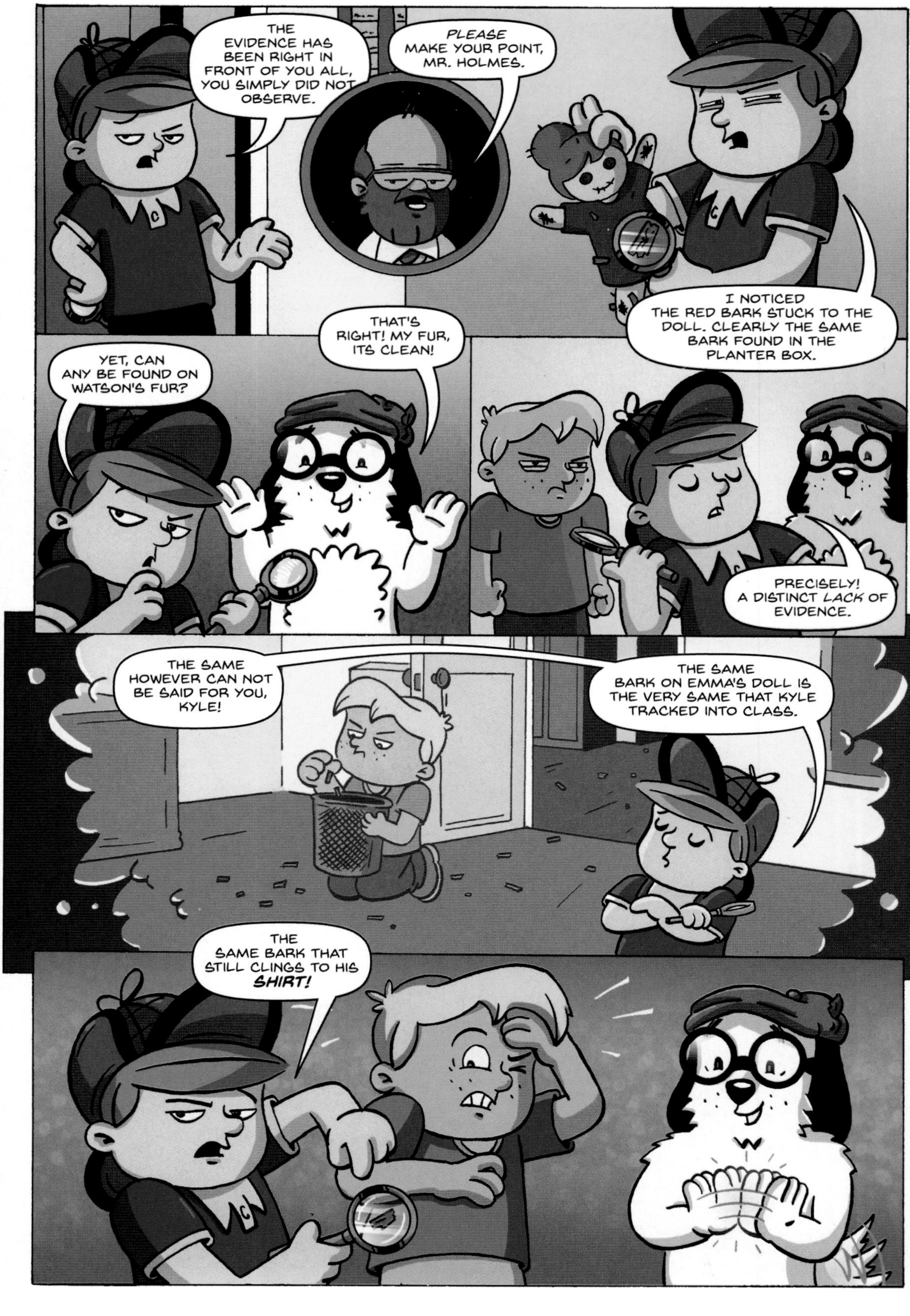
THE EVIDENCE HAS BEEN RIGHT IN FRONT OF YOU ALL, YOU SIMPLY DID NOT OBSERVE.
PLEASE MAKE YOUR POINT, MR. HOLMES.
I NOTICED THE RED BARK STUCK TO THE DOLL. CLEARLY THE SAME BARK FOUND IN THE PLANTER BOX.
YET, CAN ANY BE FOUND ON WATSON'S FUR?
THAT'S RIGHT! MY FUR, ITS CLEAN!
PRECISELY! A DISTINCT *LACK* OF EVIDENCE.
THE SAME BARK ON EMMA'S DOLL IS THE VERY SAME THAT KYLE TRACKED INTO CLASS.
THE SAME HOWEVER CAN NOT BE SAID FOR YOU, KYLE!
THE SAME BARK THAT STILL CLINGS TO HIS ***SHIRT!***

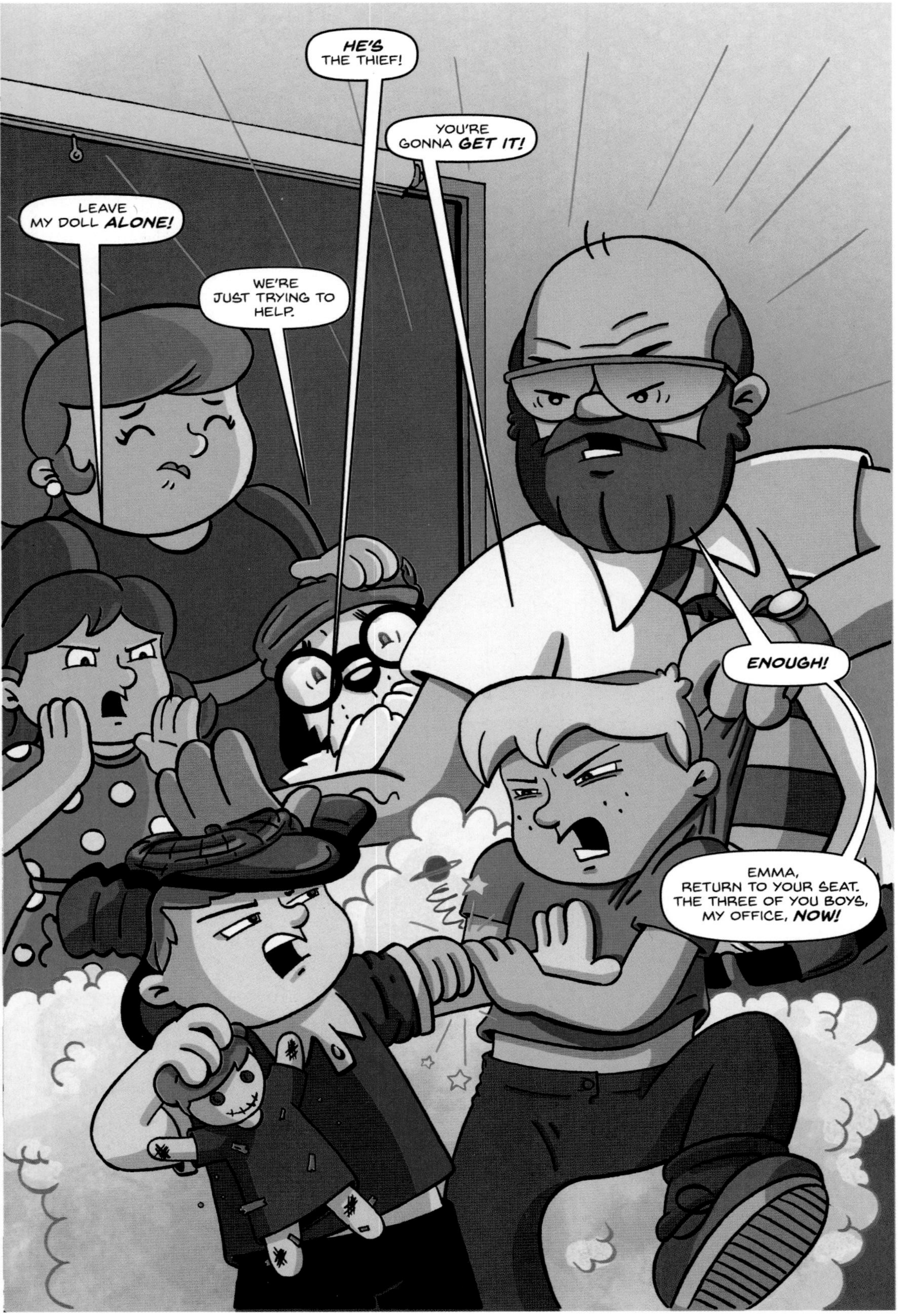
LEAVE MY DOLL ALONE!
WE'RE JUST TRYING TO HELP.
HE'S THE THIEF!
YOU'RE GONNA GET IT!
ENOUGH!
EMMA, RETURN TO YOUR SEAT. THE THREE OF YOU BOYS, MY OFFICE, NOW!

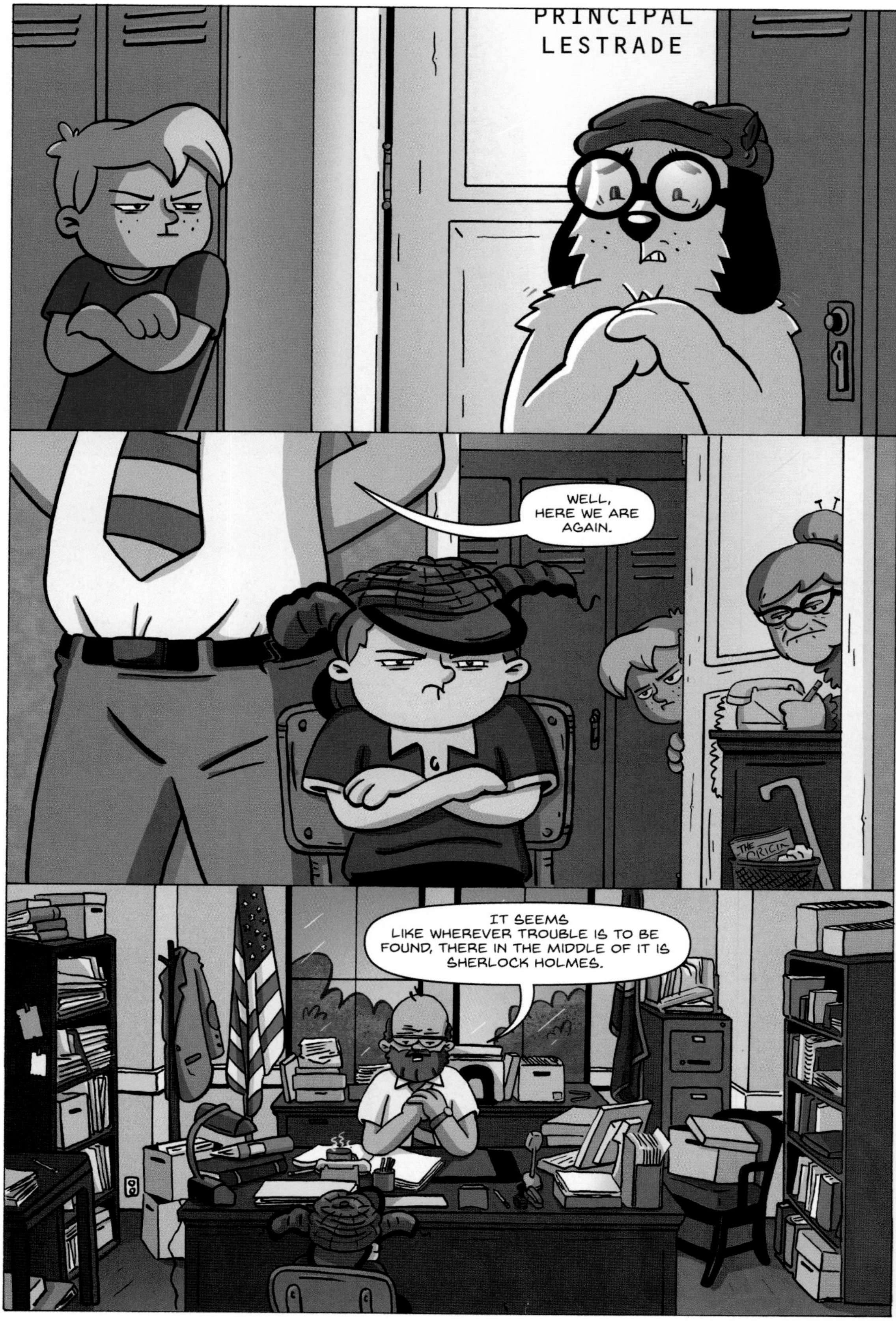
PRINCIPAL
LESTRADE
WELL, HERE WE ARE AGAIN.
IT SEEMS LIKE WHEREVER TROUBLE IS TO BE FOUND, THERE IN THE MIDDLE OF IT IS SHERLOCK HOLMES.

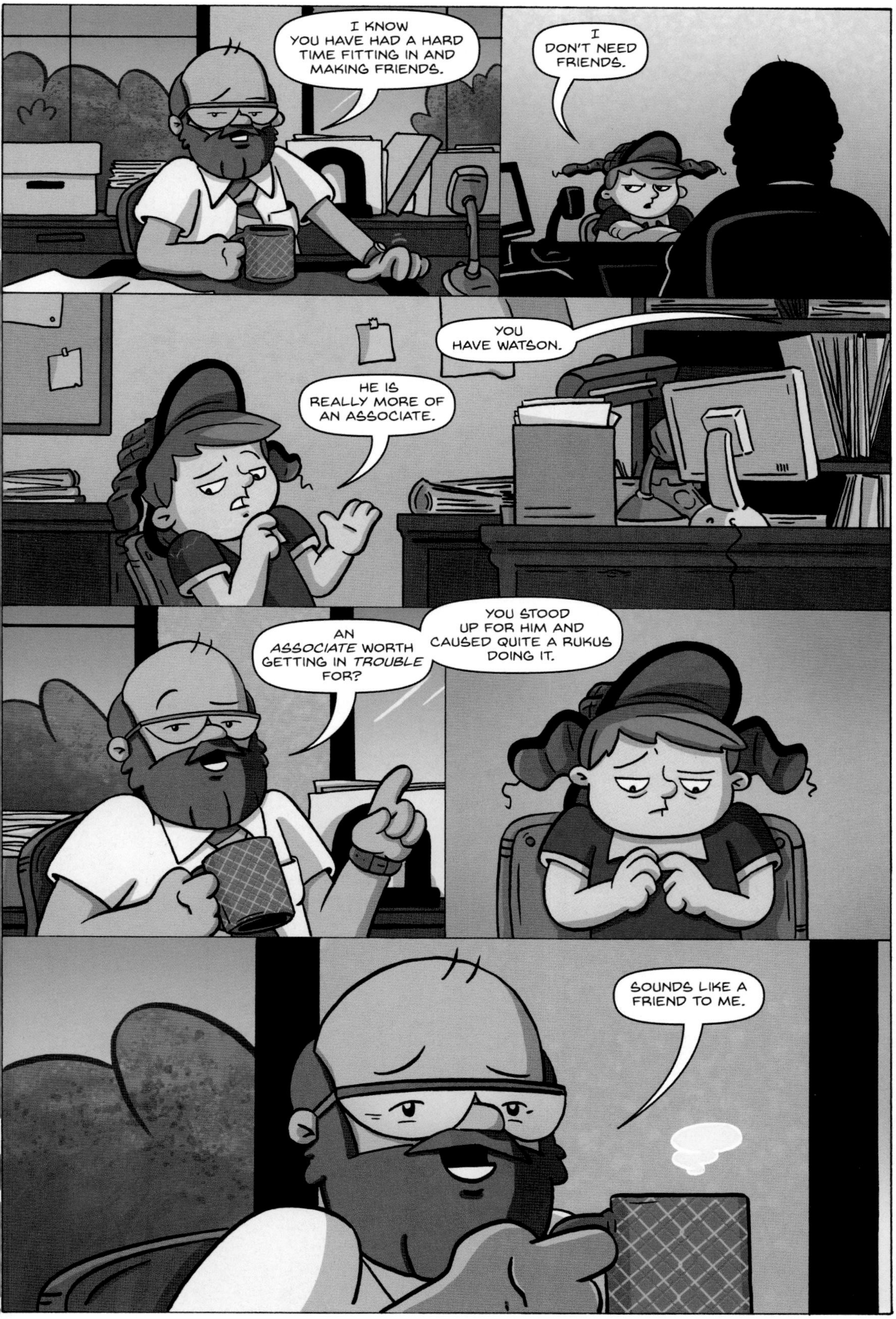
I KNOW YOU HAVE HAD A HARD TIME FITTING IN AND MAKING FRIENDS.
I DON'T NEED FRIENDS.
YOU HAVE WATSON.
HE IS REALLY MORE OF AN ASSOCIATE.
AN *ASSOCIATE* WORTH GETTING IN *TROUBLE* FOR?
YOU STOOD UP FOR HIM AND CAUSED QUITE A RUKUS DOING IT.
SOUNDS LIKE A FRIEND TO ME.

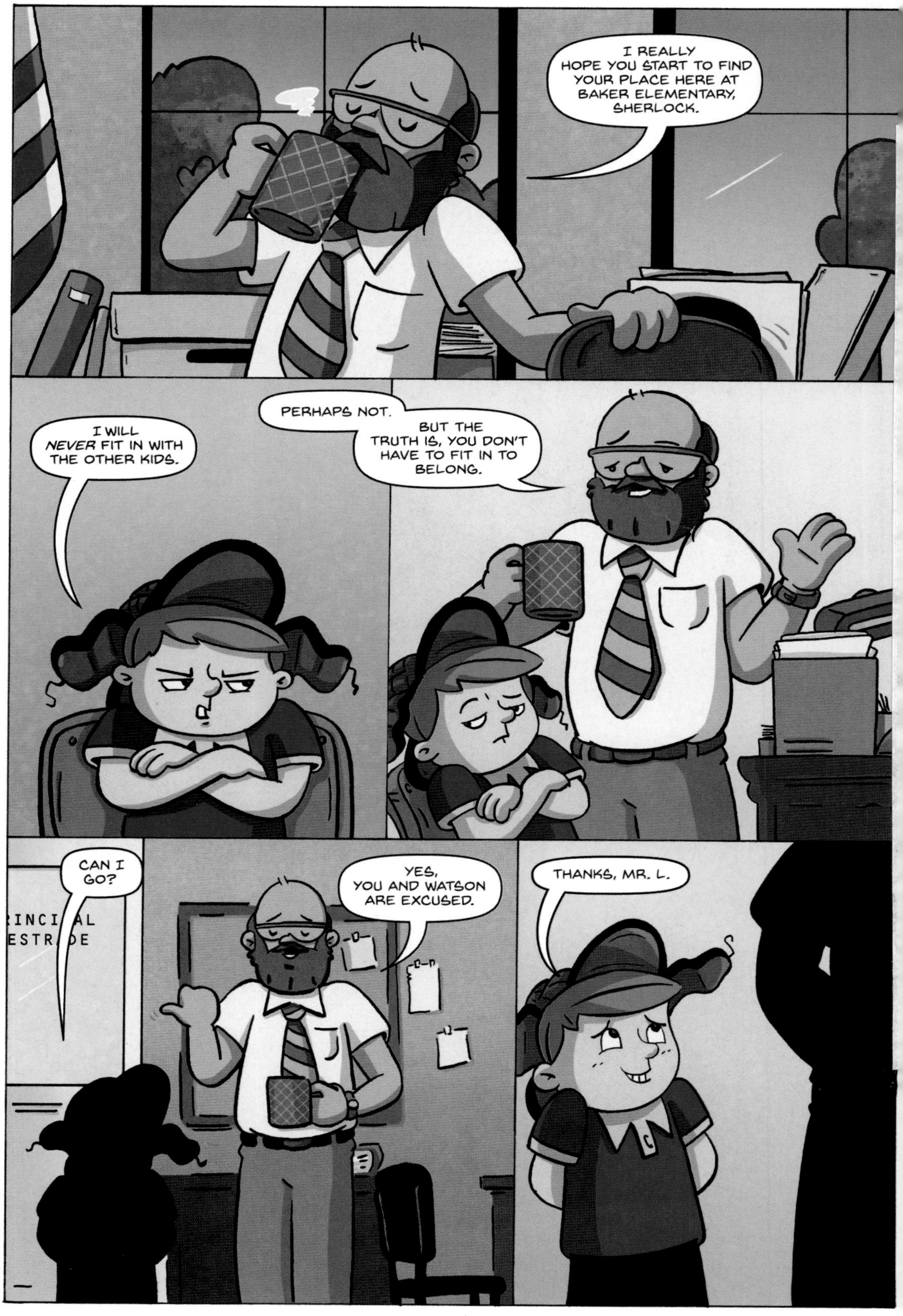
I REALLY HOPE YOU START TO FIND YOUR PLACE HERE AT BAKER ELEMENTARY, SHERLOCK.
I WILL *NEVER* FIT IN WITH THE OTHER KIDS.
PERHAPS NOT.
BUT THE TRUTH IS, YOU DON'T HAVE TO FIT IN TO BELONG.
CAN I GO?
YES, YOU AND WATSON ARE EXCUSED.
THANKS, MR. L.

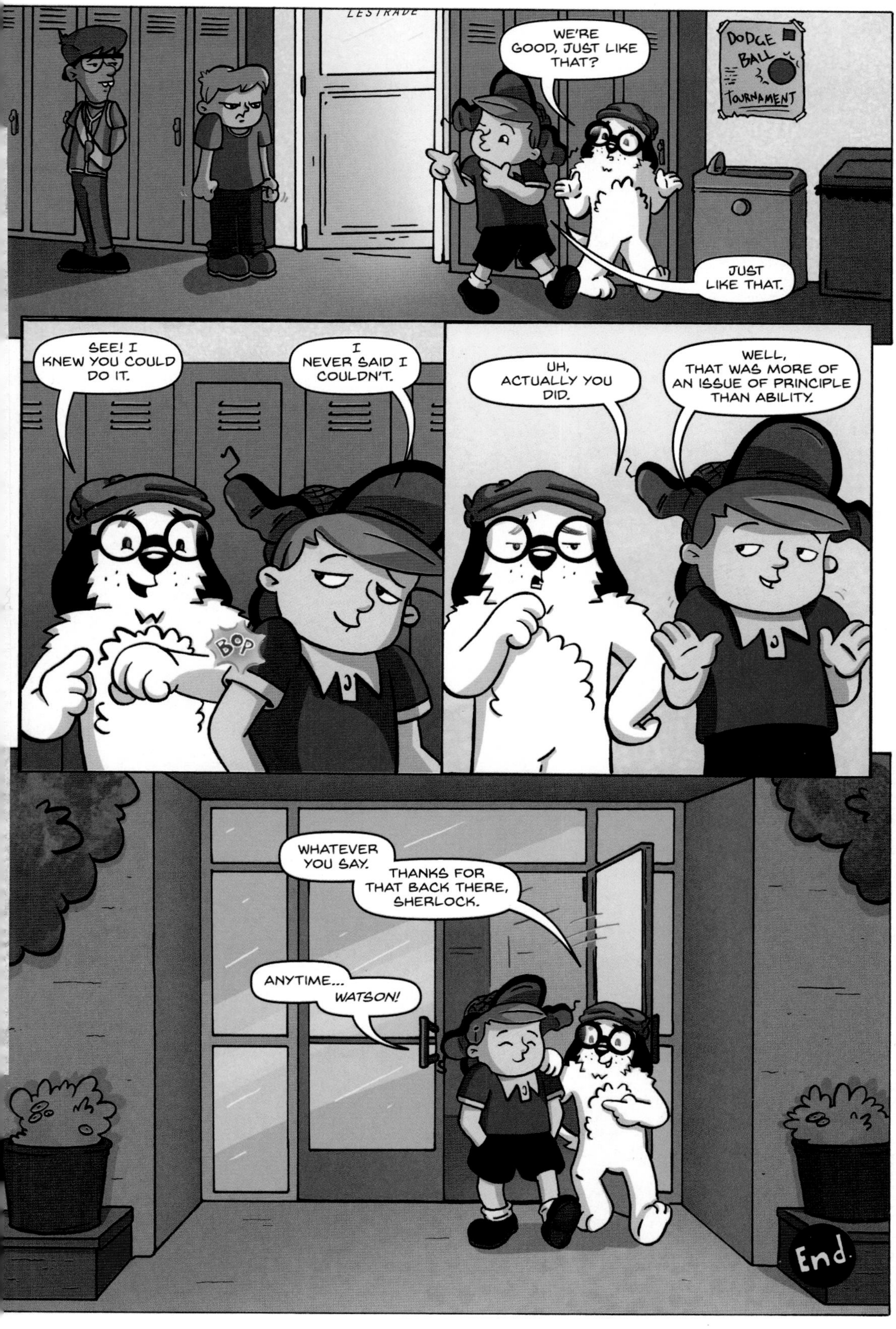
LESTRADE
WE'RE GOOD, JUST LIKE THAT?
JUST LIKE THAT.
DODGE BALL TOURNAMENT
SEE! I KNEW YOU COULD DO IT.
BOP
I NEVER SAID I COULDN'T.
UH, ACTUALLY YOU DID.
WELL, THAT WAS MORE OF AN ISSUE OF PRINCIPLE THAN ABILITY.
WHATEVER YOU SAY.
THANKS FOR THAT BACK THERE, SHERLOCK.
ANYTIME... WATSON!
End.

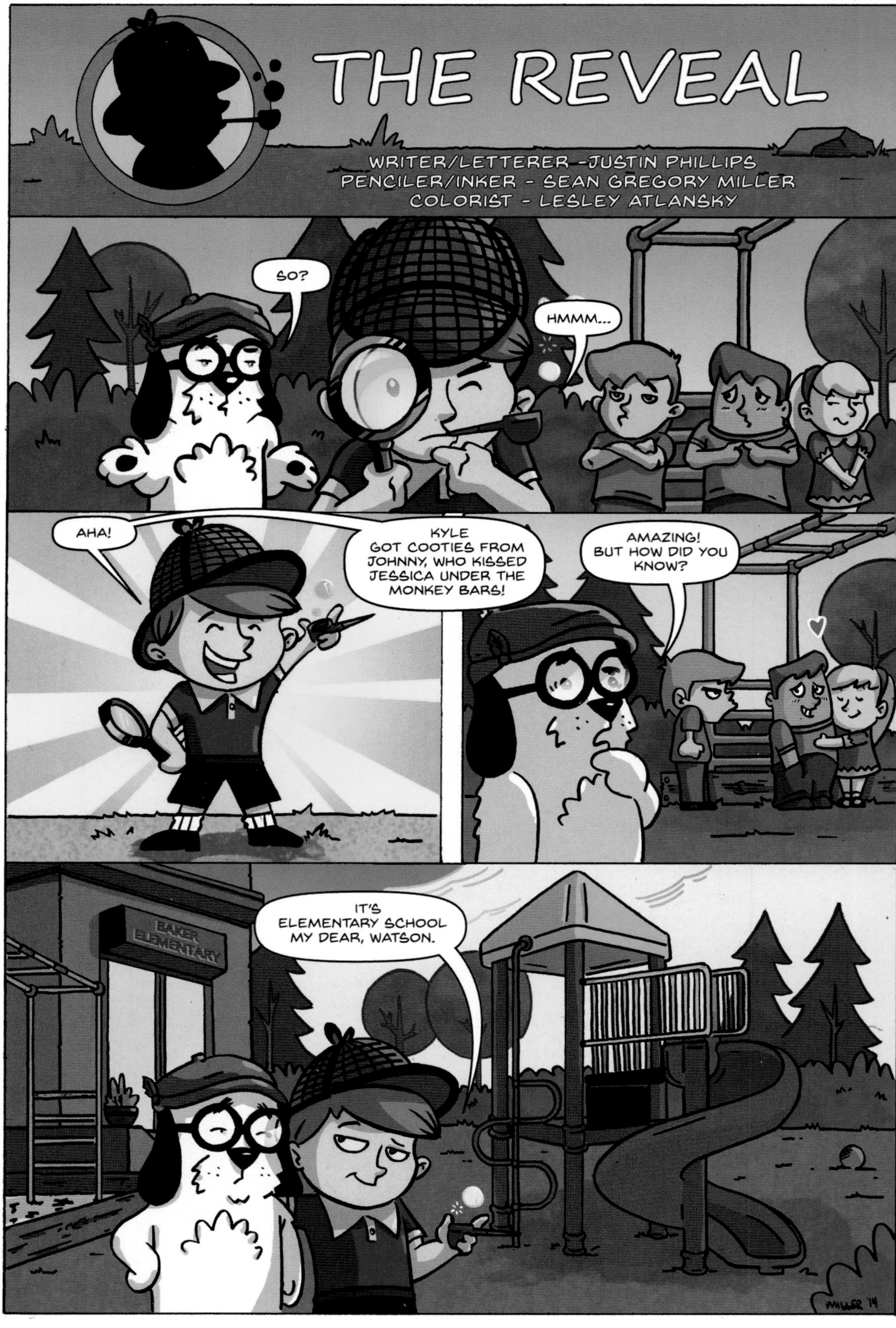
THE REVEAL
WRITER/LETTERER -JUSTIN PHILLIPS
PENCILER/INKER - SEAN GREGORY MILLER
COLORIST - LESLEY ATLANSKY
SO?
HMMM...
AHA!
KYLE GOT COOTIES FROM JOHNNY, WHO KISSED JESSICA UNDER THE MONKEY BARS!
AMAZING! BUT HOW DID YOU KNOW?
BAKER ELEMENTARY
IT'S ELEMENTARY SCHOOL MY DEAR, WATSON.
MILLER '14

LEARN TO DRAW!

LEARN TO DRAW IN SIX EASY STEPS! ALL YOU NEED IS A PENCIL, PEN, AND PAPER.

KYLE

AS ALWAYS, WE START WITH A CIRCLE!

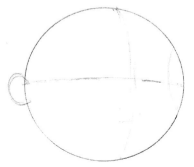

NEXT, WE ADD HIS EAR AND A FEW LINES TO INDICATE WHERE HIS EYES WILL BE,

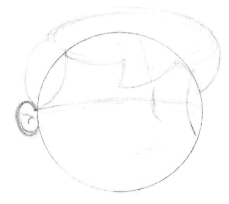

NOW WE'LL ADD HIS HAIR. REMEMBER TO KEEP EVERYTHING LIGHT AND LOOSE!

KYLE IS THE BULLY SO BE SURE TO GIVE HIM A "GRUMPY" LOOK.

YOU'RE ALMOST DONE! DARKEN THE LINES YOU WANT TO KEEP FOR YOUR DRAWING.

NOW DRAW OVER YOUR LINES WITH A PEN AND YOU'RE DONE!

YOU'VE LEARNED THE BASICS. NOW LET'S TRY SOMETHING MORE CHALLENGING!

EXPRESSIONS

SUSPICIOUS

CONTENT

SCARED/WORRIED

HAPPY

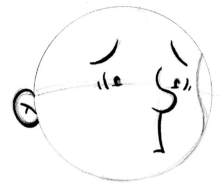

SAD/LONELY

DISGUSTED

EXPRESSIONS ON A CHARACTER'S FACE ARE A LARGE PART OF STORYTELLING! EXPRESSIONS TELL YOU WHAT A CHARACTER IS THINKING OR FELLING ABOUT A SITUATION. JUST THINK HOW BORING A STORY WOULD BE IF THE CHARACTERS ONLY MADE ONE EXPRESSION!

COLORING WITH LESLEY!

IN ISSUE #1 OF KID SHERLOCK, LESLEY TALKED ABOUT HOW IMPORTANT IT WAS TO READ THE SCRIPT TO LOOK FOR COLORING CLUES. SHE DOESN'T WANT TO COLOR SHERLOCK IN HIS SUNNY FRONT YARD WHEN HE IS SUPPOSED TO BE LOOKING FOR CLUES UNDER A FULL MOON!

THERE IS ANOTHER KIND OF CLUE TO FIND IN THE SCRIPT, AND THAT IS THE MOOD. IS WATSON SAD? IS PRINCIPAL LESTRADE ANGRY? IS KYLE UP TO NO GOOD AGAIN? LESLEY CAN USE COLOR TO HELP EMPHASIZE WHAT THEY ARE FEELING, EVEN IN THE COLORS AREN'T THE "REAL" COLORS OF THE SETTING.

WHEN EMMA REALIZES HER DOLL IS MISSING, LESLEY CHANGED THE COLOR BEHIND HER. EVERY OTHER PANEL ON THE PAGE HAS THE YELLOWS AND GREENS OF THE CLASSROOM. THE RED AND PURPLES OF THE BACKGROUND OF THIS PANEL MAKE IT STAND OUT AND REFLECT EMMA'S DESPAIR AT LOSING HER FAVORITE DOLLY.

IF YOU THINK ABOUT IT, COLOR CAN REALLY HELP SHOW MOOD. YELLOW MIGHT HELP MAKE THINGS FEEL BRIGHT AND HAPPY. REDS AND ORANGES CAN SHOW ANGER OR ACTION.

LATER, WHEN MS. HUDSON WAS COMFORTING EMMA, LESLEY USED A SOFT BLUE BACKGROUND TO HELP GIVE THE PANEL THE SAME SADNESS THAT EMMA IS FEELING.

COLORING WITH LESLEY!

ONE OF THE MOST FUN THINGS FOR
LESLEY TO COLOR IN KID SHERLOCK
IS THE CONFLICT BETWEEN SHERLOCK
AND KYLE.

LESLEY LIKES TO USE HOT COLORS
LIKE RED AND ORANGE TO MAKE
THOSE INTERACTIONS STAND OUT.

HERE IS A GREAT EXAMPLE THAT SHOWS HOW COLOR CAN CHANGE THE
MOOD OF A SCENE. FOR THE BIG CLASSROOM FIGHT, LESLEY COULD
HAVE JUST LEFT THE CLASSROOM IN ITS NORMAL COLORS (AS SEEN ON
THE LEFT).

SINCE THIS IS AN IMPORTANT SCENE THAT TAKES UP A WHOLE PAGE,
LESLEY WANTED TO REALLY MAKE IT STAND OUT. SHE ADDED THE RED
GLOW BEHIND EVERYONE AND PUT SOME RED REFLECTIONS ON PRINCI-
PAL LESTRADE'S GLASSES. THIS HELPED STRESS TO THE READER JUST
HOW MUCH TROUBLE THEY ARE IN WITH THE PRINCIPAL!

COLOR, COLOR, COLOR!

NOW IT'S YOUR
TURN TO PRACTICE COLORING
THE CAST OF CHARACTERS!

USE MARKERS OR CRAYONS
TO COLOR THIS PAGE.

YOU CAN EVEN SCAN IT ON YOUR COMPUTER
AND PRINT MULTIPULE COPIES TO
PRACTICE COLORING AGAIN
AND AGAIN!

MAZE!

HELP SHERLOCK FIND THE CLUE AT THE END OF THE MAZE!

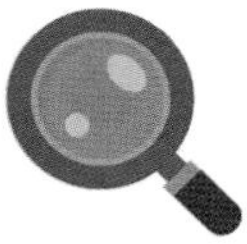

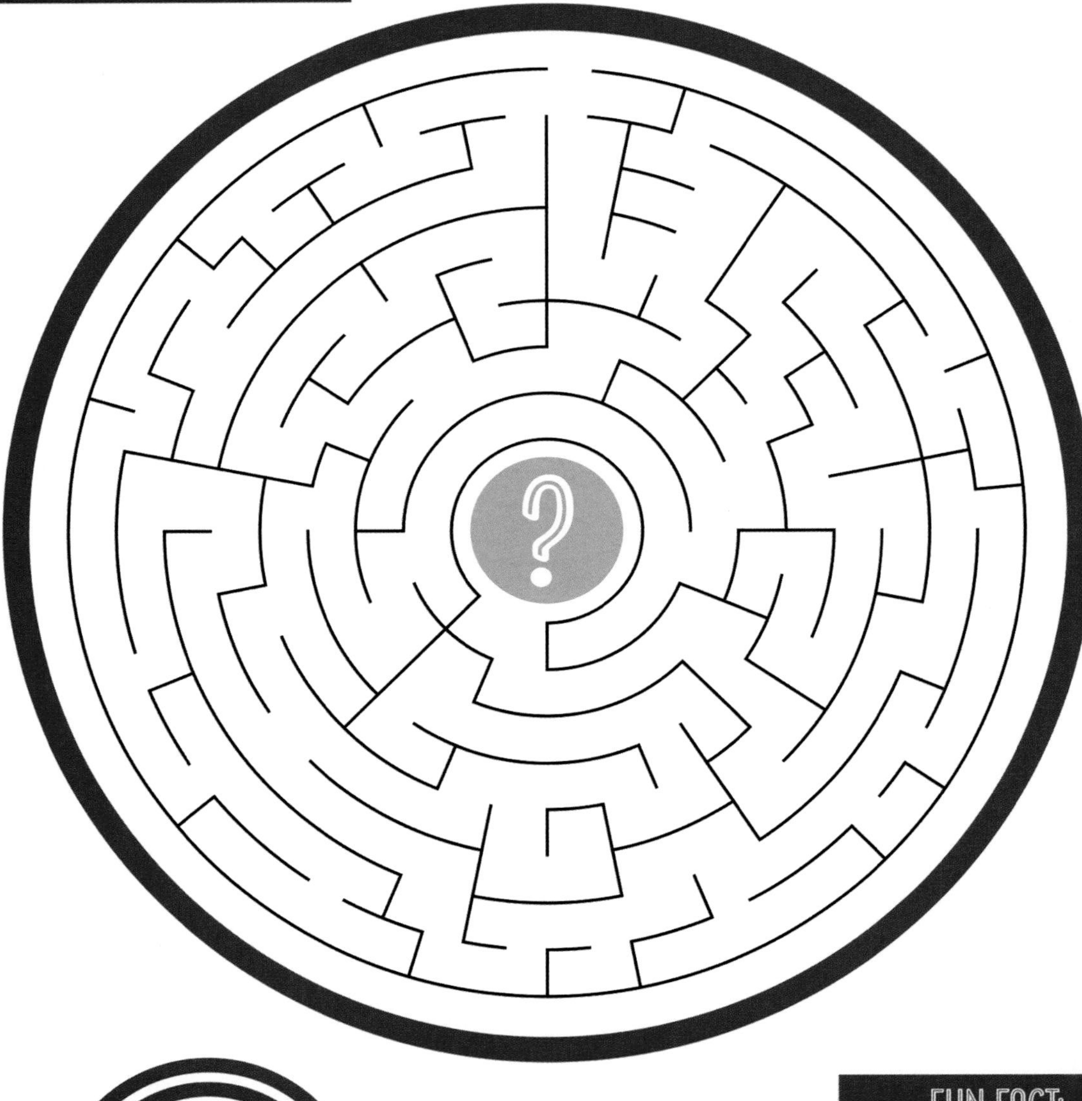
?

HINT: ACTUALLY, THERE ARE NO HINTS FOR THIS ONE. WHERE'S THE FUN IN THAT?!

FUN FACT: THE FIRST HEDGE MAZES WERE BUILT TO ENTERTAIN ROYALT

WORD SEARCH!

SEE IF YOU CAN
FIND ALL THE WORDS
FROM THIS ISSUE
HIDDEN IN THE
WORD SEARCH!

```
D V B N H D P N I F V Y
A K E D P W Q Z Y N G H
J J K S C H O O L W A V
D M U E A A L P X S A I
O Y T A I Q E C P W R M
L S S R N M W X M K K P
L T O C O M I C X Z B C
L E L H U X N C D R A W
K R V M I S S I N G R I
B Y E Z H O R Q E T K G
S Y A A V S W U D S C V
T G I I Q Q Y C Q U K J
```

COMIC

MISSING

DOLL

SEARCH

SOLVE

MYSTERY

SCHOOL

BARK

DID YOU FIND THEM ALL?

HINT:
LOOK FOR
WORDS GOING
ACROSS *AND*
UP AND DOWN!

FAN ART!

CHECK OUT THESE PICTURES FROM OUR FANS!
(WE HAVE THOSE)

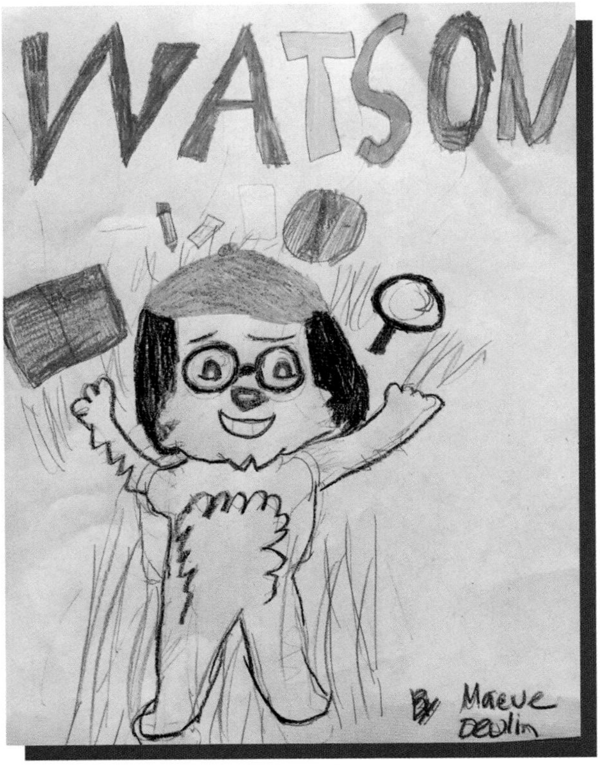
WATSON
By Maeve Devlin

WATSON BY MAEVE
AGE 9
FROM ASHLAND, MA.

SHERLOCK BY FIONA
AGE 5
FROM ASHLAND, MA.

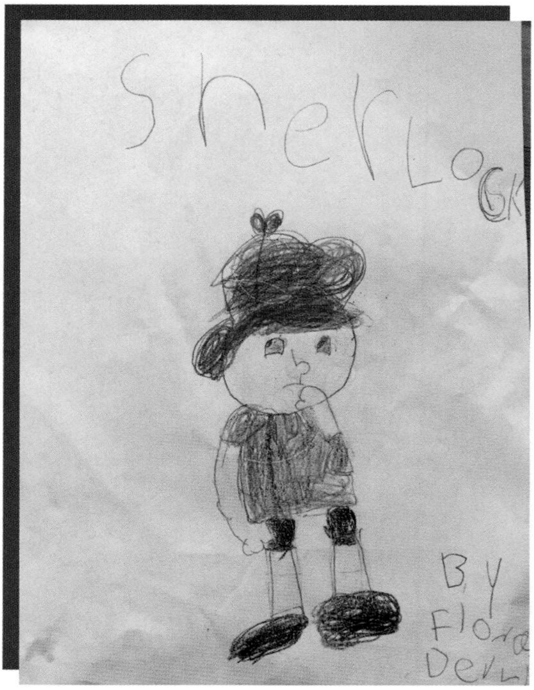
SherLock
By

IF YOU HAVE ANY ART THAT YOU WOULD LIKE TO SHARE OR WOULD LIKE TO SEND US A LETTER, YOU CAN!

WE'D LOVE TO HEAR FROM YOU!

YOU CAN REACH US AT:
KIDSHERLOCKANDWATSON@GMAIL.COM

Kid Sherlock

CASE FILE 3:
"Missing Equipment"

THE CREATIVE TEAM

Written
and lettered by
JUSTIN PHILLIPS

Art by
SEAN GREGORY MILLER

Colors by
LESLEY ATLANSKY

Kid Sherlock

CREATED BY JUSTIN PHILLIPS AND SEAN GREGORY MILLER
BASED ON CHARACTERS BY SIR ARTHUR CONAN DOYLE

Bryan Seaton: Publisher/ CEO • **Shawn Gabborin:** Editor In Chief • **Jason Martin:** Publisher-Danger Zone • **Nicole D'Andria:** Marketing Director/Editor
Jim Dietz: Social Media Manager • **Danielle Davison:** Executive Administrator • **Chad Cicconi:** Moriarty's Understudy • **Shawn Pryor:** President of Creator Relations
KID SHERLOCK #3, August, 2017. Copyright Justin Phillips, 2017. Published by Action Lab Entertainment. All rights reserved. All characters are fictional. Any likeness to anyone living or dead is purely coincidental. No part of this publication may be reproduced or transmitted without permission, except for review purposes. Printed in Canada. First Printing.

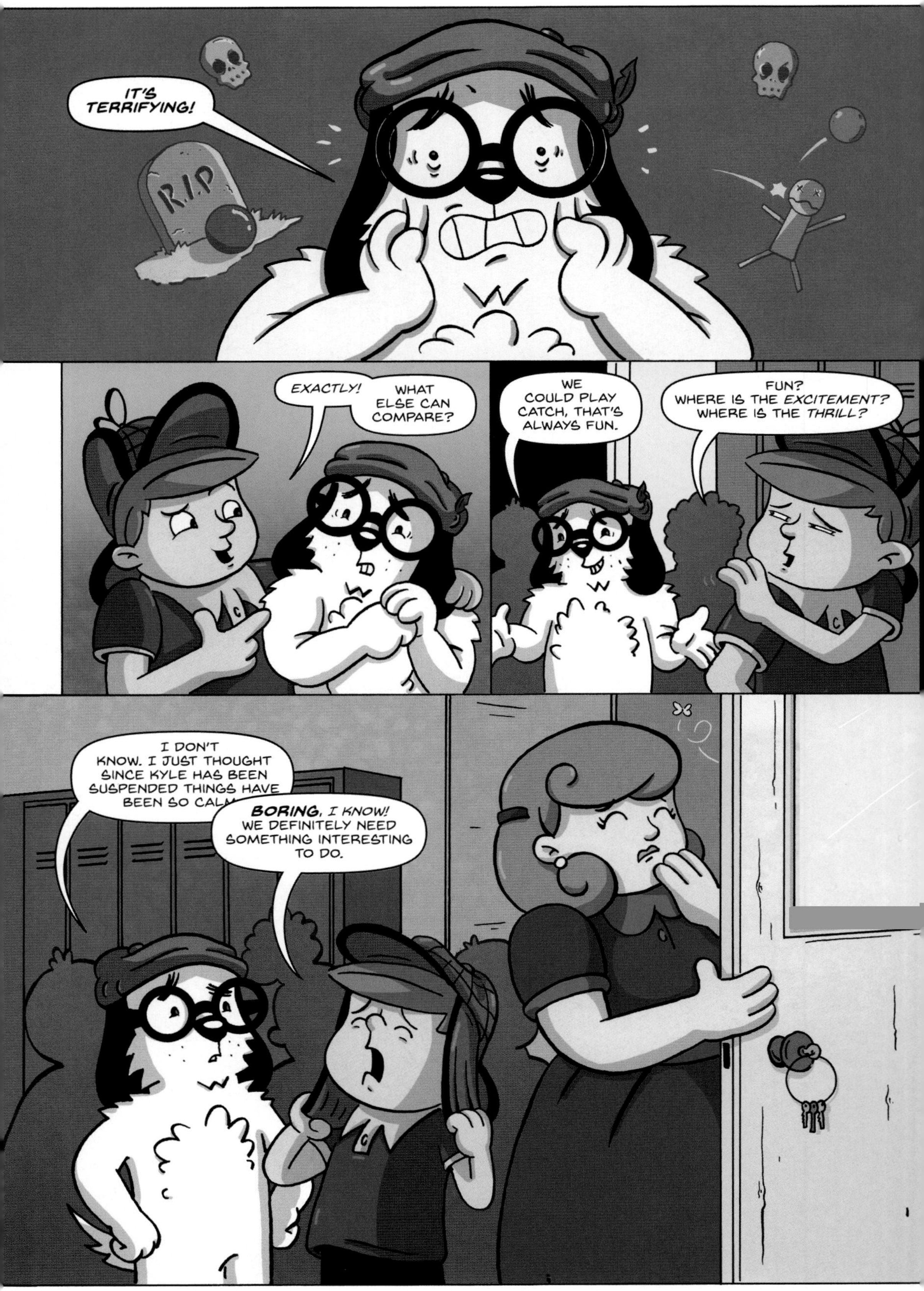
IT'S TERRIFYING!
R.I.P.
EXACTLY! WHAT ELSE CAN COMPARE?
WE COULD PLAY CATCH, THAT'S ALWAYS FUN.
FUN? WHERE IS THE *EXCITEMENT?* WHERE IS THE *THRILL?*
I DON'T KNOW. I JUST THOUGHT SINCE KYLE HAS BEEN SUSPENDED THINGS HAVE BEEN SO CALM
BORING, *I KNOW!* WE DEFINITELY NEED SOMETHING INTERESTING TO DO.

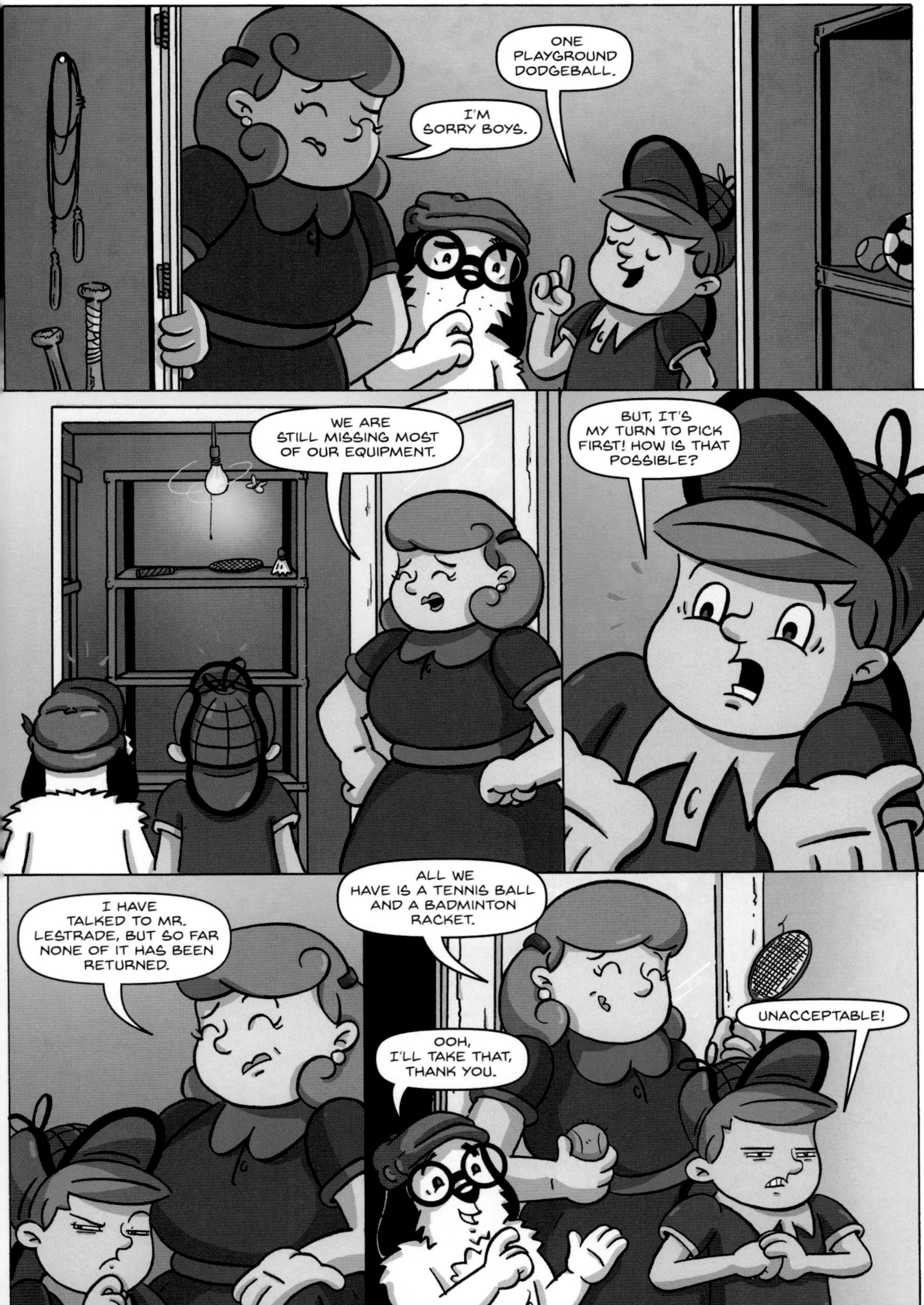
I'M SORRY BOYS.
ONE PLAYGROUND DODGEBALL.
WE ARE STILL MISSING MOST OF OUR EQUIPMENT.
BUT, IT'S MY TURN TO PICK FIRST! HOW IS THAT POSSIBLE?
I HAVE TALKED TO MR. LESTRADE, BUT SO FAR NONE OF IT HAS BEEN RETURNED.
ALL WE HAVE IS A TENNIS BALL AND A BADMINTON RACKET.
UNACCEPTABLE!
OOH, I'LL TAKE THAT, THANK YOU.

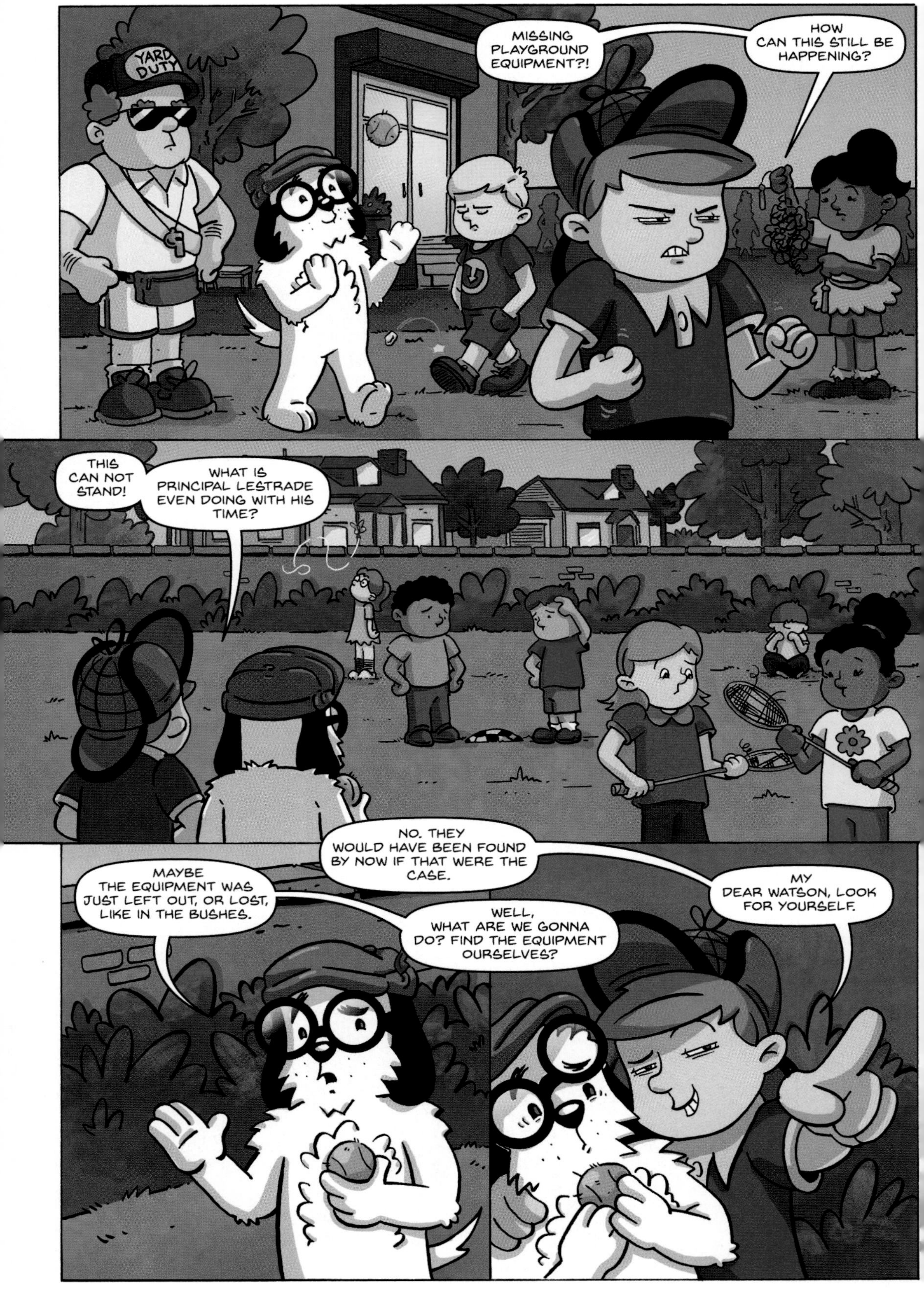
MISSING PLAYGROUND EQUIPMENT?!
HOW CAN THIS STILL BE HAPPENING?
YARD DUTY
THIS CAN NOT STAND!
WHAT IS PRINCIPAL LESTRADE EVEN DOING WITH HIS TIME?
MAYBE THE EQUIPMENT WAS JUST LEFT OUT, OR LOST, LIKE IN THE BUSHES.
NO. THEY WOULD HAVE BEEN FOUND BY NOW IF THAT WERE THE CASE.
WELL, WHAT ARE WE GONNA DO? FIND THE EQUIPMENT OURSELVES?
MY DEAR WATSON, LOOK FOR YOURSELF.

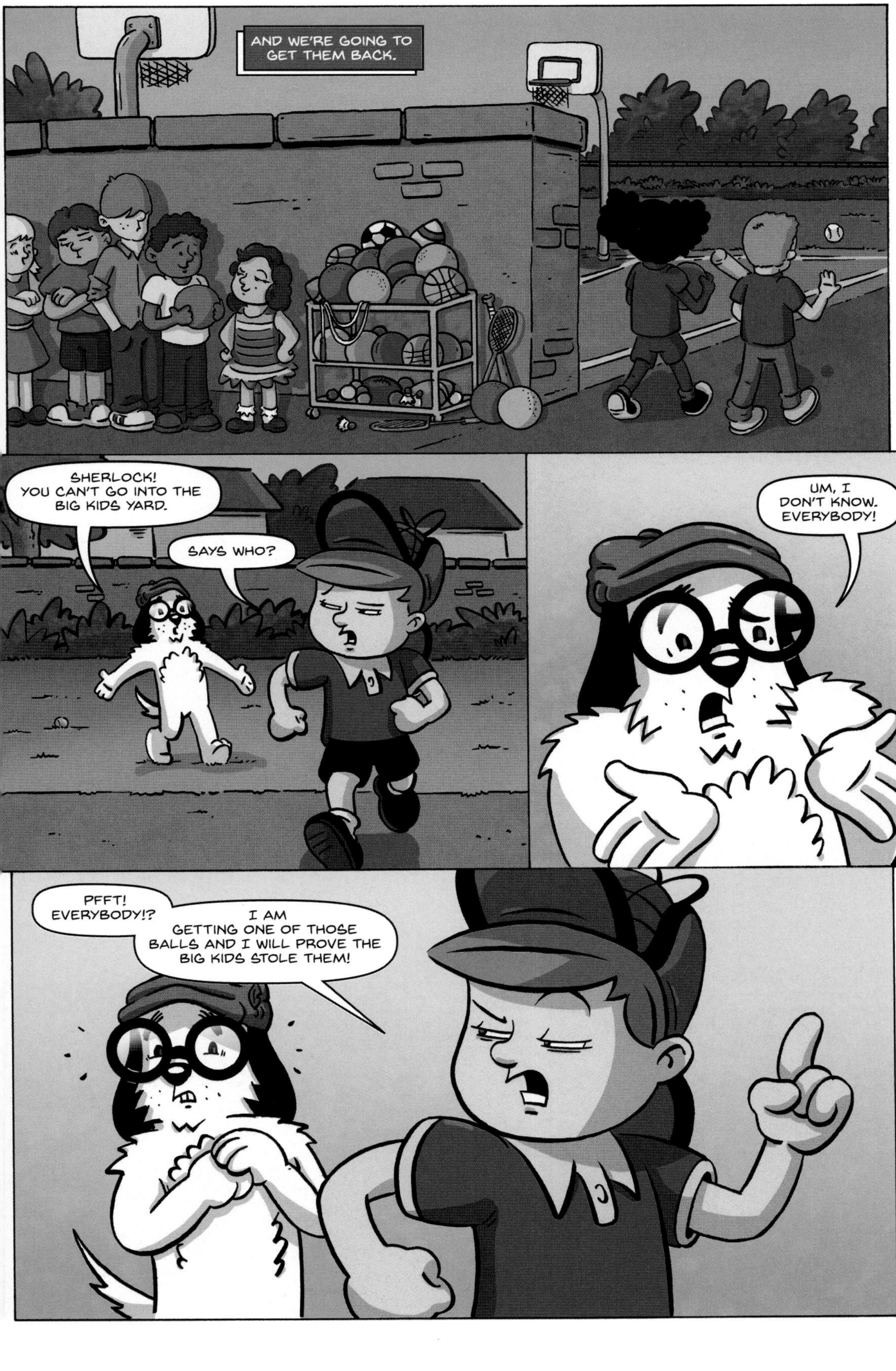
AND WE'RE GOING TO GET THEM BACK.
SHERLOCK! YOU CAN'T GO INTO THE BIG KIDS YARD.
SAYS WHO?
UM, I DON'T KNOW. EVERYBODY!
PFFT! EVERYBODY!?
I AM GETTING ONE OF THOSE BALLS AND I WILL PROVE THE BIG KIDS STOLE THEM!

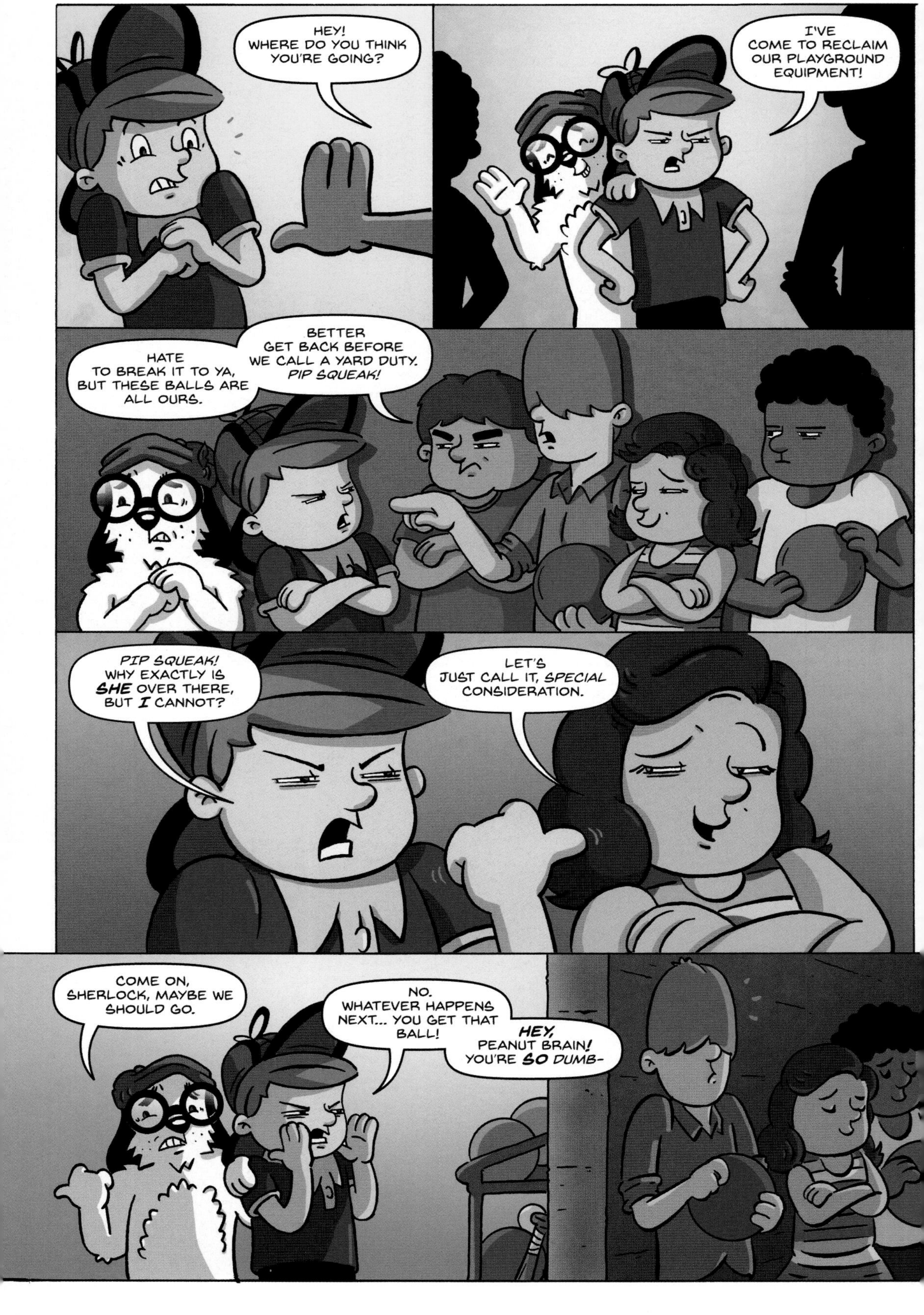
HEY! WHERE DO YOU THINK YOU'RE GOING?
I'VE COME TO RECLAIM OUR PLAYGROUND EQUIPMENT!
HATE TO BREAK IT TO YA, BUT THESE BALLS ARE ALL OURS.
BETTER GET BACK BEFORE WE CALL A YARD DUTY. PIP SQUEAK!
PIP SQUEAK! WHY EXACTLY IS SHE OVER THERE, BUT I CANNOT?
LET'S JUST CALL IT, SPECIAL CONSIDERATION.
COME ON, SHERLOCK, MAYBE WE SHOULD GO.
NO. WHATEVER HAPPENS NEXT... YOU GET THAT BALL!
HEY, PEANUT BRAIN! YOU'RE SO DUMB-

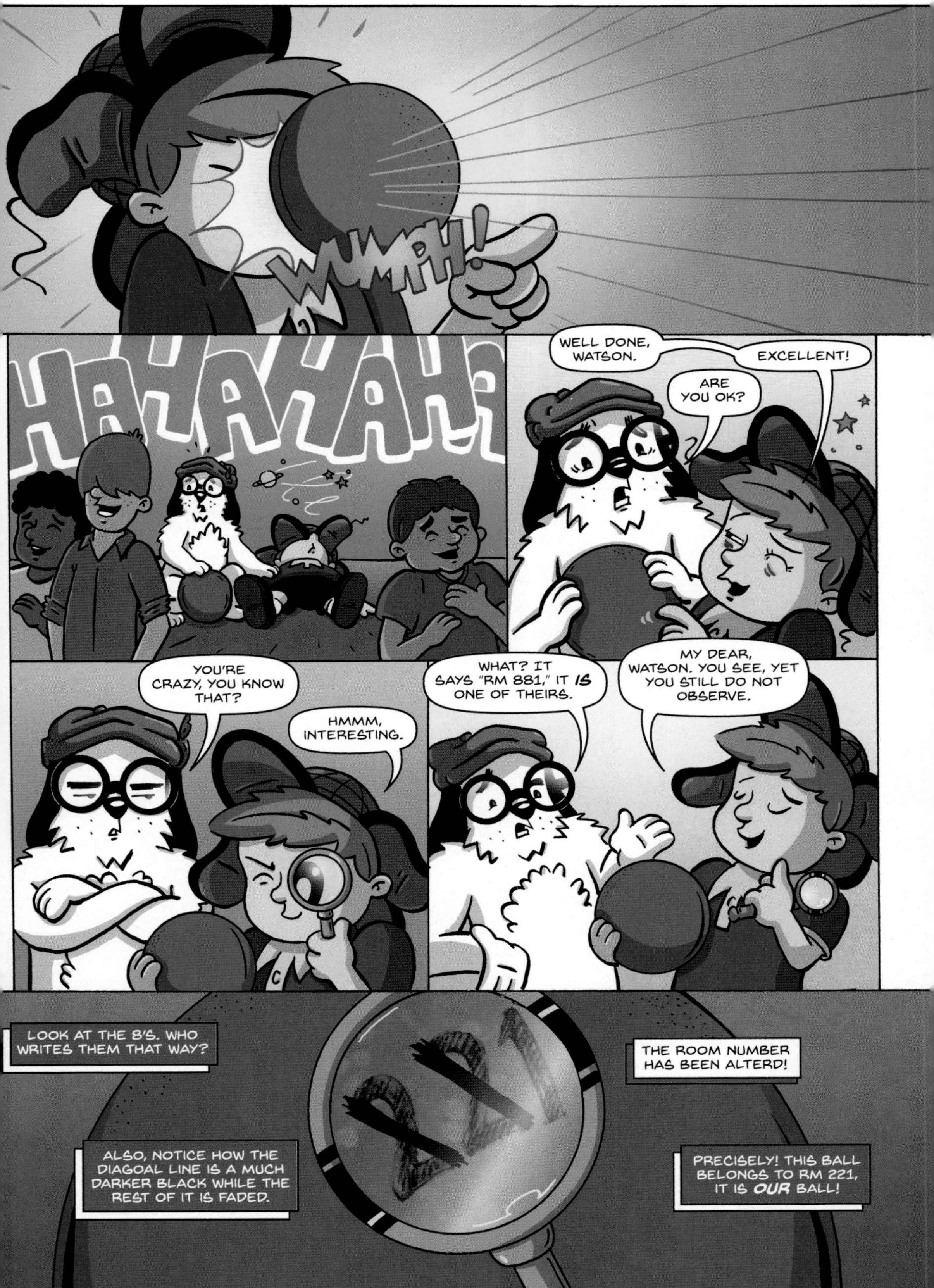
WUMPH!
HAHAHAHAH
WELL DONE, WATSON.
EXCELLENT!
ARE YOU OK?
YOU'RE CRAZY, YOU KNOW THAT?
HMMM, INTERESTING.
WHAT? IT SAYS "RM 881," IT IS ONE OF THEIRS.
MY DEAR, WATSON. YOU SEE, YET YOU STILL DO NOT OBSERVE.
LOOK AT THE 8'S. WHO WRITES THEM THAT WAY?
THE ROOM NUMBER HAS BEEN ALTERD!
ALSO, NOTICE HOW THE DIAGOAL LINE IS A MUCH DARKER BLACK WHILE THE REST OF IT IS FADED.
PRECISELY! THIS BALL BELONGS TO RM 221, IT IS OUR BALL!

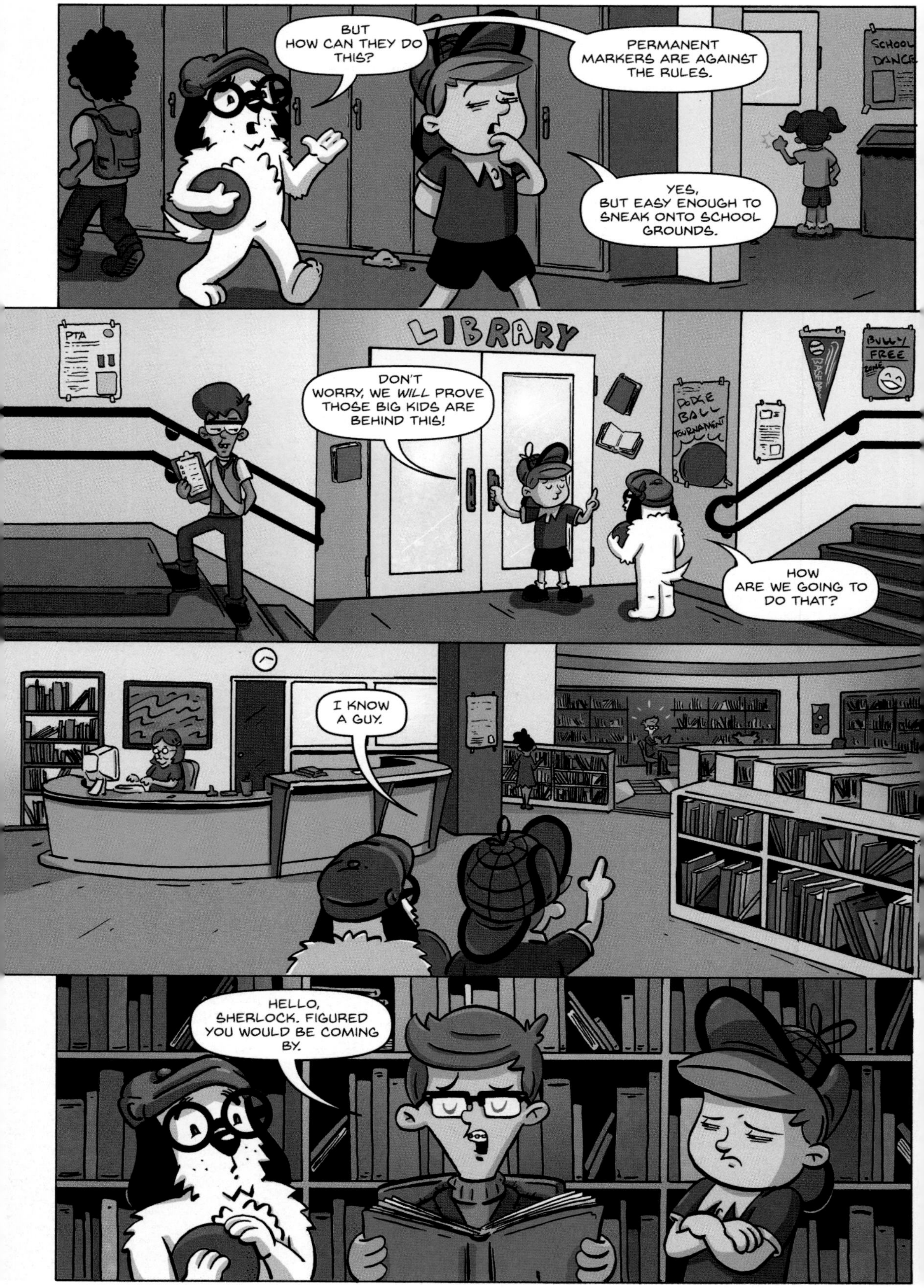
BUT HOW CAN THEY DO THIS?
PERMANENT MARKERS ARE AGAINST THE RULES.
SCHOOL DANCE
YES, BUT EASY ENOUGH TO SNEAK ONTO SCHOOL GROUNDS.
PTA
LIBRARY
BULLY FREE ZONE
BASEBALL
DODGE BALL TOURNAMENT
DON'T WORRY, WE *WILL* PROVE THOSE BIG KIDS ARE BEHIND THIS!
HOW ARE WE GOING TO DO THAT?
I KNOW A GUY.
HELLO, SHERLOCK. FIGURED YOU WOULD BE COMING BY.

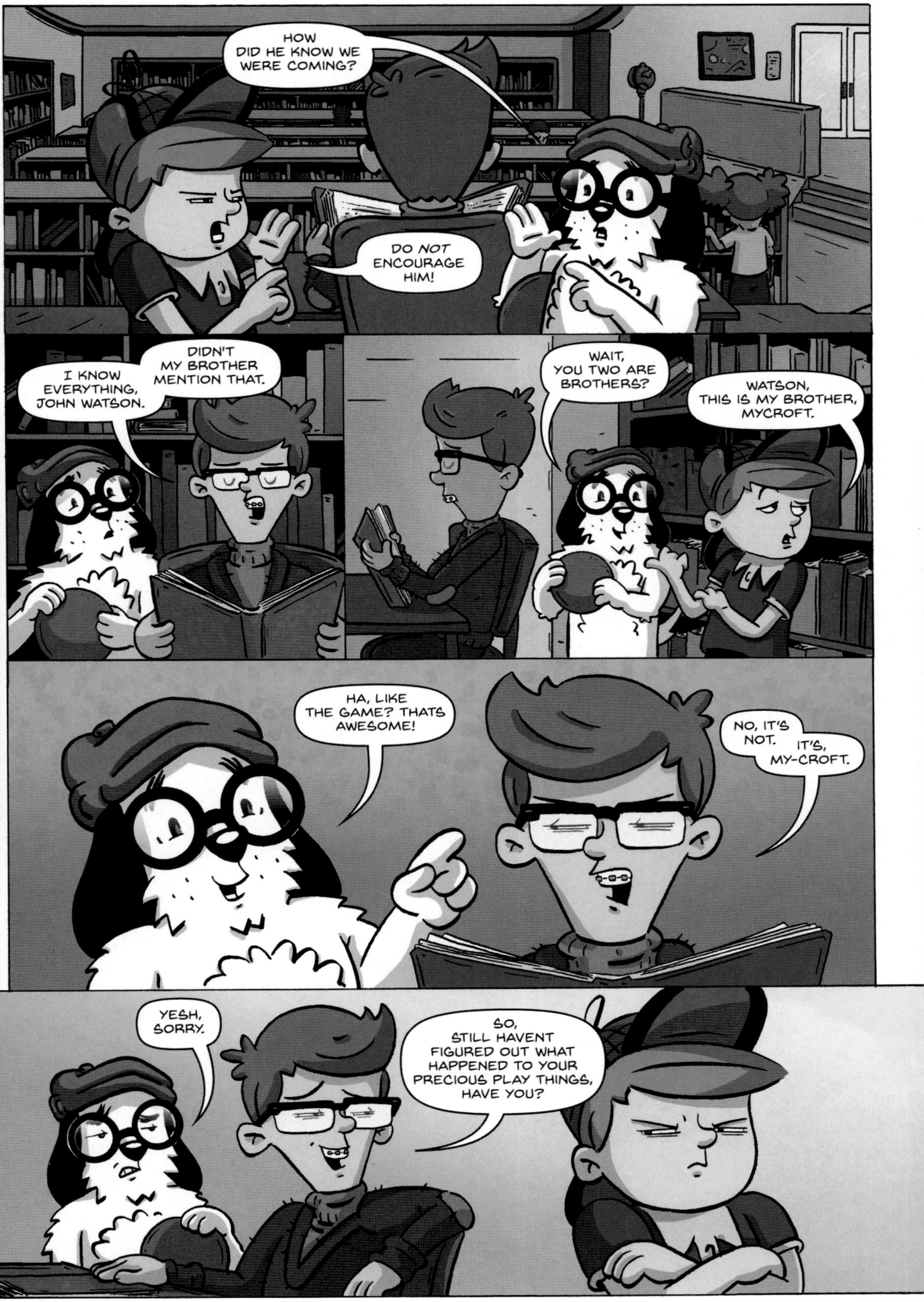
HOW DID HE KNOW WE WERE COMING?
DO NOT ENCOURAGE HIM!
I KNOW EVERYTHING, JOHN WATSON.
DIDN'T MY BROTHER MENTION THAT.
WAIT, YOU TWO ARE BROTHERS?
WATSON, THIS IS MY BROTHER, MYCROFT.
HA, LIKE THE GAME? THATS AWESOME!
NO, IT'S NOT.
IT'S, MY-CROFT.
YESH, SORRY.
SO, STILL HAVENT FIGURED OUT WHAT HAPPENED TO YOUR PRECIOUS PLAY THINGS, HAVE YOU?

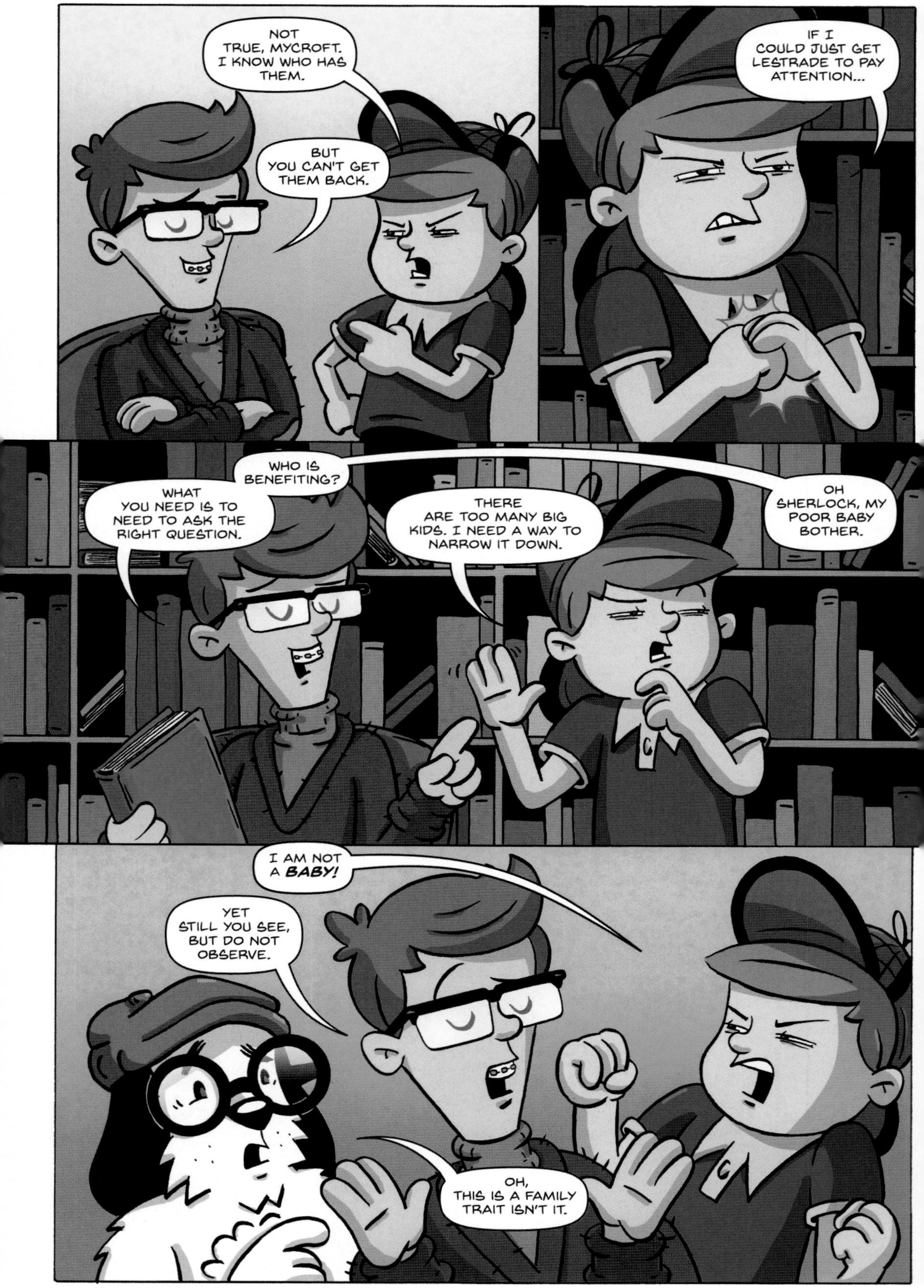
NOT TRUE, MYCROFT. I KNOW WHO HAS THEM.
BUT YOU CAN'T GET THEM BACK.
IF I COULD JUST GET LESTRADE TO PAY ATTENTION...
WHO IS BENEFITING?
WHAT YOU NEED IS TO NEED TO ASK THE RIGHT QUESTION.
THERE ARE TOO MANY BIG KIDS. I NEED A WAY TO NARROW IT DOWN.
OH SHERLOCK, MY POOR BABY BOTHER.
I AM NOT A ***BABY!***
YET STILL YOU SEE, BUT DO NOT OBSERVE.
OH, THIS IS A FAMILY TRAIT ISN'T IT.

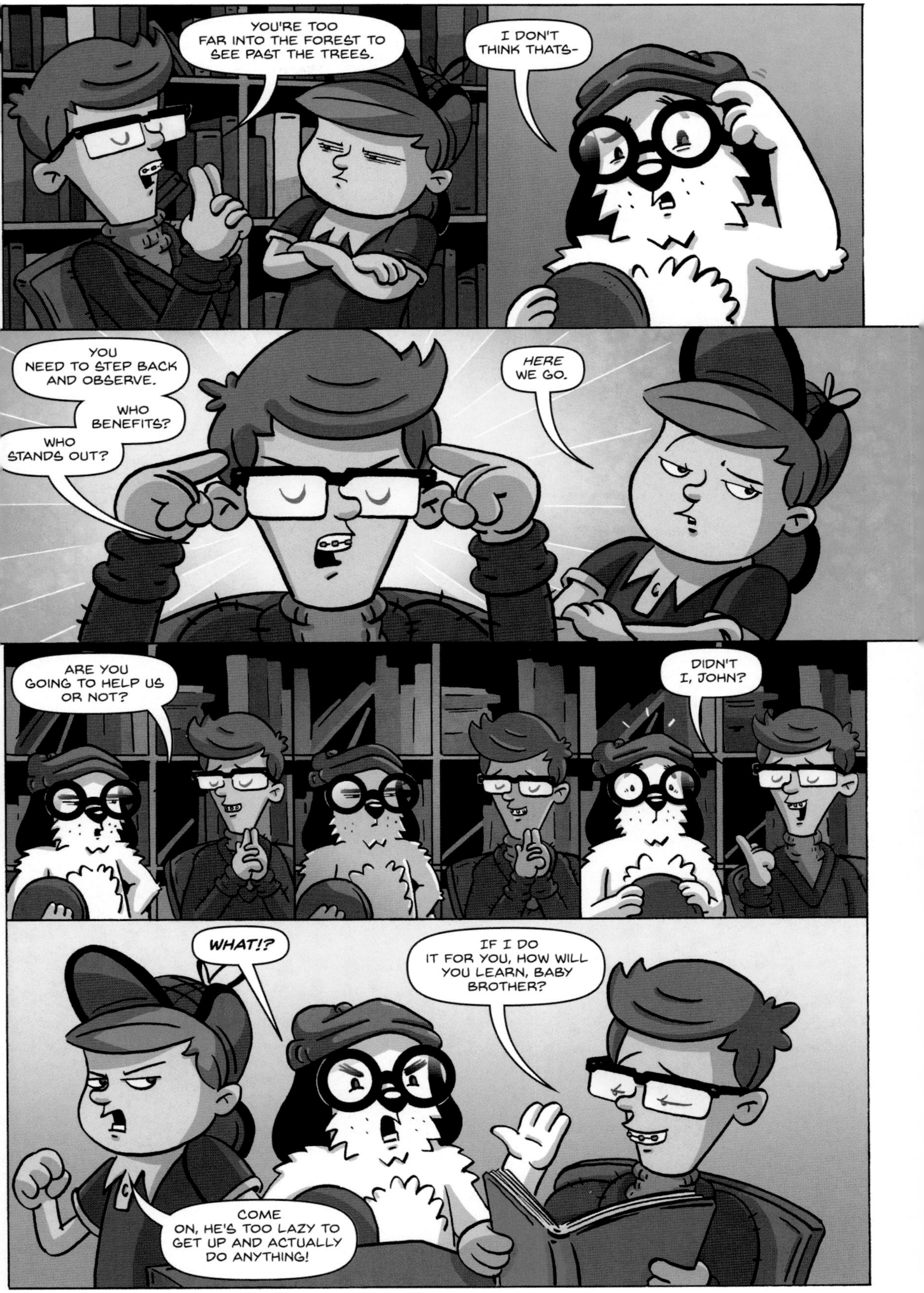
YOU'RE TOO FAR INTO THE FOREST TO SEE PAST THE TREES.
I DON'T THINK THATS-
YOU NEED TO STEP BACK AND OBSERVE.
WHO BENEFITS?
WHO STANDS OUT?
HERE WE GO.
ARE YOU GOING TO HELP US OR NOT?
DIDN'T I, JOHN?
WHAT!?
IF I DO IT FOR YOU, HOW WILL YOU LEARN, BABY BROTHER?
COME ON, HE'S TOO LAZY TO GET UP AND ACTUALLY DO ANYTHING!

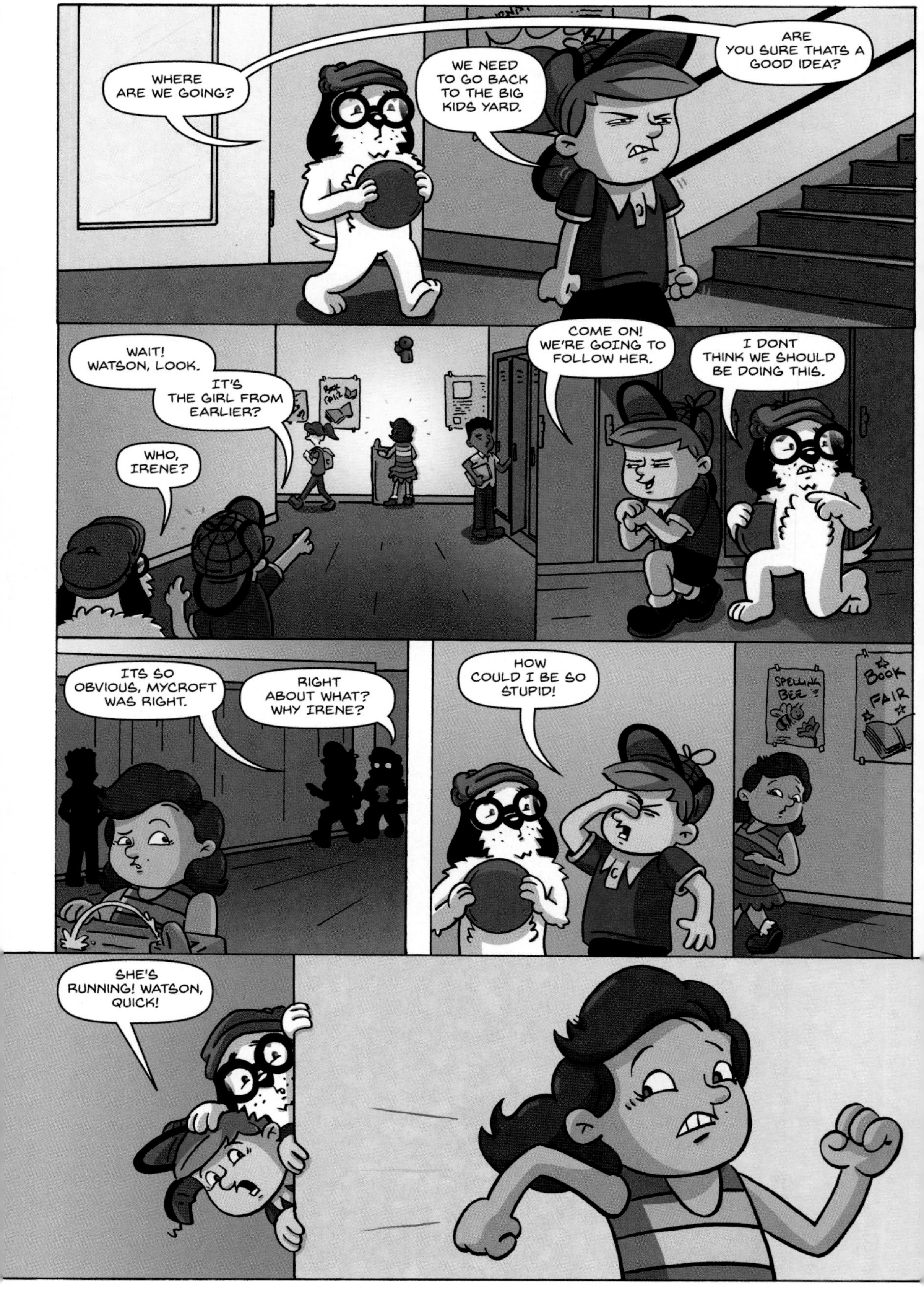
WHERE ARE WE GOING?
WE NEED TO GO BACK TO THE BIG KIDS YARD.
ARE YOU SURE THATS A GOOD IDEA?
WAIT! WATSON, LOOK.
IT'S THE GIRL FROM EARLIER?
WHO, IRENE?
COME ON! WE'RE GOING TO FOLLOW HER.
I DONT THINK WE SHOULD BE DOING THIS.
ITS SO OBVIOUS, MYCROFT WAS RIGHT.
RIGHT ABOUT WHAT? WHY IRENE?
HOW COULD I BE SO STUPID!
SPELLING BEE
BOOK FAIR
SHE'S RUNNING! WATSON, QUICK!

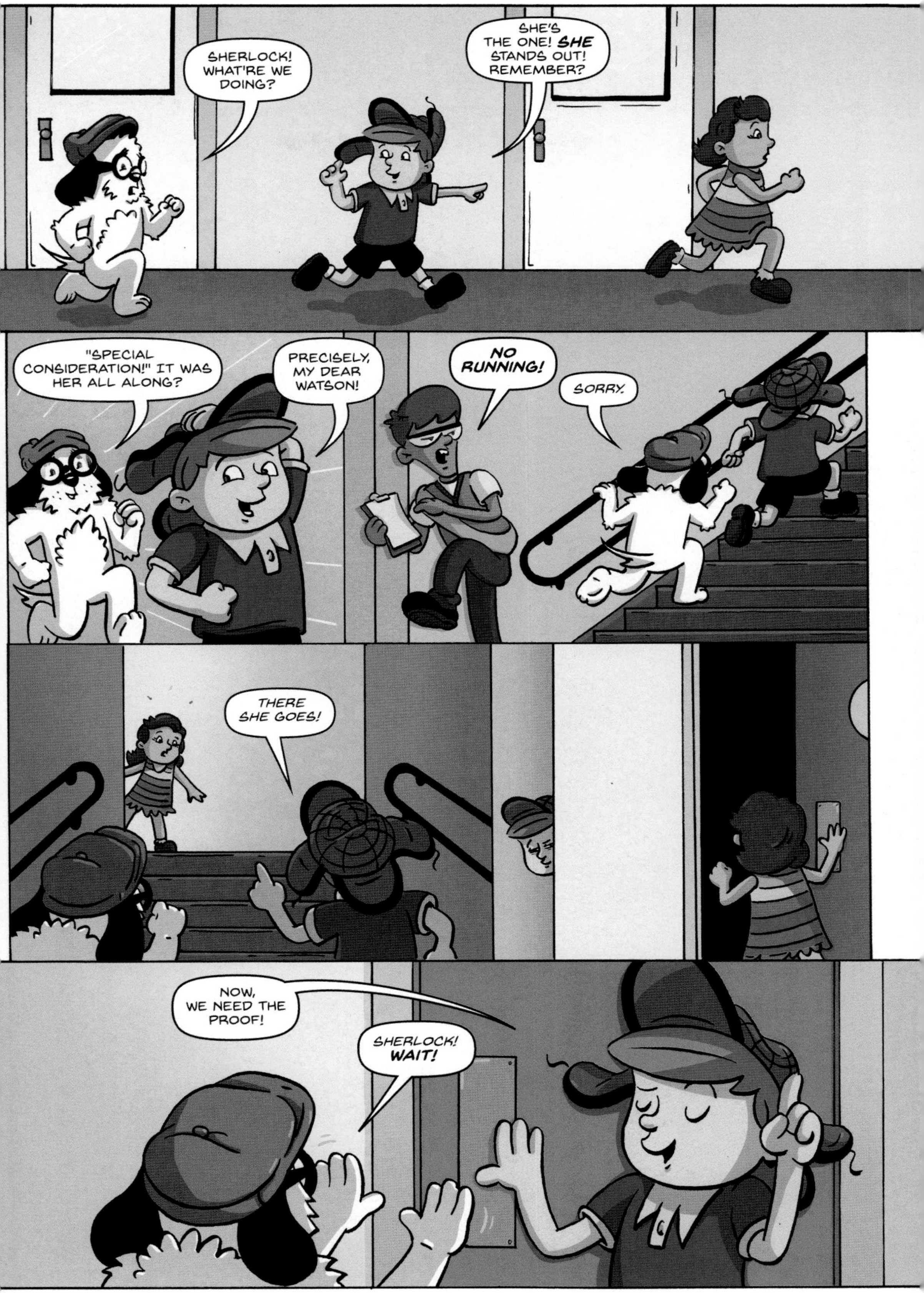
SHERLOCK! WHAT'RE WE DOING?
SHE'S THE ONE! SHE STANDS OUT! REMEMBER?
"SPECIAL CONSIDERATION!" IT WAS HER ALL ALONG?
PRECISELY, MY DEAR WATSON!
NO RUNNING!
SORRY.
THERE SHE GOES!
NOW, WE NEED THE PROOF!
SHERLOCK! WAIT!

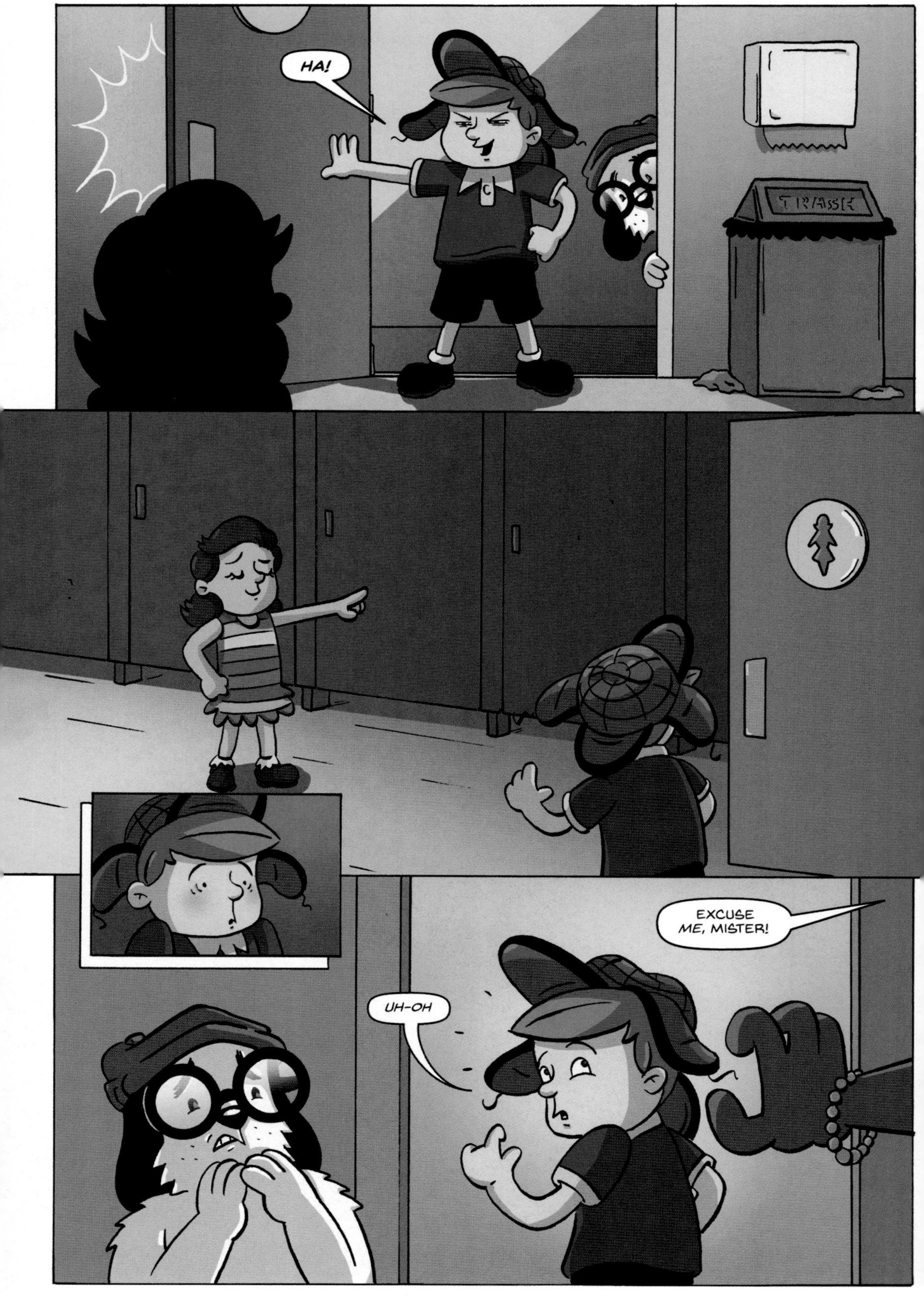
HA!
TRASH
EXCUSE ME, MISTER!
UH-OH

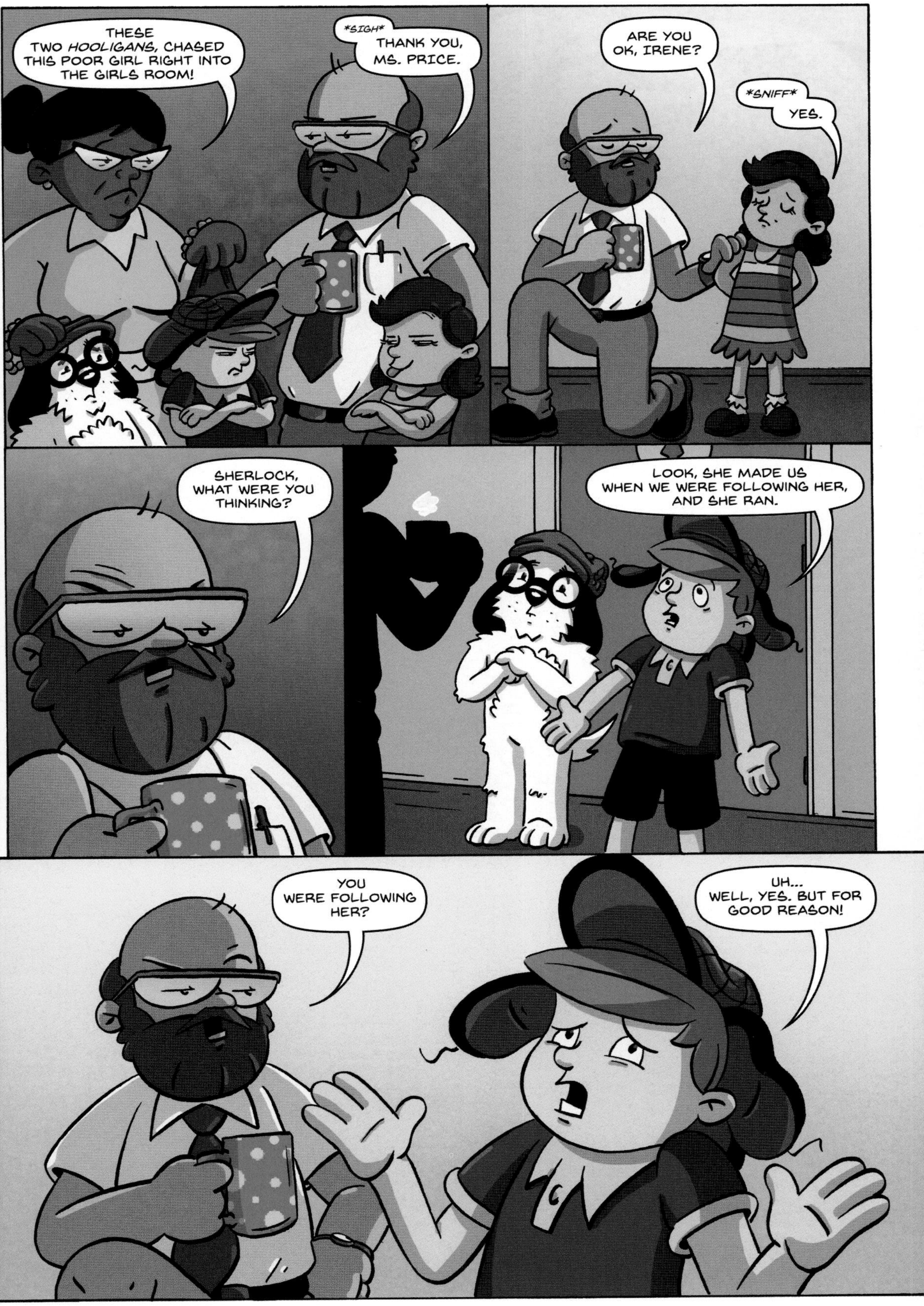
THESE TWO *HOOLIGANS*, CHASED THIS POOR GIRL RIGHT INTO THE GIRLS ROOM!
SIGH
THANK YOU, MS. PRICE.
ARE YOU OK, IRENE?
SNIFF
YES.
SHERLOCK, WHAT WERE YOU THINKING?
LOOK, SHE MADE US WHEN WE WERE FOLLOWING HER, AND SHE RAN.
YOU WERE FOLLOWING HER?
UH... WELL, YES. BUT FOR GOOD REASON!

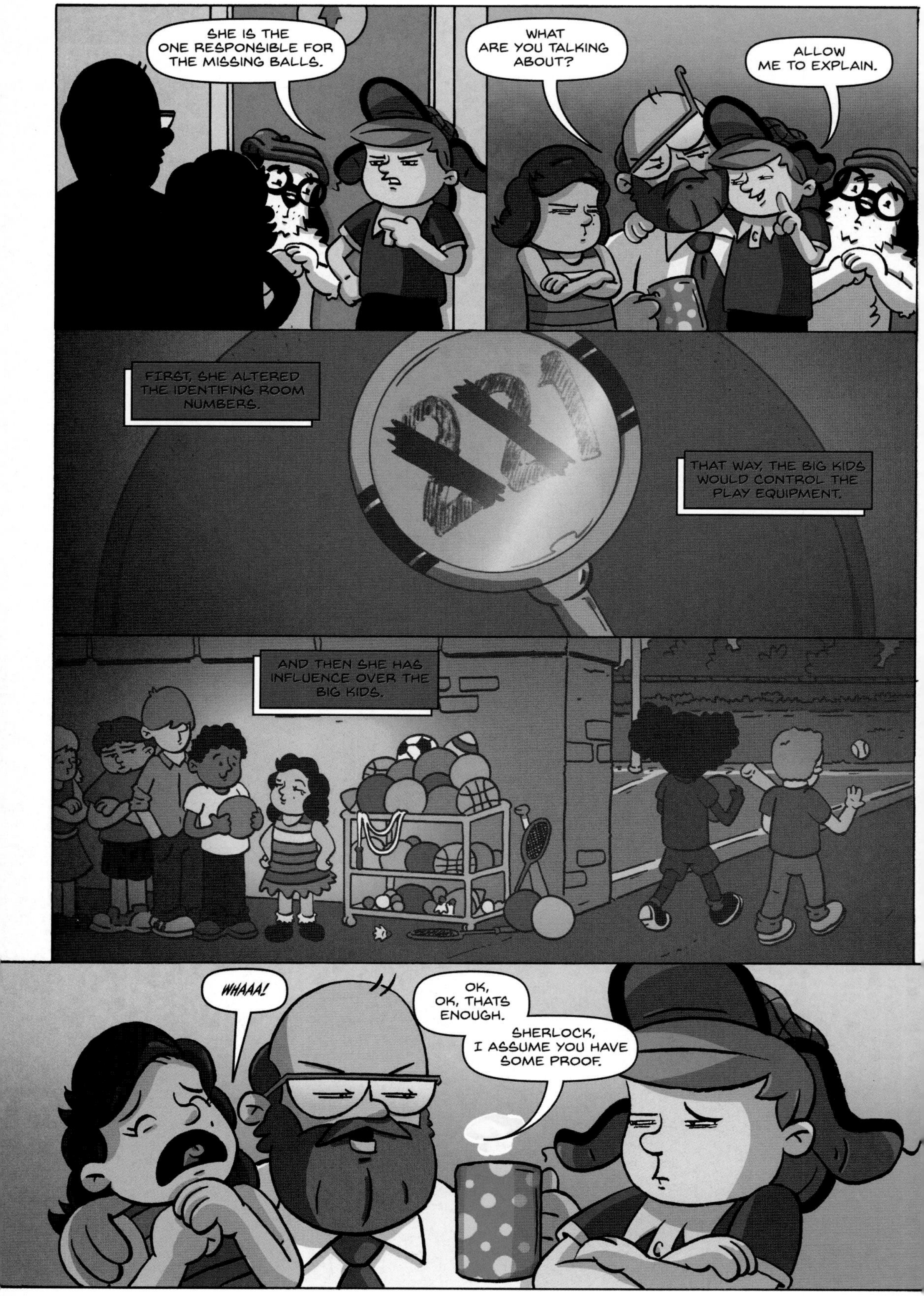
SHE IS THE ONE RESPONSIBLE FOR THE MISSING BALLS.
WHAT ARE YOU TALKING ABOUT?
ALLOW ME TO EXPLAIN.
FIRST, SHE ALTERED THE IDENTIFING ROOM NUMBERS.
THAT WAY, THE BIG KIDS WOULD CONTROL THE PLAY EQUIPMENT.
AND THEN SHE HAS INFLUENCE OVER THE BIG KIDS.
WHAAA!
OK, OK, THATS ENOUGH.
SHERLOCK, I ASSUME YOU HAVE SOME PROOF.

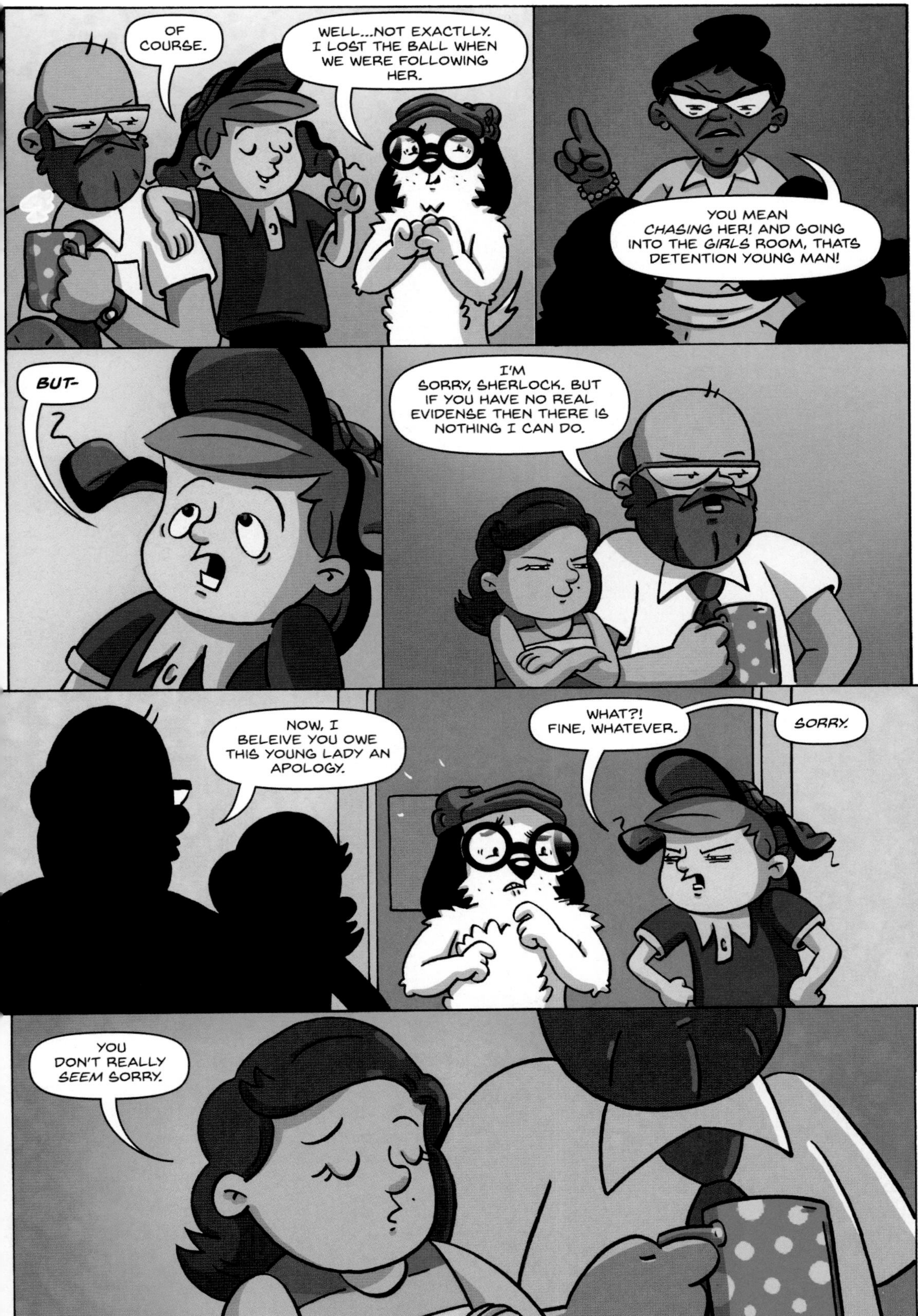
OF COURSE.
WELL...NOT EXACTLLY. I LOST THE BALL WHEN WE WERE FOLLOWING HER.
YOU MEAN CHASING HER! AND GOING INTO THE GIRLS ROOM, THATS DETENTION YOUNG MAN!
BUT-
I'M SORRY, SHERLOCK. BUT IF YOU HAVE NO REAL EVIDENSE THEN THERE IS NOTHING I CAN DO.
NOW, I BELEIVE YOU OWE THIS YOUNG LADY AN APOLOGY.
WHAT?! FINE, WHATEVER.
SORRY.
YOU DON'T REALLY SEEM SORRY.

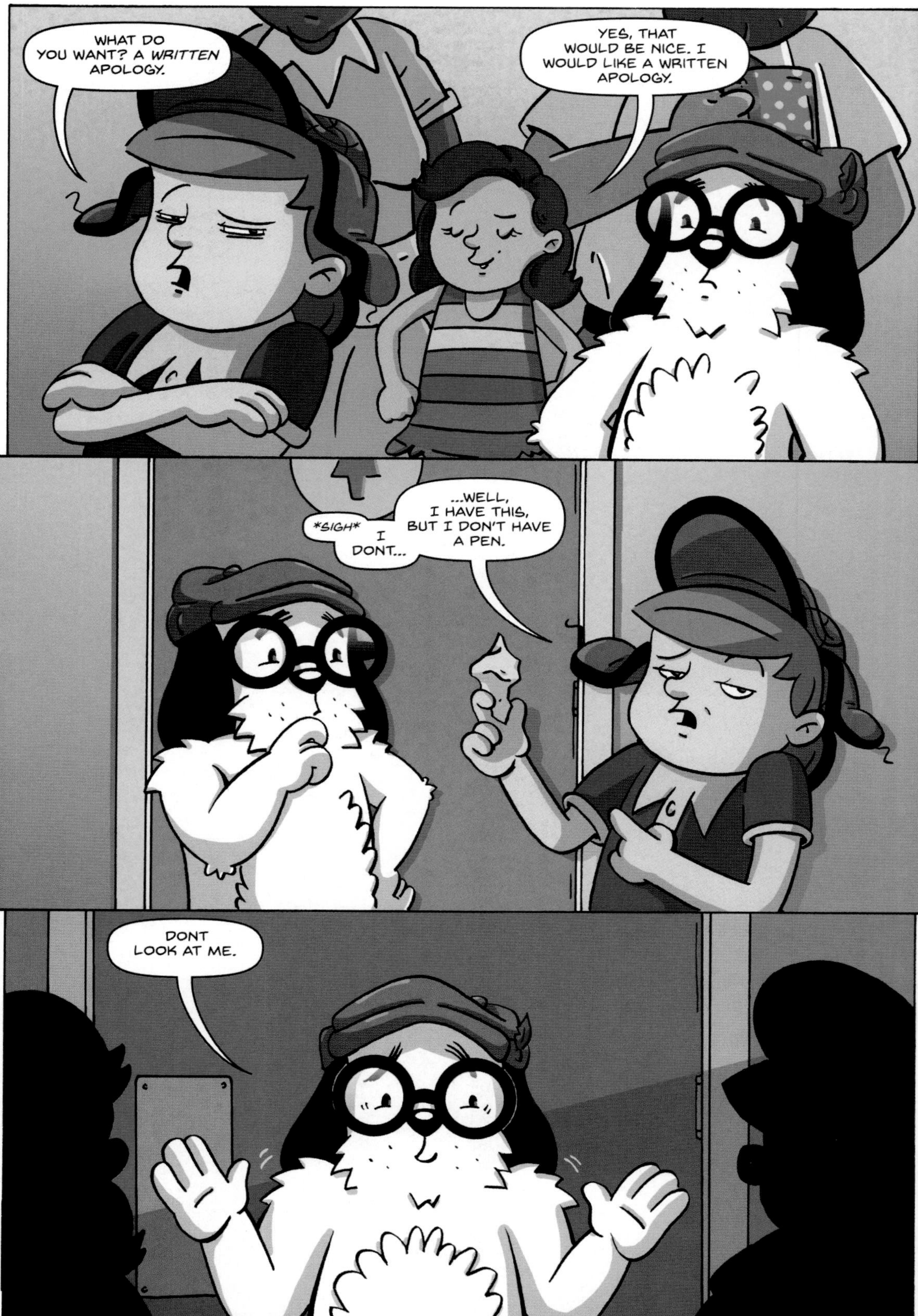
WHAT DO YOU WANT? A *WRITTEN* APOLOGY.
YES, THAT WOULD BE NICE. I WOULD LIKE A WRITTEN APOLOGY.
SIGH I DONT...
...WELL, I HAVE THIS, BUT I DON'T HAVE A PEN.
DONT LOOK AT ME.

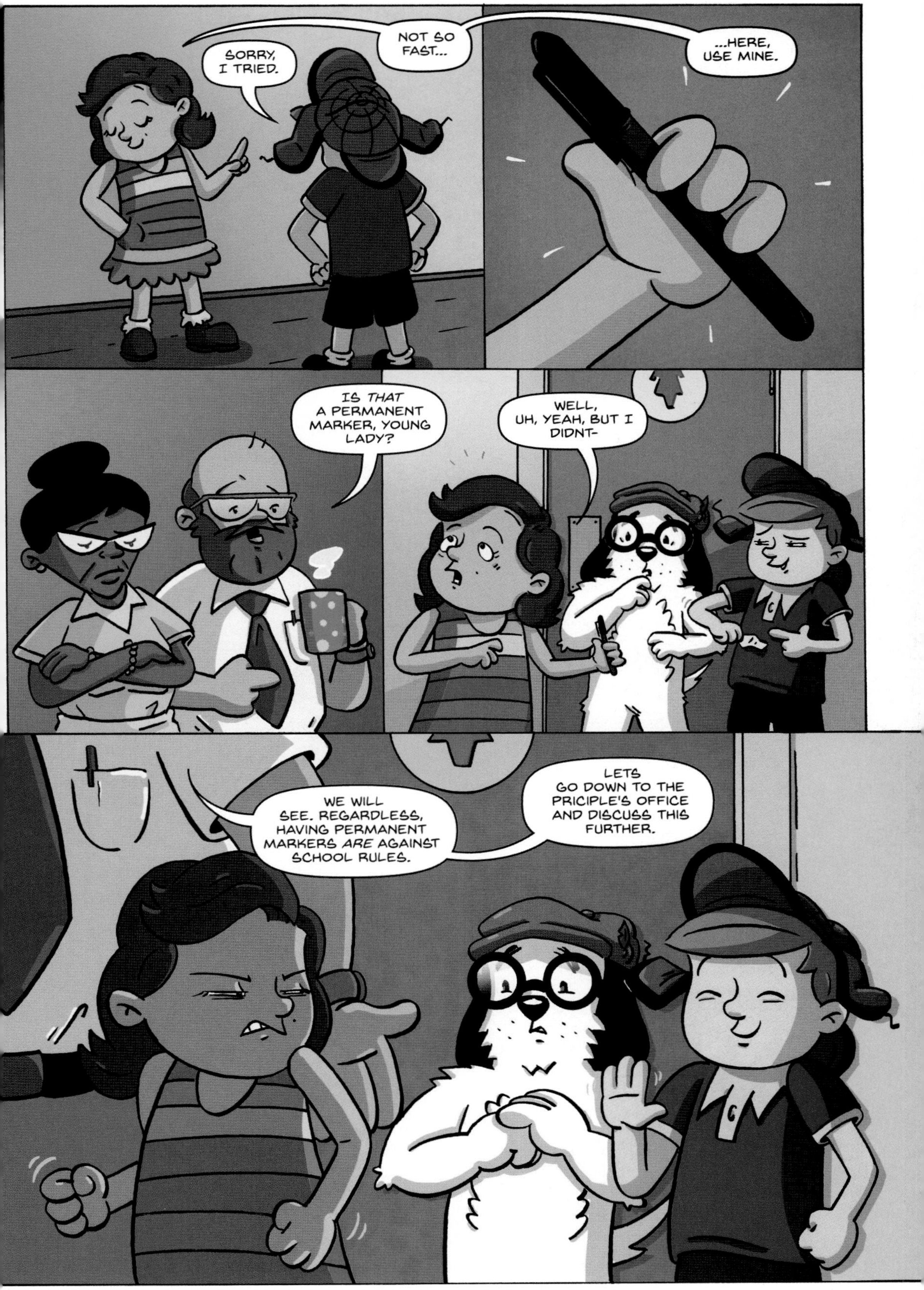
SORRY, I TRIED.
NOT SO FAST...
...HERE, USE MINE.
IS *THAT* A PERMANENT MARKER, YOUNG LADY?
WELL, UH, YEAH, BUT I DIDNT-
WE WILL SEE. REGARDLESS, HAVING PERMANENT MARKERS *ARE* AGAINST SCHOOL RULES.
LETS GO DOWN TO THE PRICIPLE'S OFFICE AND DISCUSS THIS FURTHER.

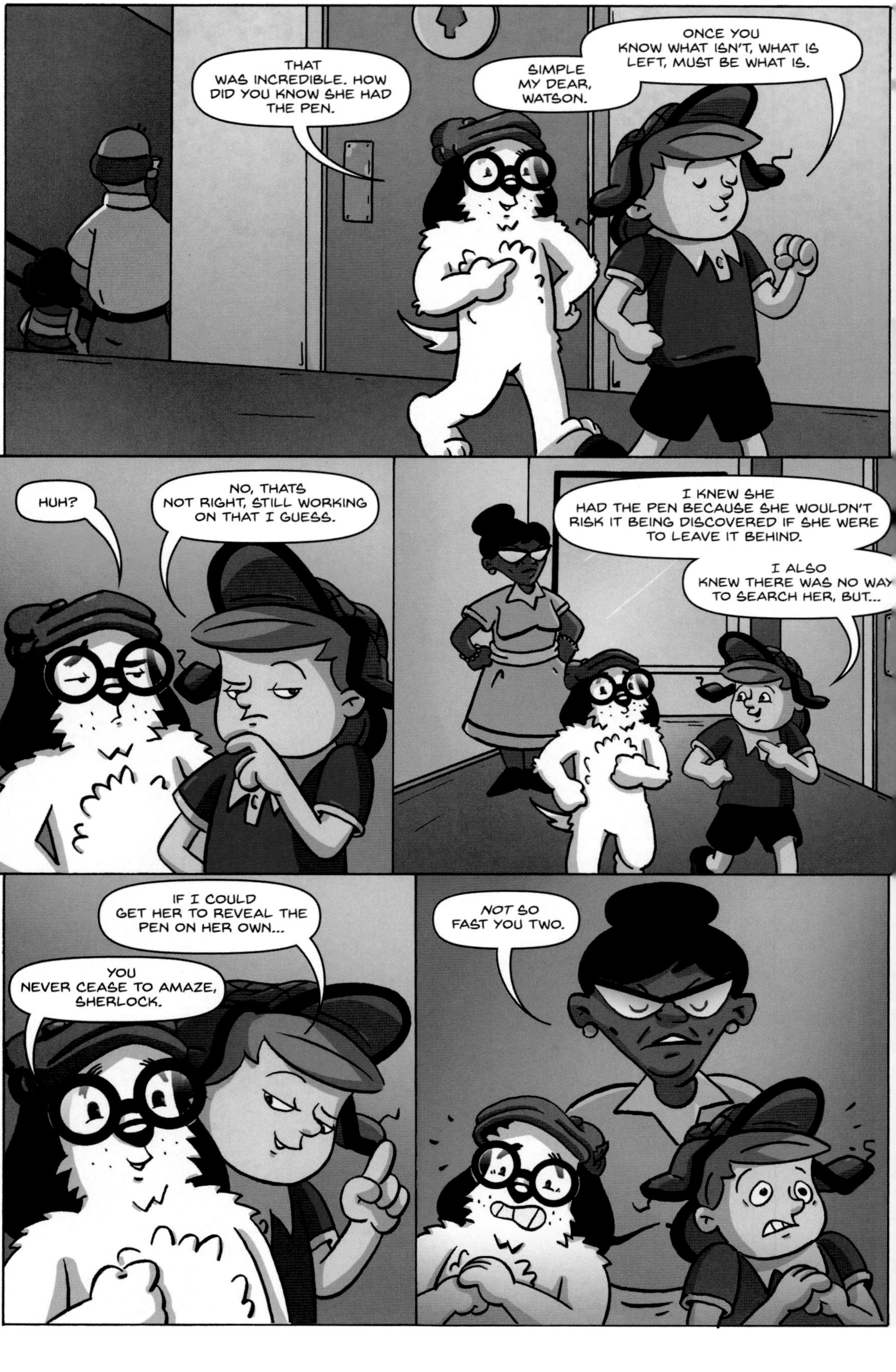
THAT WAS INCREDIBLE. HOW DID YOU KNOW SHE HAD THE PEN.
SIMPLE MY DEAR, WATSON.
ONCE YOU KNOW WHAT ISN'T, WHAT IS LEFT, MUST BE WHAT IS.
HUH?
NO, THATS NOT RIGHT, STILL WORKING ON THAT I GUESS.
I KNEW SHE HAD THE PEN BECAUSE SHE WOULDN'T RISK IT BEING DISCOVERED IF SHE WERE TO LEAVE IT BEHIND.
I ALSO KNEW THERE WAS NO WAY TO SEARCH HER, BUT...
IF I COULD GET HER TO REVEAL THE PEN ON HER OWN...
YOU NEVER CEASE TO AMAZE, SHERLOCK.
NOT SO FAST YOU TWO.

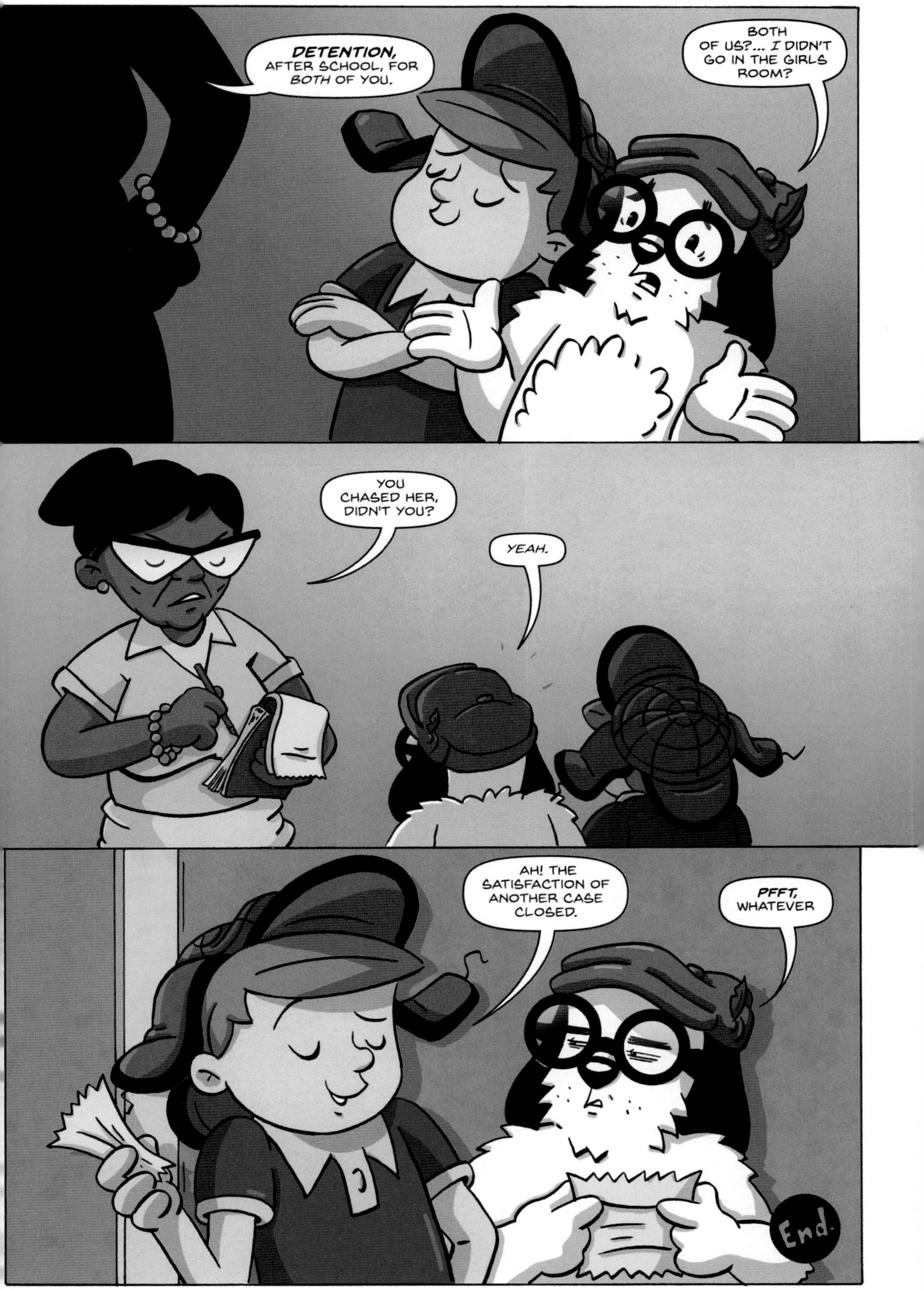
DETENTION, AFTER SCHOOL, FOR BOTH OF YOU.
BOTH OF US?... I DIDN'T GO IN THE GIRLS ROOM?
YOU CHASED HER, DIDN'T YOU?
YEAH.
AH! THE SATISFACTION OF ANOTHER CASE CLOSED.
PFFT, WHATEVER
End.

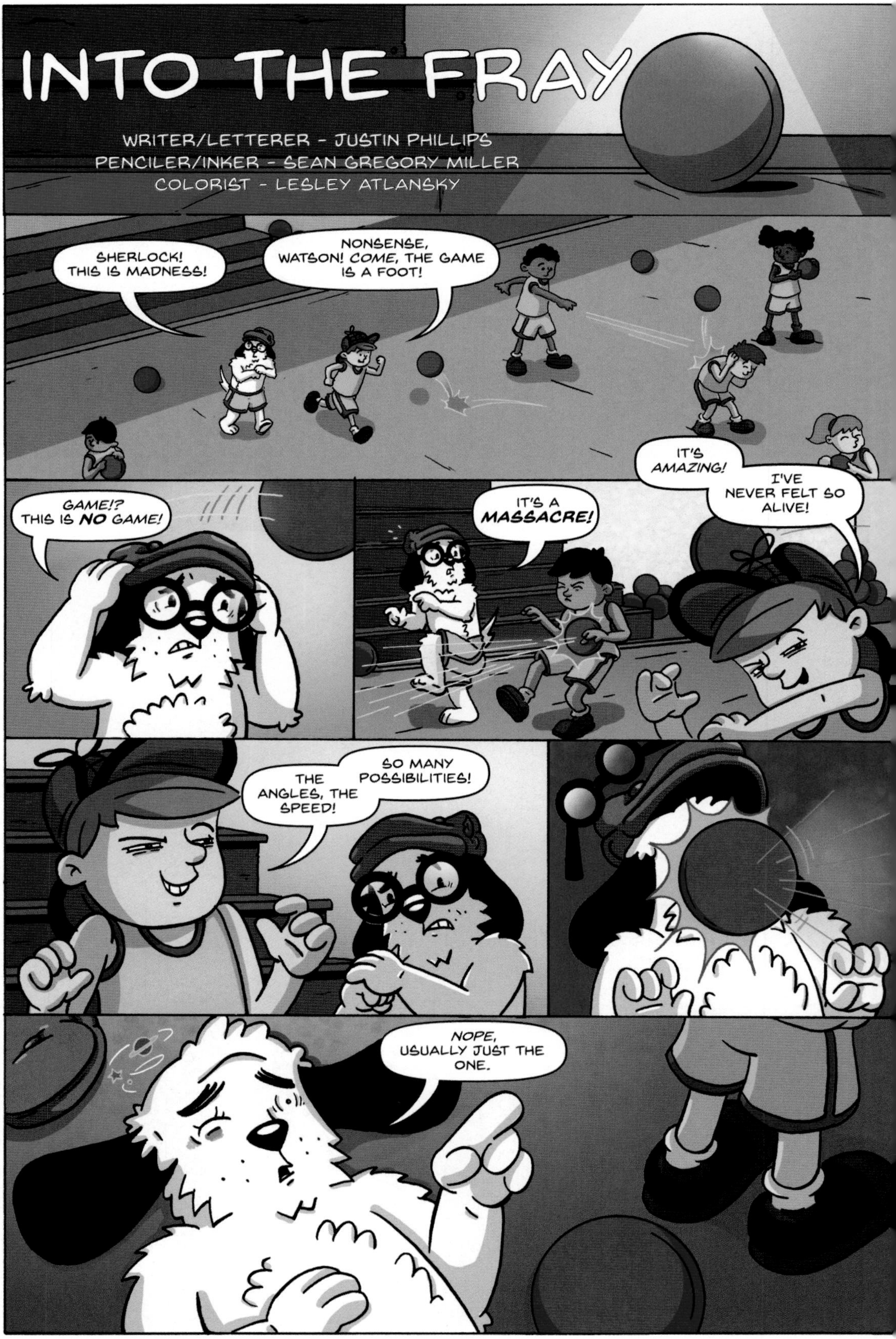
INTO THE FRAY
WRITER/LETTERER - JUSTIN PHILLIPS
PENCILER/INKER - SEAN GREGORY MILLER
COLORIST - LESLEY ATLANSKY
SHERLOCK! THIS IS MADNESS!
NONSENSE, WATSON! COME, THE GAME IS A FOOT!
GAME!? THIS IS NO GAME!
IT'S A MASSACRE!
IT'S AMAZING!
I'VE NEVER FELT SO ALIVE!
THE ANGLES, THE SPEED!
SO MANY POSSIBILITIES!
NOPE, USUALLY JUST THE ONE.

LEARN TO DRAW!

LEARN TO DRAW IN SIX EASY STEPS! ALL YOU NEED IS A PENCIL, PEN, AND PAPER.

LESTRADE

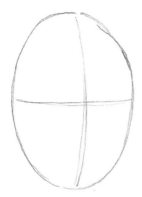

DO DRAW LESTRADE, FIRST START WITH AN OVAL!

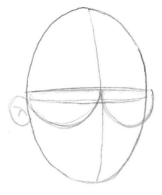

NEXT, ADD HIS EAR AND HALF CIRCLES FOR HIS GLASSES.

START TO ADD OTHER ROUGH SHAPES FOR HIS HAIR AND MUSTACHE.

LESTRADE IS A SERIOUS GUY, SO I ALWAYS KEEP HIS EXPRESSIONS SIMPLE!

FILL HIM OUT BY ADDING HIS BEARD AND SMALL DETAILS.

NOW YOU'RE READY TO INK!

LEARN TO DRAW!

TRY THESE BASIC EXERCISES AND YOU CAN BE A COMIC ARTIST TOO!

HANDS

1.

2.

3.

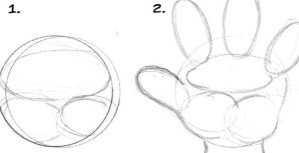

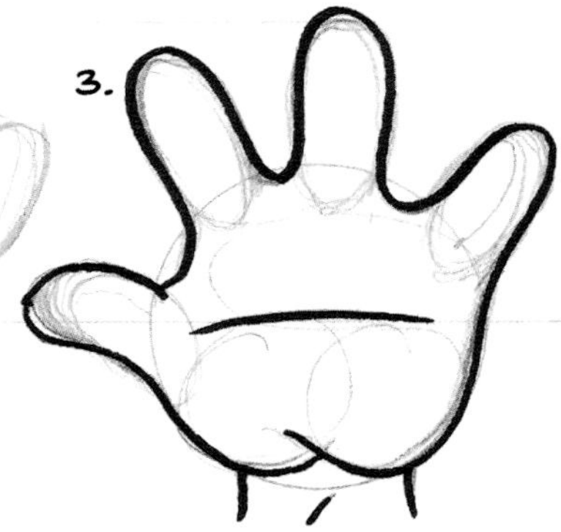

DRAWING HANDS IS AN IMPORTANT PART OF SHOWING A CHARACTERS PERSONALITY! AS ALWAYS, START WITH SIMPLE SHAPES AND BUILD FROM THERE.

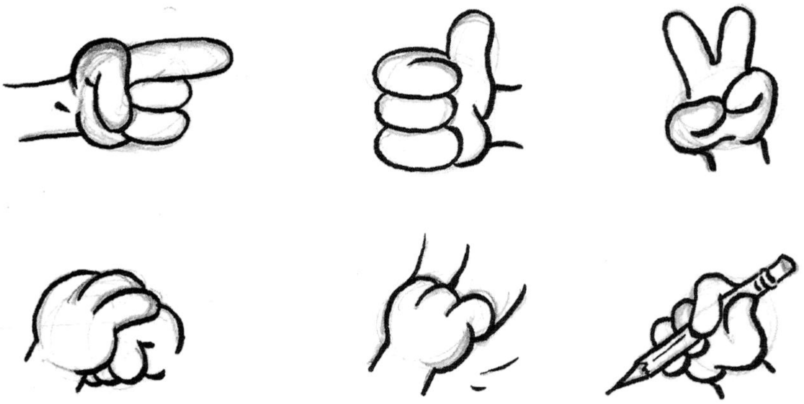

ONCE YOU GET THE BASIC SHAPES DOWN, YOU CAN START TO TRY MORE COMPLICATED GESTURES!

ADDING PROPS AND "MOTION LINES" CAN ADD A LOT OF HUMOR TO YOUR CHARACTERS TOO. GIVE IT A TRY!

COLORING WITH LESLEY!

LESLEY USES THE COMPUTER TO COLOR KID SHERLOCK. SHE ALSO LIKES TO PAINT, AND ONE OF HER FAVORITE THINGS TO DO IS EXPERIMENT WITH DIFFERENT PAINTBRUSHES THAT ARE FOR THE COMPUTER!

LESLEY USES A PRETTY NORMAL BRUSH TO DO ALL THE COLORING ON THE PEOPLE (AND DOG!).

SHE LIKES TO USE THIS SPECIAL BRUSH TO COLOR A LOT OF THE SCENERY. YOU MAY ALSO SEE IT ADDING TEXTURE TO EMPTY BACKGROUND PANELS.

HERE IS A PANEL FROM THIS ISSUE. IT LOOKS FUNNY BECAUSE THEY ONLY COLOR YOU ARE SEEING IS THE TEXTURE FROM THE SPECIAL BRUSH. THIS BRUSH GIVES THE EFFECT OF SHOWING DIFFERENT SHADES OF GREEN IN THE GRASS AND TREES WITHOUT COLORING EVERY SINGLE BLADE AND LEAF!

HERE IS THE SAME PANEL WITH ALL THE COLORS.

COLORING WITH LESLEY!

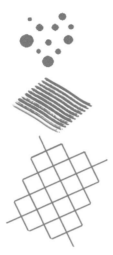

ANOTHER PLACE LESLEY HAS USED SPECIAL BRUSHES IS ON PRINCIPAL LESTRADE'S COFFEE MUG. SHE LIKES TO IMAGINE THAT OVER THE YEARS HE HAS RECEIVED MANY MUGS AS GIFTS FROM STUDENTS. HE PRACTICALLY HAS A DIFFERENT MUG FOR EACH DAY OF THE WEEK!

FOR EACH ISSUE, LESLEY HAS COLORED THE PRINCIPAL'S MUG A DIFFERENT COLOR AND PATTERN.

SHHH! HERE IS A SNEAK PEEK AT HIS MUG FROM UPCOMING ISSUE #4!

YOU CAN SEE ANOTHER USE OF A SPECIAL BRUSH IN THE BUSHES BEHIND PRINCIPAL LESTRADE. LESLEY ADDED SOME RED SPECKLES ON THE BUSH. THEY CAN BE BERRIES, FLOWERS, OR WHATEVER ELSE YOU IMAGINE!

COLOR, COLOR, COLOR!

NOW IT'S YOUR
TURN TO PACTICE COLORING,
AND JUST IN TIME!
KYLE IS AT IT AGAIN!

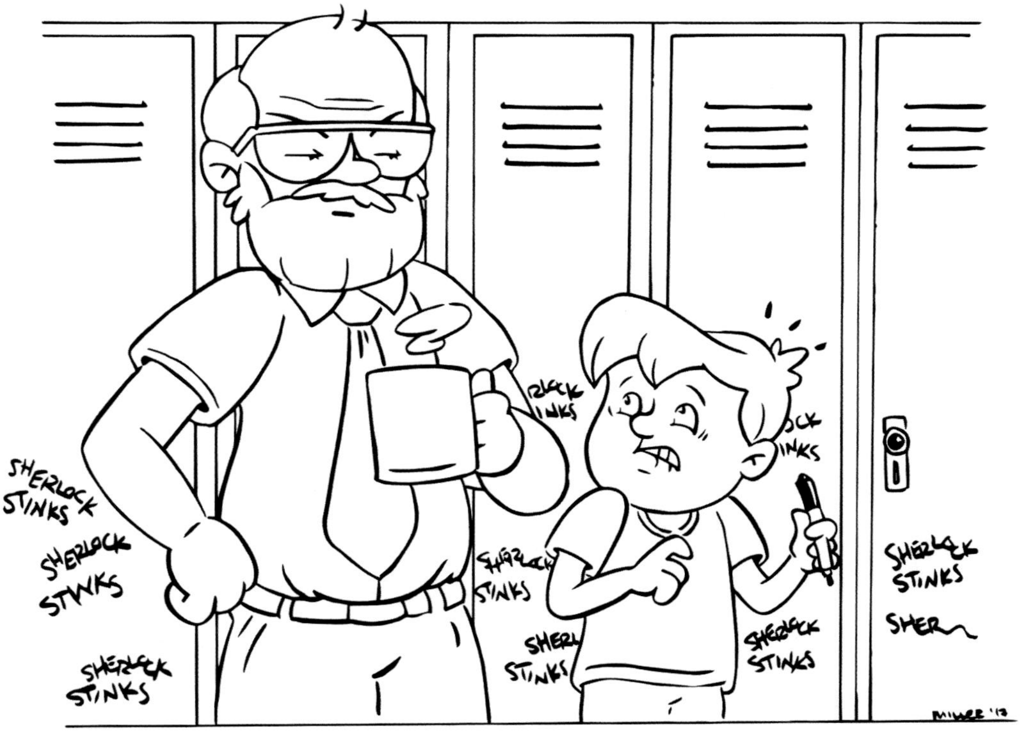
SHERLOCK STINKS
SHERLOCK STINKS
SHERLOCK STINKS
SHERLOCK STINKS
SHERLOCK STINKS
SHER

USE MARKERS OR CRAYONS
TO COLOR THIS PAGE.

YOU CAN EVEN SCAN IT ON YOUR COMPUTER
AND PRINT MULTIPULE COPIES TO
PRACTICE COLORING AGAIN
AND AGAIN!

MAZE!

HELP SHERLOCK
FIND THE CLUE AT THE
END OF THE MAZE!

THIS
ONE IS EXTRA
TRICKY, SO TAKE
YOUR TIME!
THINK YOU CAN
DO IT?

FUN FACT:
SCIENTISTS HAVE
USED MAZES TO STUD[Y]
ANIMALS SINCE 1882

WORD SEARCH!

SEE IF YOU CAN
FIND ALL THE WORDS
FROM THIS ISSUE
HIDDEN IN THE
WORD SEARCH!

```
R Q J Q J F Z M L Y E Y
Z O U E S O L V E S S T
M A M P I F S T S D S S
A E P L H D K E T D Z E
R O R A I O S Q R Z L K
K V O Y A D T U A T J I
E L P G N G O I D U G D
R M E R Y E L P E D U S
O N Q O Z B E M B R V O
P W B U R A N E U R H K
S W M N P L H N H X G H
G F H D P L Z T A E G D
```

PLAYGROUND

KIDS

SOLVE

MARKER

LESTRADE

DODGEBALL

EQUIPMENT

STOLEN

JUMPROPE

DID YOU FIND THEM ALL?

HINT:
LOOK FOR
WORDS GOING
ACROSS *AND*
UP AND DOWN!

FAN ART!

CHECK OUT
THESE PICTURES FROM
OUR FANS!
(WE HAVE THOSE)

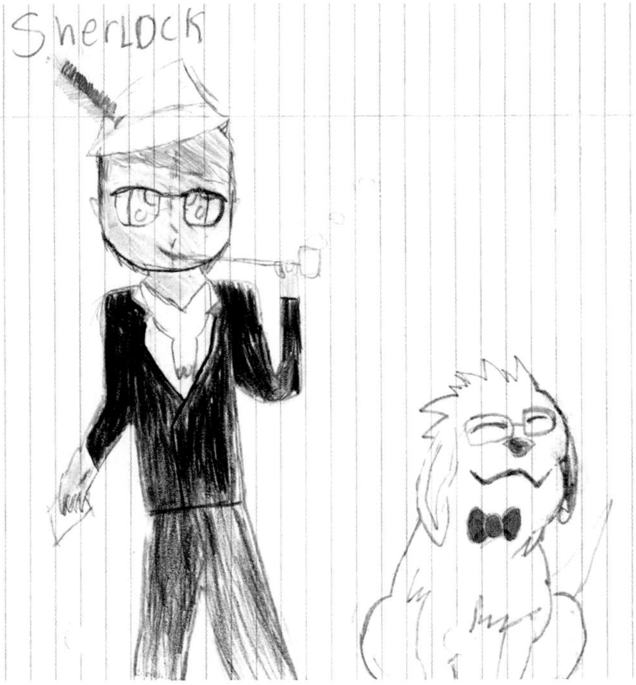
SherLOCK

SHERLOCK & WATSON BY XIAO MIAO
AGE 12
FROM PORTLAND, OR.

COOL REDESIGN, XIAO MIAO!

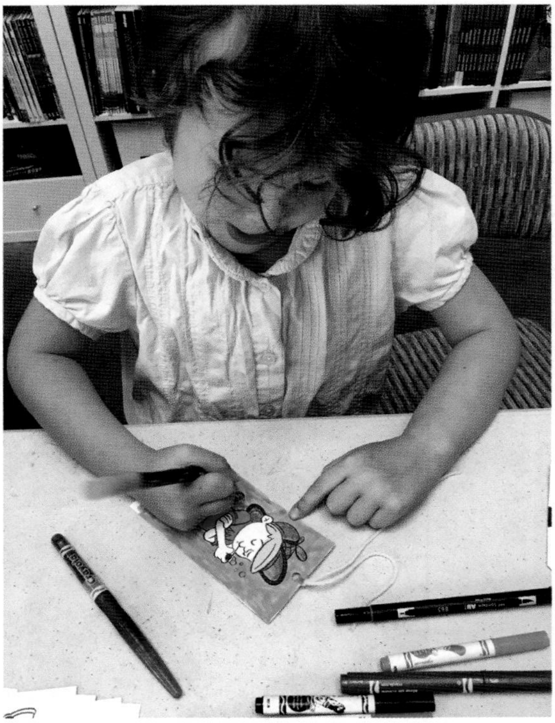

SHERLOCK BY KESTREL
AGE 5
FROM PORTLAND, OR.

FROM
COLORING WITH LESLEY
AT BOOKS WITH PICTURES

IF YOU HAVE
ANY ART THAT YOU
WOULD LIKE TO SHARE
OR WOULD LIKE TO
SEND US A LETTER,
YOU CAN!

WE'D LOVE
TO HEAR FROM YOU!

YOU CAN REACH US AT:
KIDSHERLOCKANDWATSON@GMAIL.COM

Kid Sherlock

CASE FILE 4:
"The Tripper"

THE
CREATIVE TEAM

Written
and lettered by
JUSTIN PHILLIPS

Art by
SEAN GREGORY MILLER

Colors by
LESLEY ATLANSKY

CREATED BY JUSTIN PHILLIPS AND SEAN GREGORY MILLER
BASED ON CHARACTERS BY SIR ARTHUR CONAN DOYLE

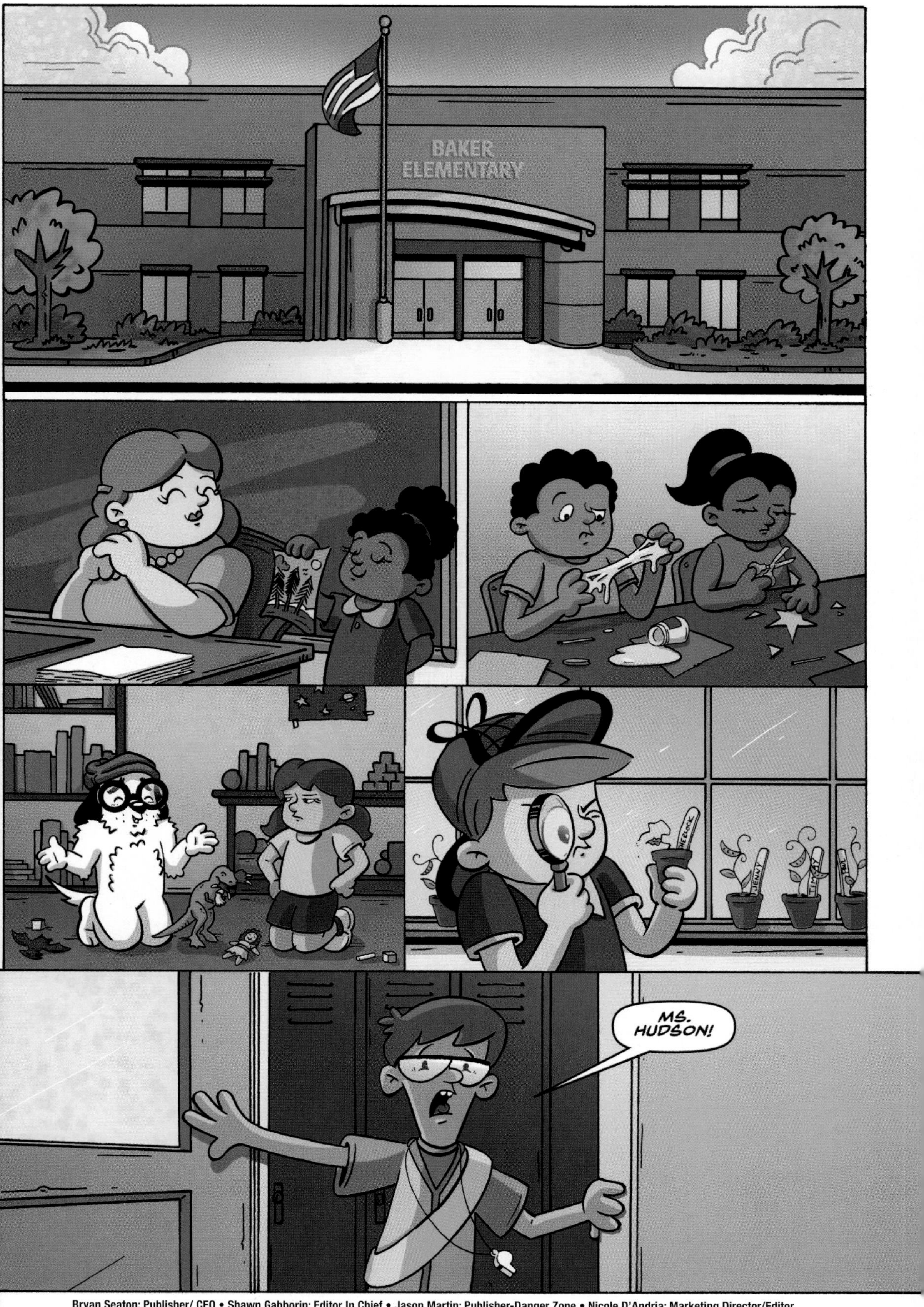
BAKER ELEMENTARY
SHERLOCK
JENNY
TIMMY
MS. HUDSON!

Bryan Seaton: Publisher/ CEO • Shawn Gabborin: Editor In Chief • Jason Martin: Publisher-Danger Zone • Nicole D'Andria: Marketing Director/Editor
Jim Dietz: Social Media Manager • Danielle Davison: Executive Administrator • Chad Cicconi: Moriarty's Understudy • Shawn Pryor: President of Creator Relations

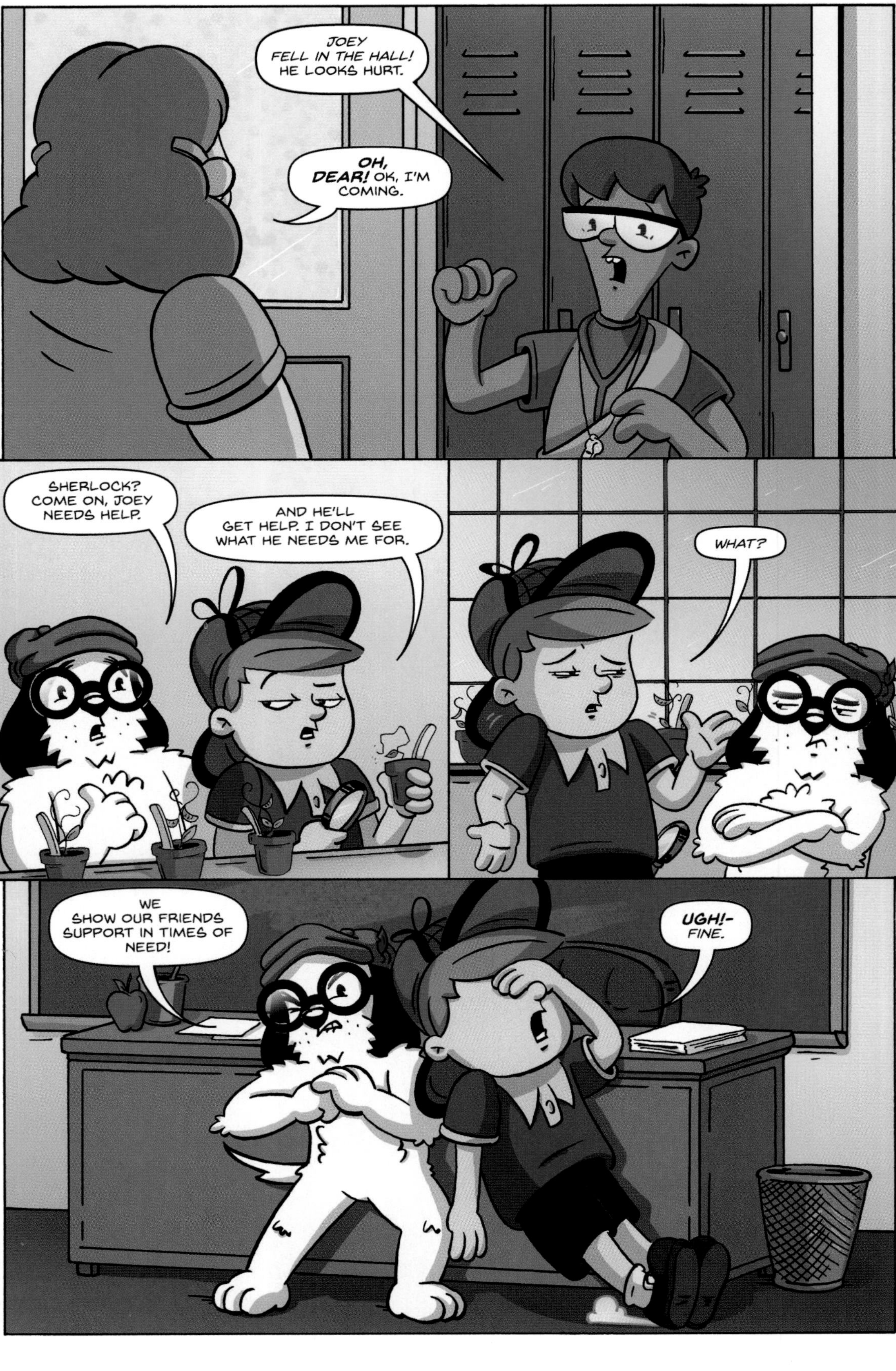
JOEY FELL IN THE HALL! HE LOOKS HURT.
OH, DEAR! OK, I'M COMING.
SHERLOCK? COME ON, JOEY NEEDS HELP.
AND HE'LL GET HELP. I DON'T SEE WHAT HE NEEDS ME FOR.
WHAT?
WE SHOW OUR FRIENDS SUPPORT IN TIMES OF NEED!
UGH!- FINE.

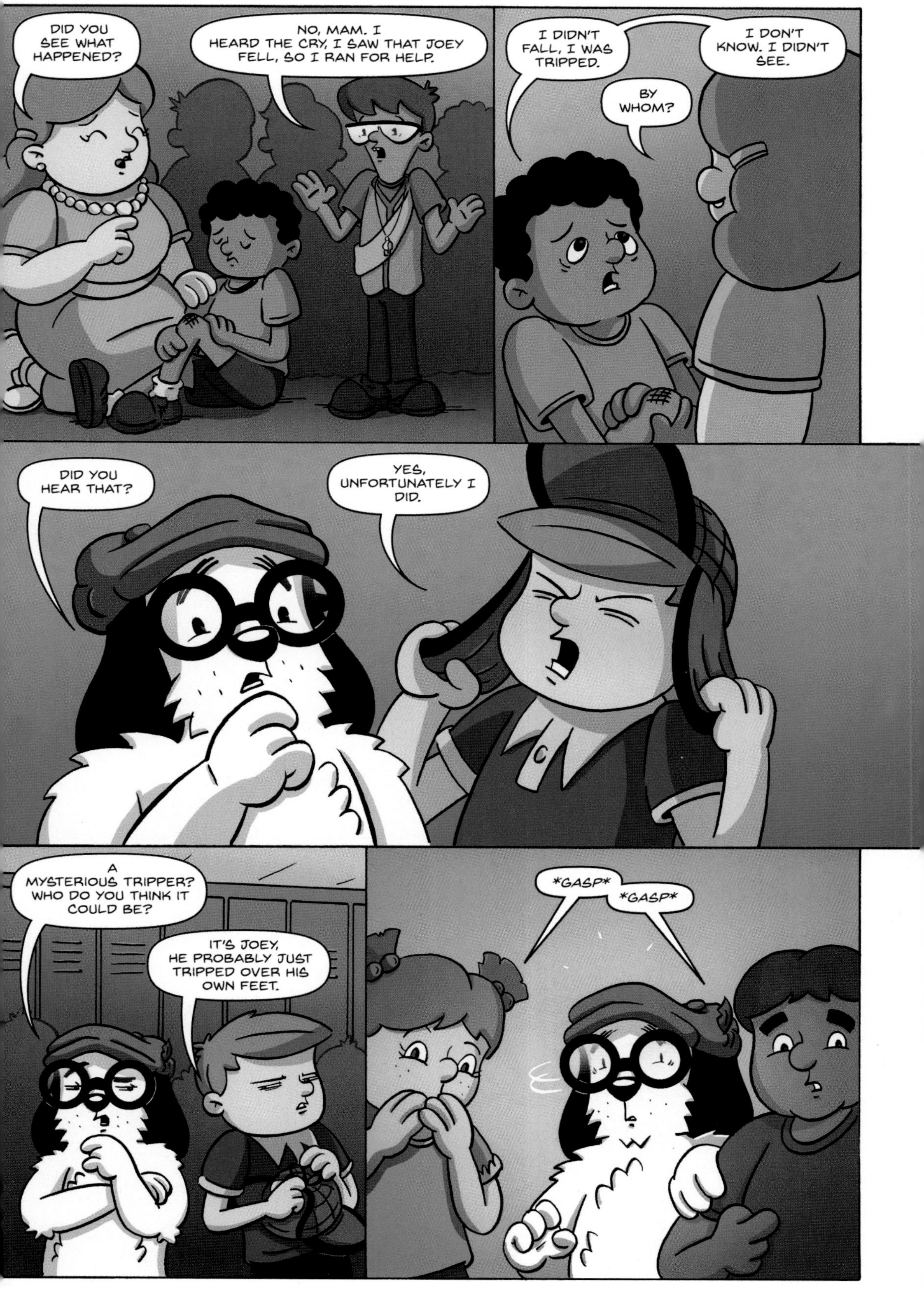
DID YOU SEE WHAT HAPPENED?
NO, MAM. I HEARD THE CRY, I SAW THAT JOEY FELL, SO I RAN FOR HELP.
I DIDN'T FALL, I WAS TRIPPED.
BY WHOM?
I DON'T KNOW. I DIDN'T SEE.
DID YOU HEAR THAT?
YES, UNFORTUNATELY I DID.
A MYSTERIOUS TRIPPER? WHO DO YOU THINK IT COULD BE?
IT'S JOEY, HE PROBABLY JUST TRIPPED OVER HIS OWN FEET.
GASP
GASP

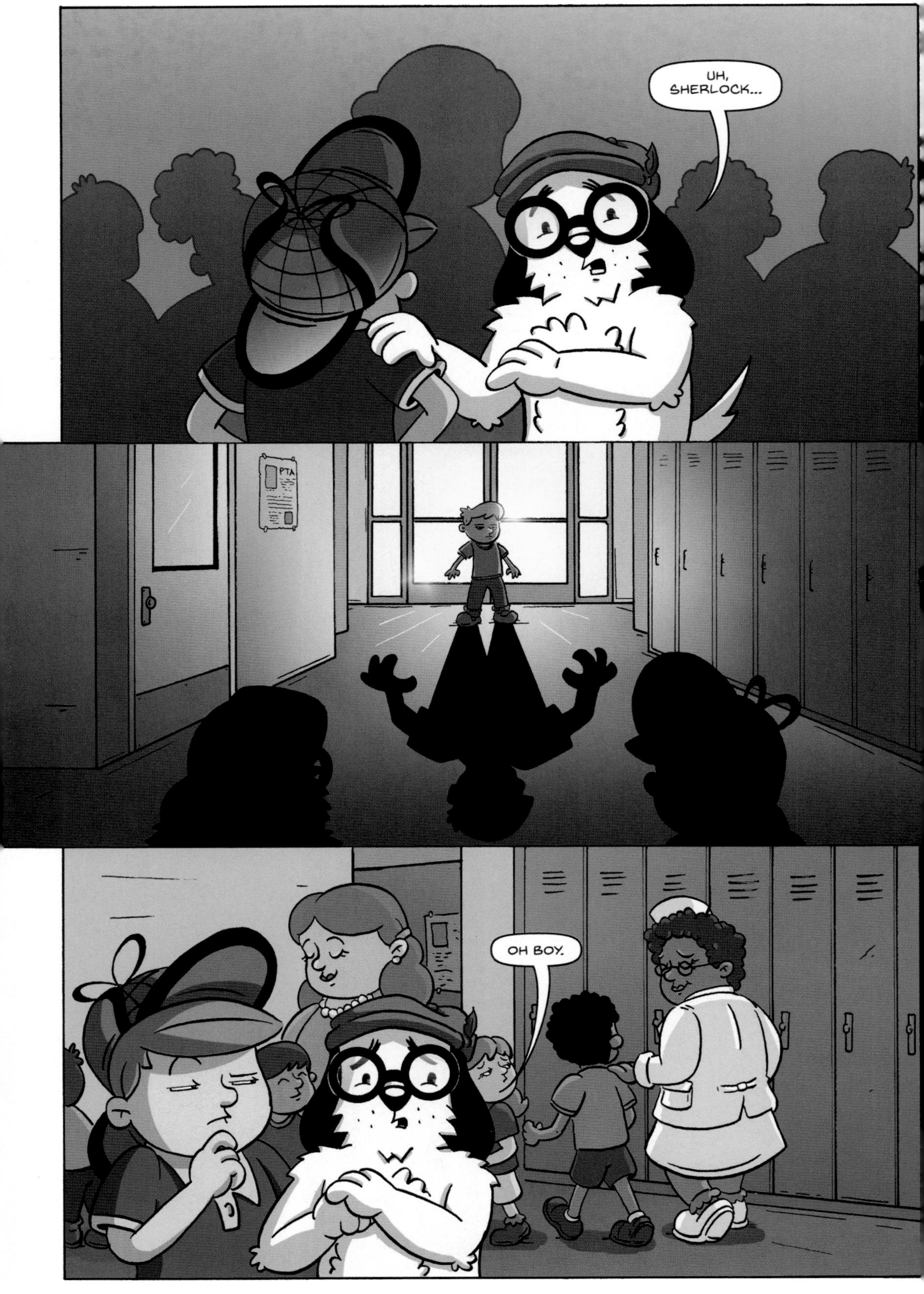
UH, SHERLOCK...
PTA
OH BOY.

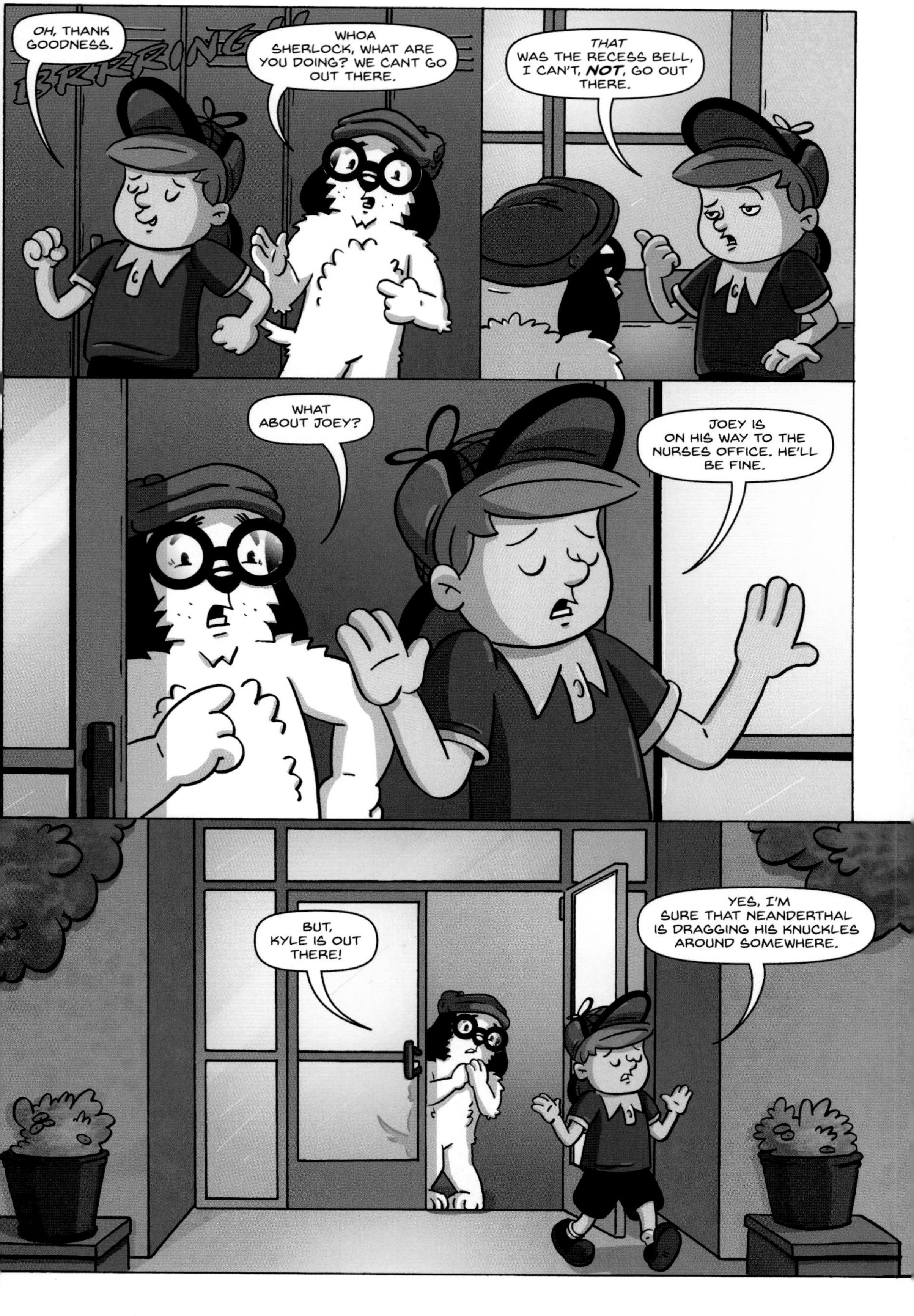

OH, THANK GOODNESS.
BRRRING!!
WHOA SHERLOCK, WHAT ARE YOU DOING? WE CANT GO OUT THERE.
THAT WAS THE RECESS BELL, I CAN'T, NOT, GO OUT THERE.
WHAT ABOUT JOEY?
JOEY IS ON HIS WAY TO THE NURSES OFFICE. HE'LL BE FINE.
BUT, KYLE IS OUT THERE!
YES, I'M SURE THAT NEANDERTHAL IS DRAGGING HIS KNUCKLES AROUND SOMEWHERE.

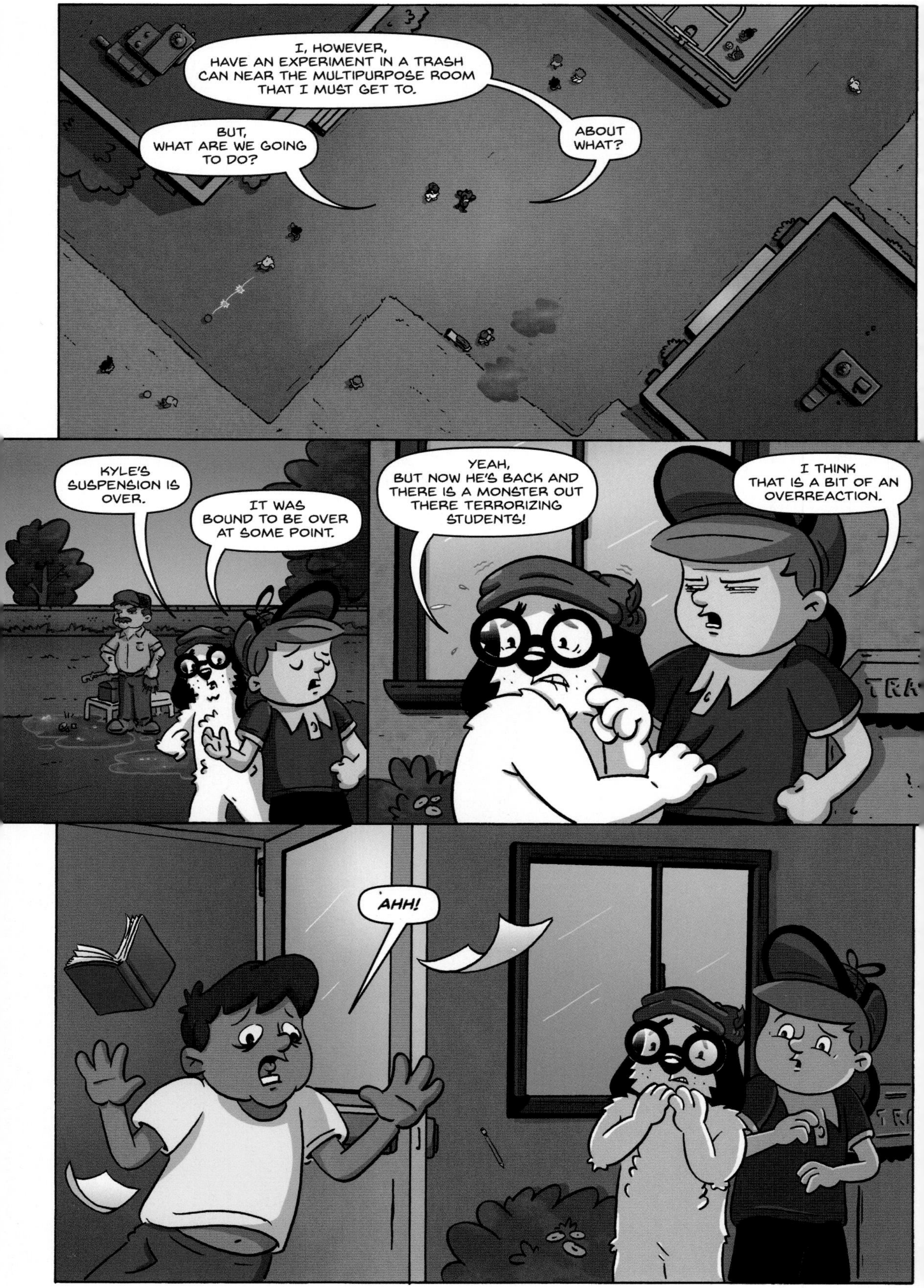
I, HOWEVER, HAVE AN EXPERIMENT IN A TRASH CAN NEAR THE MULTIPURPOSE ROOM THAT I MUST GET TO.
BUT, WHAT ARE WE GOING TO DO?
ABOUT WHAT?
KYLE'S SUSPENSION IS OVER.
IT WAS BOUND TO BE OVER AT SOME POINT.
YEAH, BUT NOW HE'S BACK AND THERE IS A MONSTER OUT THERE TERRORIZING STUDENTS!
I THINK THAT IS A BIT OF AN OVERREACTION.
AHH!

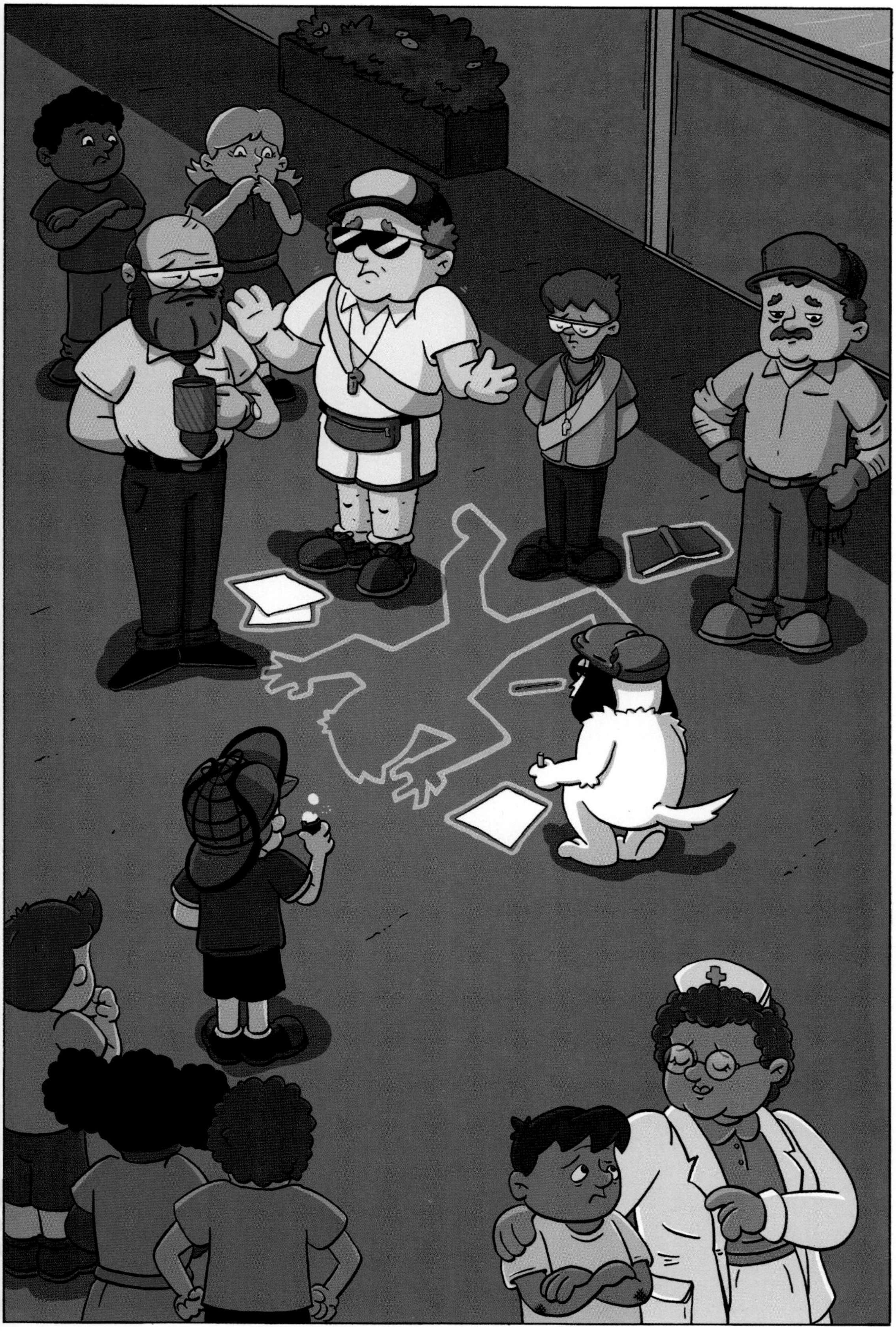

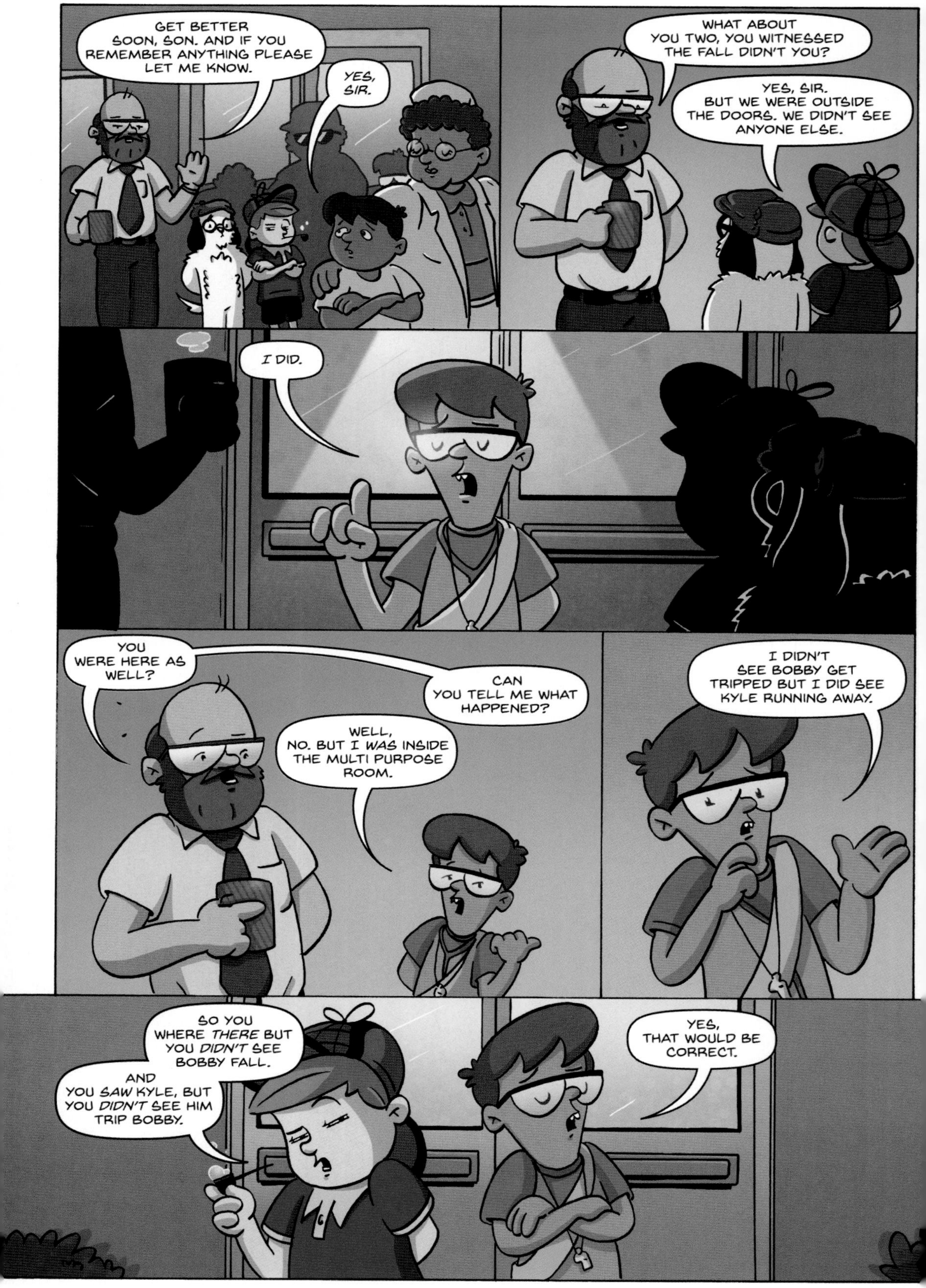
GET BETTER SOON, SON. AND IF YOU REMEMBER ANYTHING PLEASE LET ME KNOW.
YES, SIR.
WHAT ABOUT YOU TWO, YOU WITNESSED THE FALL DIDN'T YOU?
YES, SIR. BUT WE WERE OUTSIDE THE DOORS. WE DIDN'T SEE ANYONE ELSE.
I DID.
YOU WERE HERE AS WELL?
CAN YOU TELL ME WHAT HAPPENED?
WELL, NO. BUT I *WAS* INSIDE THE MULTI PURPOSE ROOM.
I DIDN'T SEE BOBBY GET TRIPPED BUT I DID SEE KYLE RUNNING AWAY.
SO YOU WHERE *THERE* BUT YOU *DIDN'T* SEE BOBBY FALL.
AND YOU SAW KYLE, BUT YOU *DIDN'T* SEE HIM TRIP BOBBY.
YES, THAT WOULD BE CORRECT.

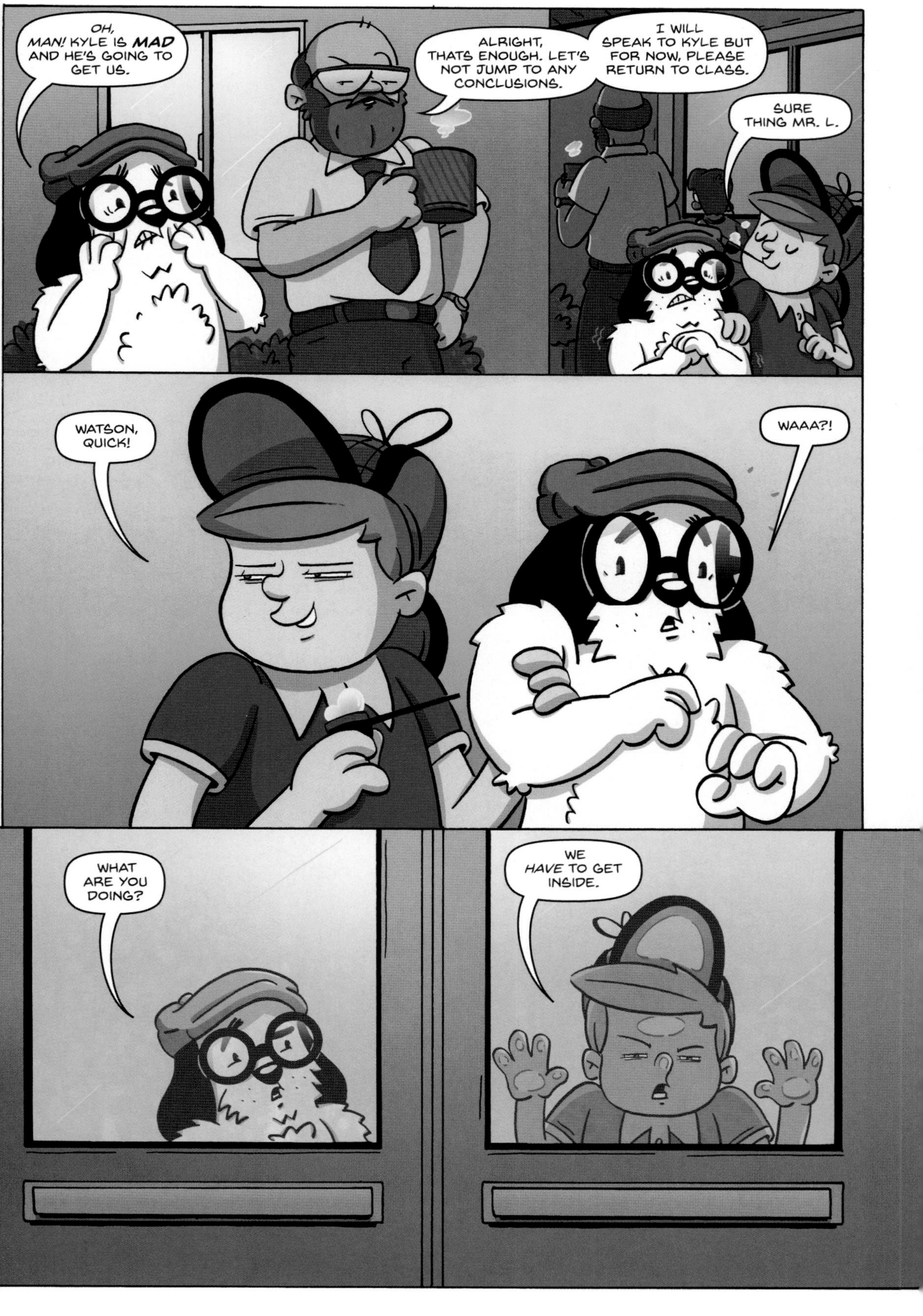
OH, MAN! KYLE IS MAD AND HE'S GOING TO GET US.
ALRIGHT, THATS ENOUGH. LET'S NOT JUMP TO ANY CONCLUSIONS.
I WILL SPEAK TO KYLE BUT FOR NOW, PLEASE RETURN TO CLASS.
SURE THING MR. L.
WATSON, QUICK!
WAAA?!
WHAT ARE YOU DOING?
WE HAVE TO GET INSIDE.

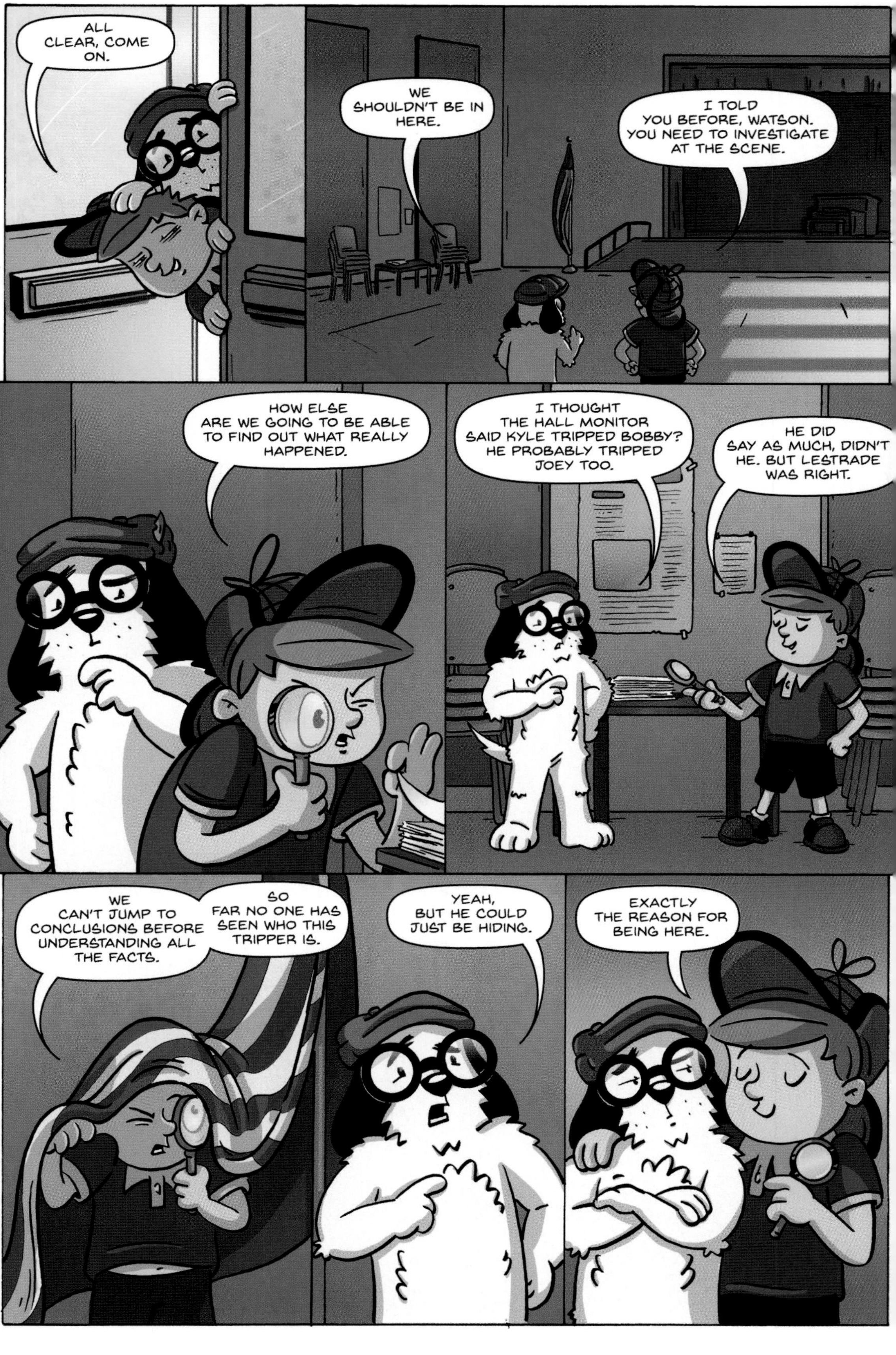
ALL CLEAR, COME ON.
WE SHOULDN'T BE IN HERE.
I TOLD YOU BEFORE, WATSON. YOU NEED TO INVESTIGATE AT THE SCENE.
HOW ELSE ARE WE GOING TO BE ABLE TO FIND OUT WHAT REALLY HAPPENED.
I THOUGHT THE HALL MONITOR SAID KYLE TRIPPED BOBBY? HE PROBABLY TRIPPED JOEY TOO.
HE DID SAY AS MUCH, DIDN'T HE. BUT LESTRADE WAS RIGHT.
WE CAN'T JUMP TO CONCLUSIONS BEFORE UNDERSTANDING ALL THE FACTS.
SO FAR NO ONE HAS SEEN WHO THIS TRIPPER IS.
YEAH, BUT HE COULD JUST BE HIDING.
EXACTLY THE REASON FOR BEING HERE.

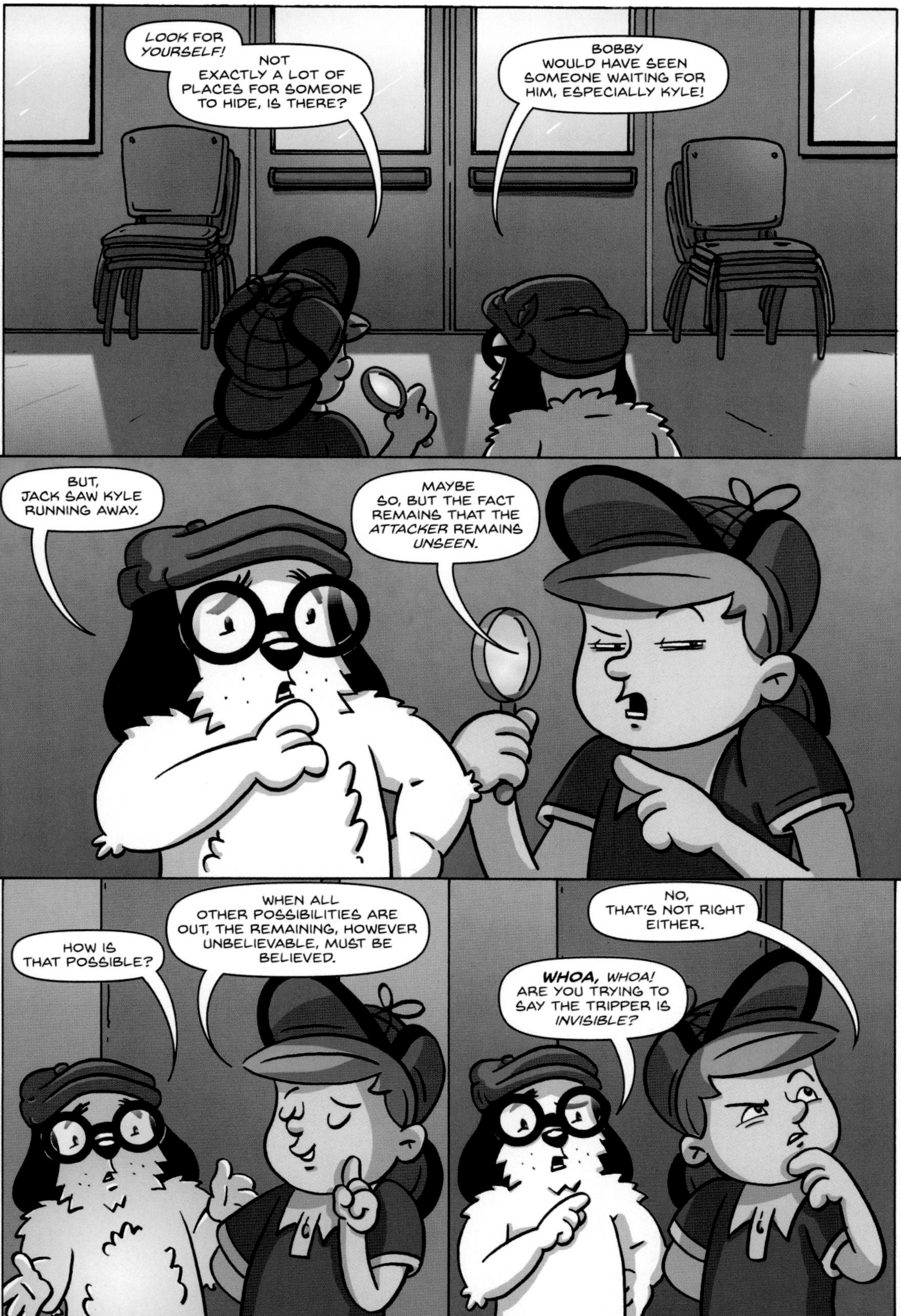
LOOK FOR YOURSELF!
NOT EXACTLY A LOT OF PLACES FOR SOMEONE TO HIDE, IS THERE?
BOBBY WOULD HAVE SEEN SOMEONE WAITING FOR HIM, ESPECIALLY KYLE!
BUT, JACK SAW KYLE RUNNING AWAY.
MAYBE SO, BUT THE FACT REMAINS THAT THE ATTACKER REMAINS UNSEEN.
HOW IS THAT POSSIBLE?
WHEN ALL OTHER POSSIBILITIES ARE OUT, THE REMAINING, HOWEVER UNBELIEVABLE, MUST BE BELIEVED.
WHOA, WHOA! ARE YOU TRYING TO SAY THE TRIPPER IS INVISIBLE?
NO, THAT'S NOT RIGHT EITHER.

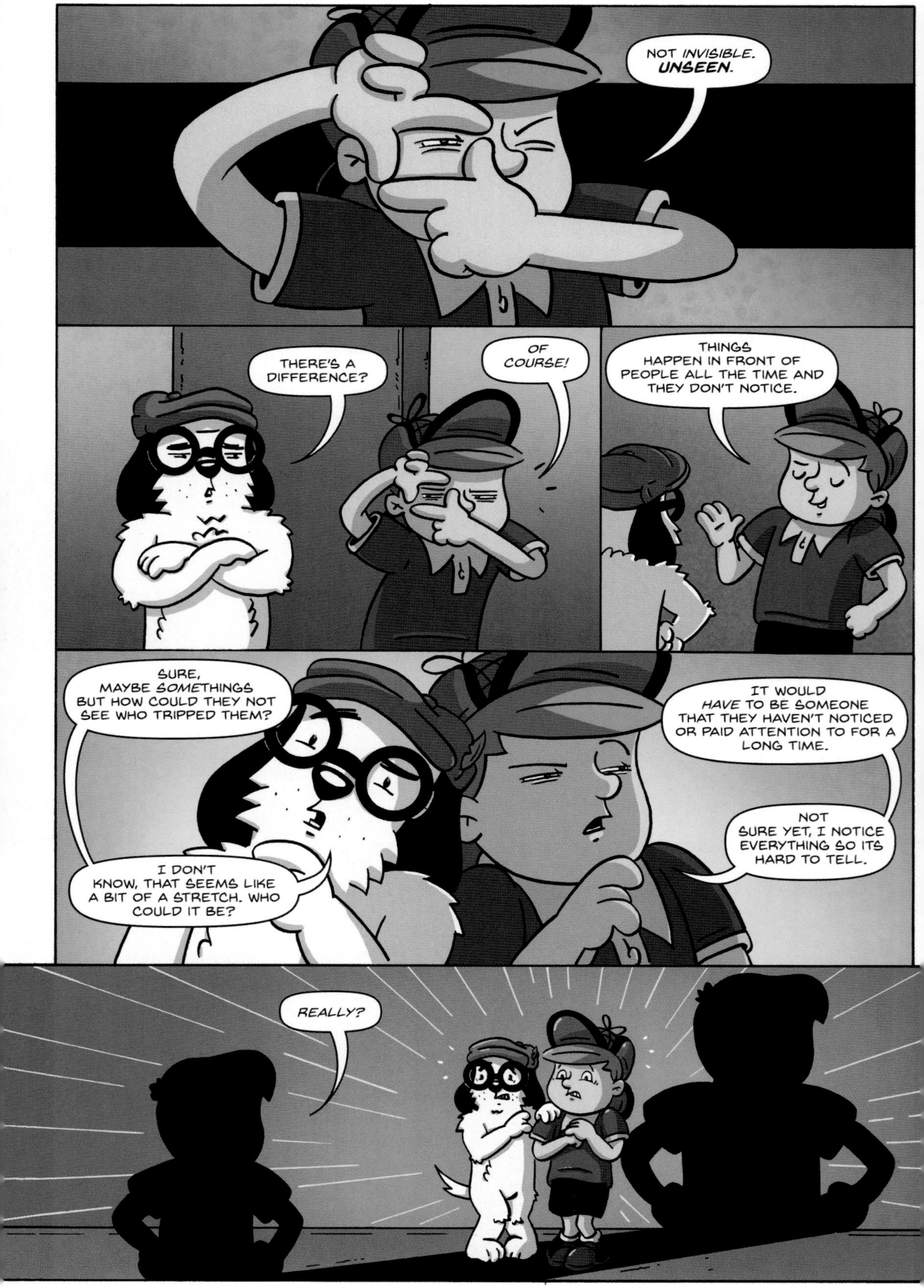

NOT INVISIBLE. UNSEEN.
THERE'S A DIFFERENCE?
OF COURSE!
THINGS HAPPEN IN FRONT OF PEOPLE ALL THE TIME AND THEY DON'T NOTICE.
SURE, MAYBE SOMETHINGS BUT HOW COULD THEY NOT SEE WHO TRIPPED THEM?
IT WOULD HAVE TO BE SOMEONE THAT THEY HAVEN'T NOTICED OR PAID ATTENTION TO FOR A LONG TIME.
I DON'T KNOW, THAT SEEMS LIKE A BIT OF A STRETCH. WHO COULD IT BE?
NOT SURE YET, I NOTICE EVERYTHING SO ITS HARD TO TELL.
REALLY?

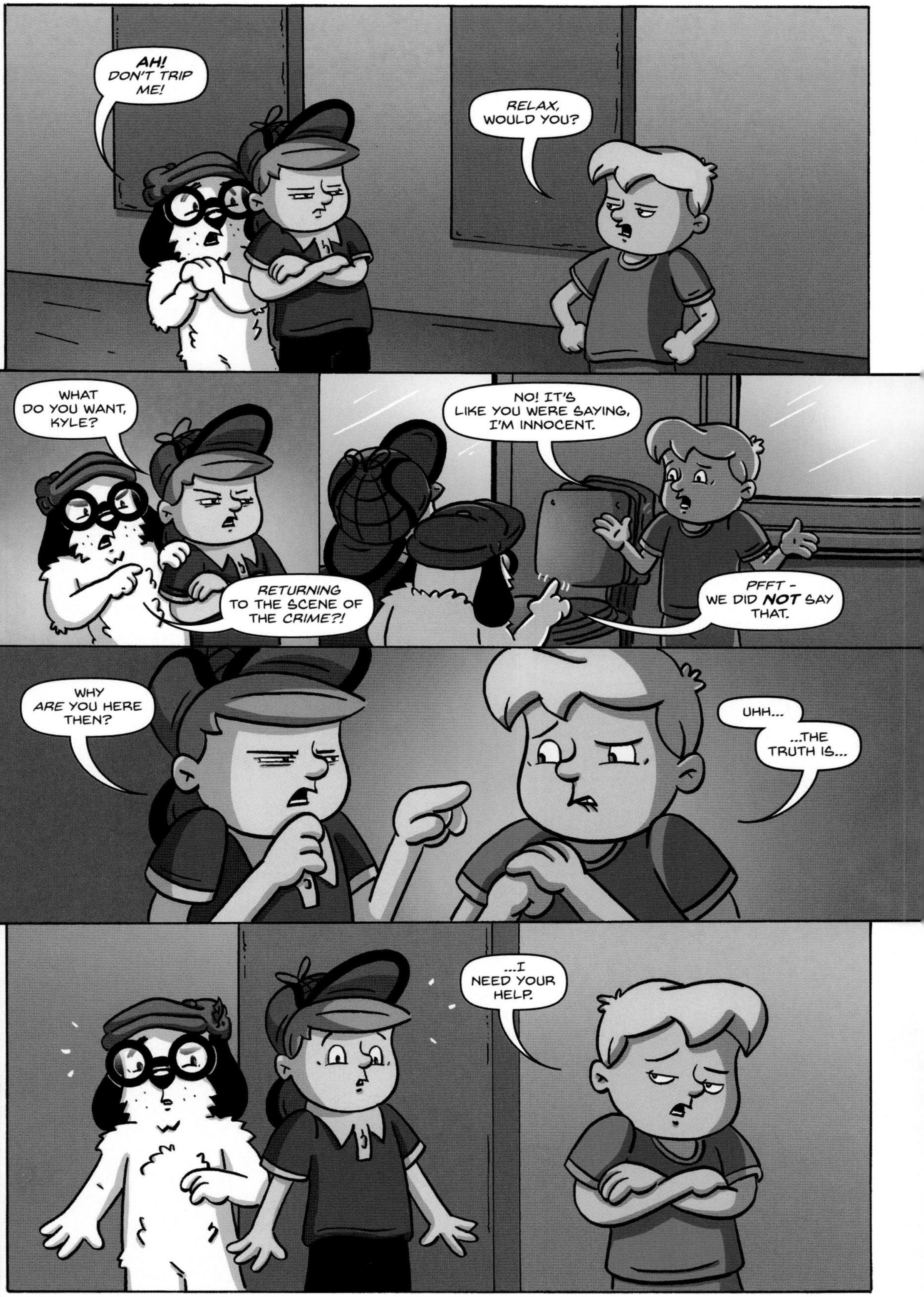
AH! DON'T TRIP ME!
RELAX, WOULD YOU?
WHAT DO YOU WANT, KYLE?
RETURNING TO THE SCENE OF THE CRIME?!
NO! IT'S LIKE YOU WERE SAYING, I'M INNOCENT.
PFFT - WE DID NOT SAY THAT.
WHY ARE YOU HERE THEN?
UHH...
...THE TRUTH IS...
...I NEED YOUR HELP.

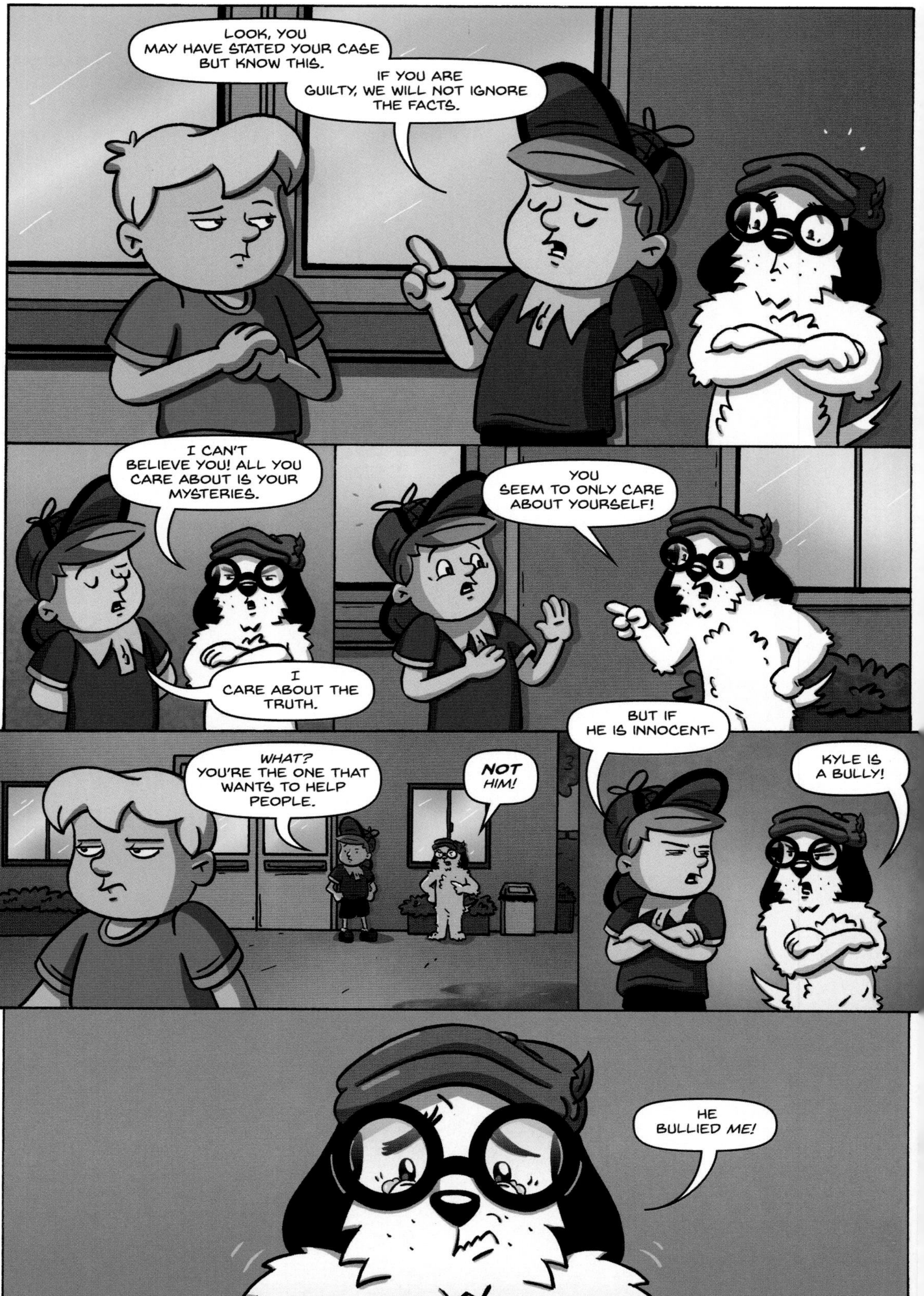
LOOK, YOU MAY HAVE STATED YOUR CASE BUT KNOW THIS.
IF YOU ARE GUILTY, WE WILL NOT IGNORE THE FACTS.
I CAN'T BELIEVE YOU! ALL YOU CARE ABOUT IS YOUR MYSTERIES.
I CARE ABOUT THE TRUTH.
YOU SEEM TO ONLY CARE ABOUT YOURSELF!
WHAT? YOU'RE THE ONE THAT WANTS TO HELP PEOPLE.
NOT *HIM!*
BUT IF HE IS INNOCENT-
KYLE IS A BULLY!
HE BULLIED *ME!*

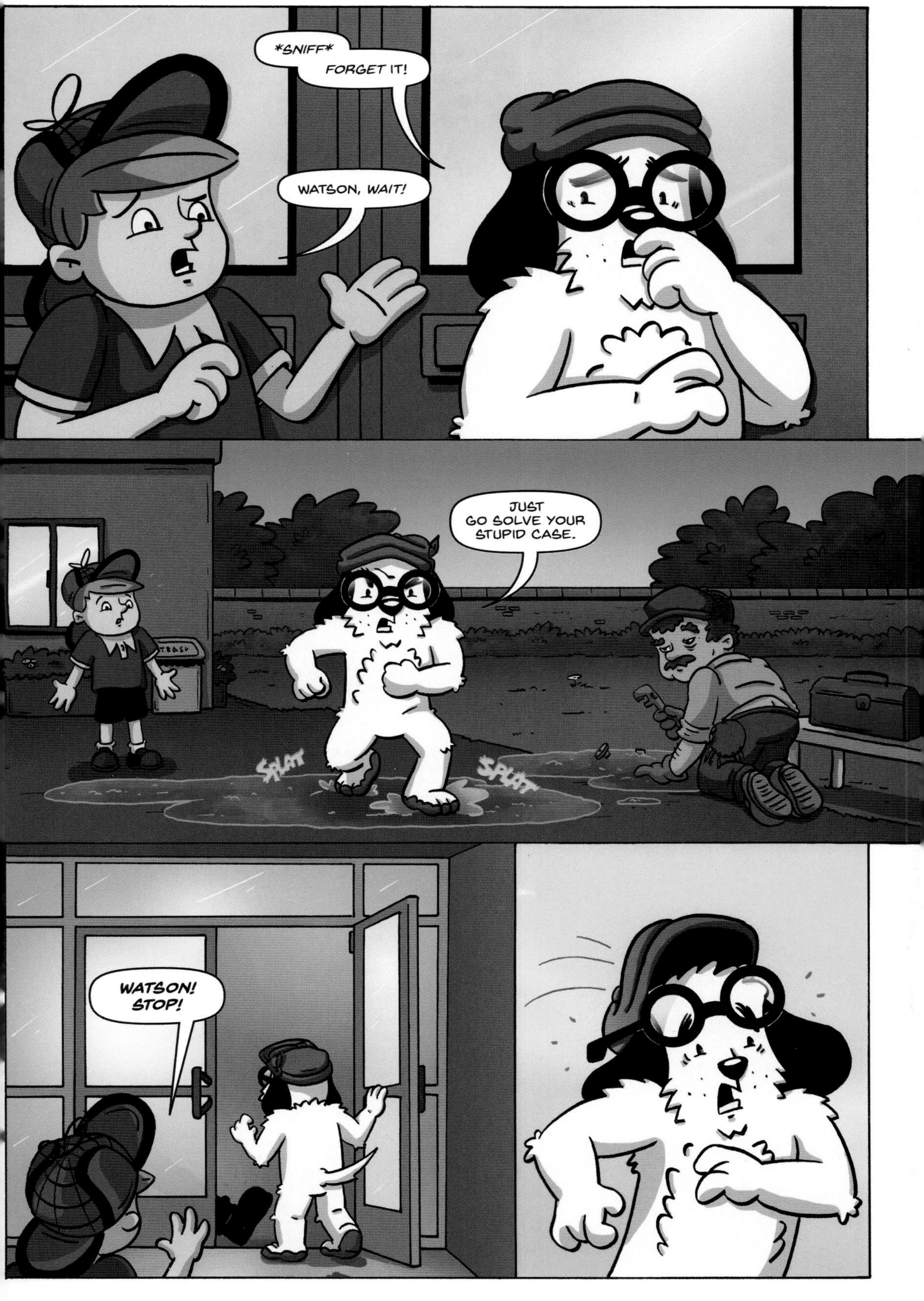
SNIFF
FORGET IT!
WATSON, WAIT!
JUST GO SOLVE YOUR STUPID CASE.
SPLAT
SPLAT
WATSON! STOP!

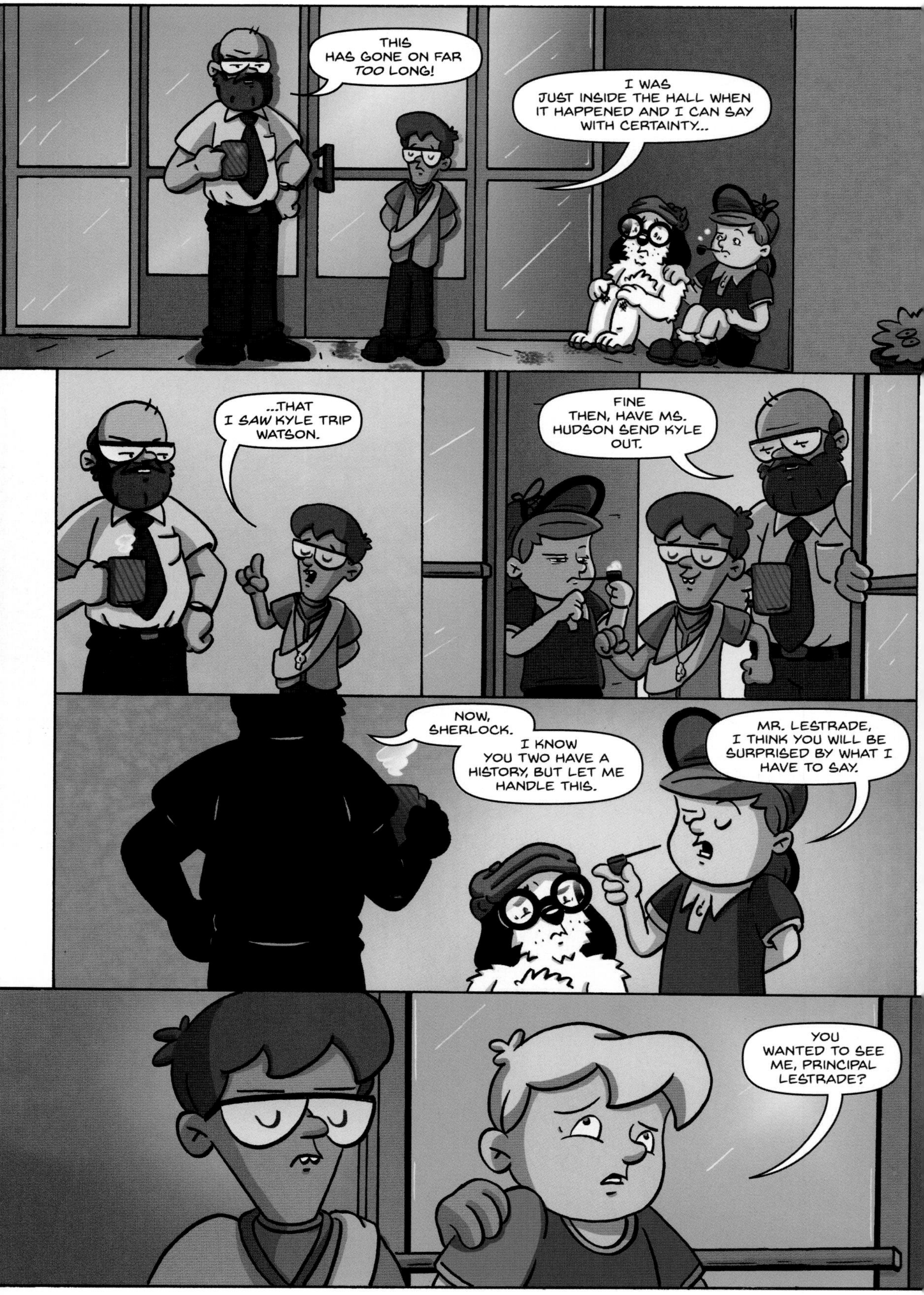
THIS HAS GONE ON FAR *TOO* LONG!
I WAS JUST INSIDE THE HALL WHEN IT HAPPENED AND I CAN SAY WITH CERTAINTY...
...THAT I *SAW* KYLE TRIP WATSON.
FINE THEN, HAVE MS. HUDSON SEND KYLE OUT.
NOW, SHERLOCK.
I KNOW YOU TWO HAVE A HISTORY, BUT LET ME HANDLE THIS.
MR. LESTRADE, I THINK YOU WILL BE SURPRISED BY WHAT I HAVE TO SAY.
YOU WANTED TO SEE ME, PRINCIPAL LESTRADE?

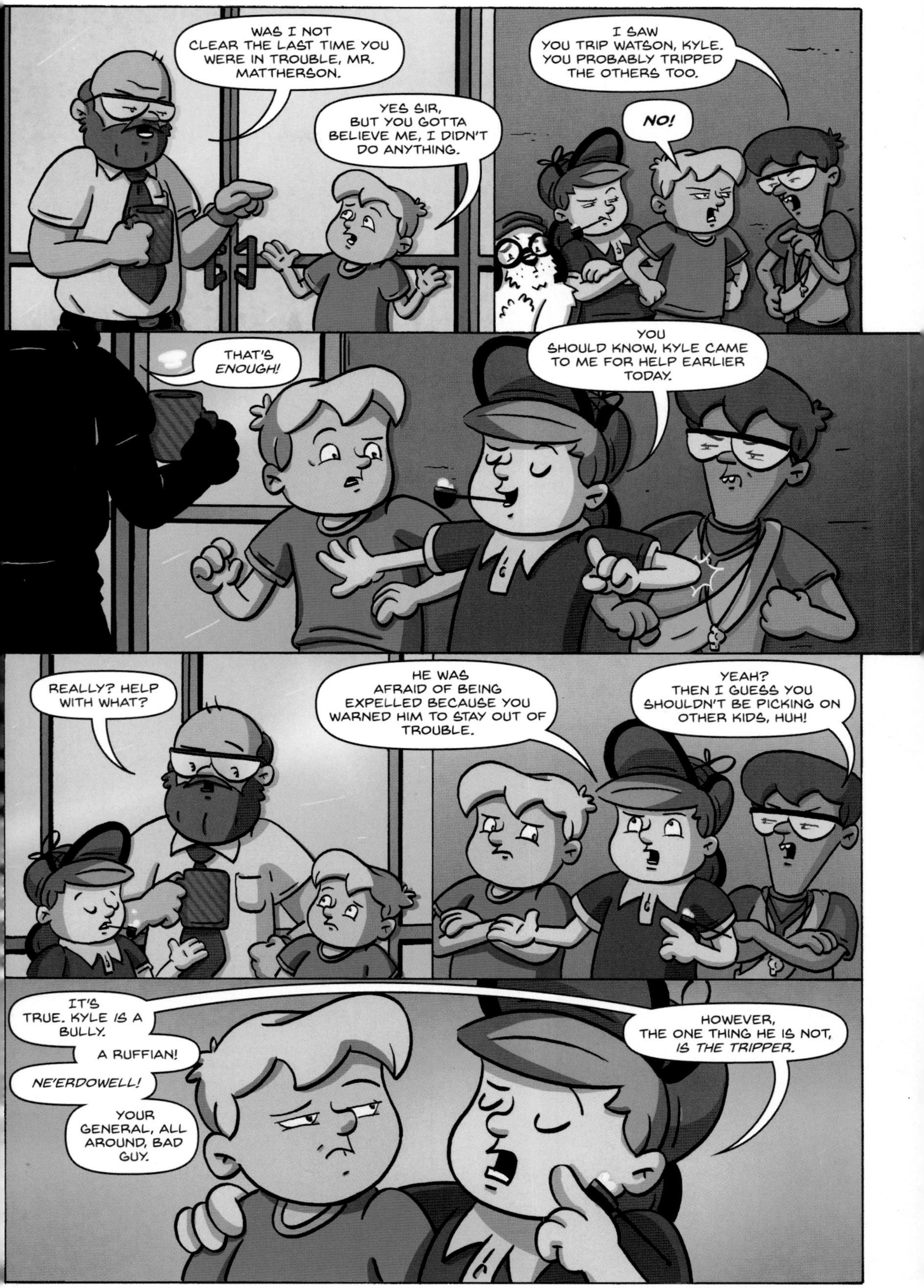
WAS I NOT CLEAR THE LAST TIME YOU WERE IN TROUBLE, MR. MATTHERSON.
YES SIR, BUT YOU GOTTA BELIEVE ME, I DIDN'T DO ANYTHING.
I SAW YOU TRIP WATSON, KYLE. YOU PROBABLY TRIPPED THE OTHERS TOO.
NO!
THAT'S ENOUGH!
YOU SHOULD KNOW, KYLE CAME TO ME FOR HELP EARLIER TODAY.
REALLY? HELP WITH WHAT?
HE WAS AFRAID OF BEING EXPELLED BECAUSE YOU WARNED HIM TO STAY OUT OF TROUBLE.
YEAH? THEN I GUESS YOU SHOULDN'T BE PICKING ON OTHER KIDS, HUH!
IT'S TRUE. KYLE IS A BULLY.
A RUFFIAN!
NE'ERDOWELL!
YOUR GENERAL, ALL AROUND, BAD GUY.
HOWEVER, THE ONE THING HE IS NOT, IS THE TRIPPER.

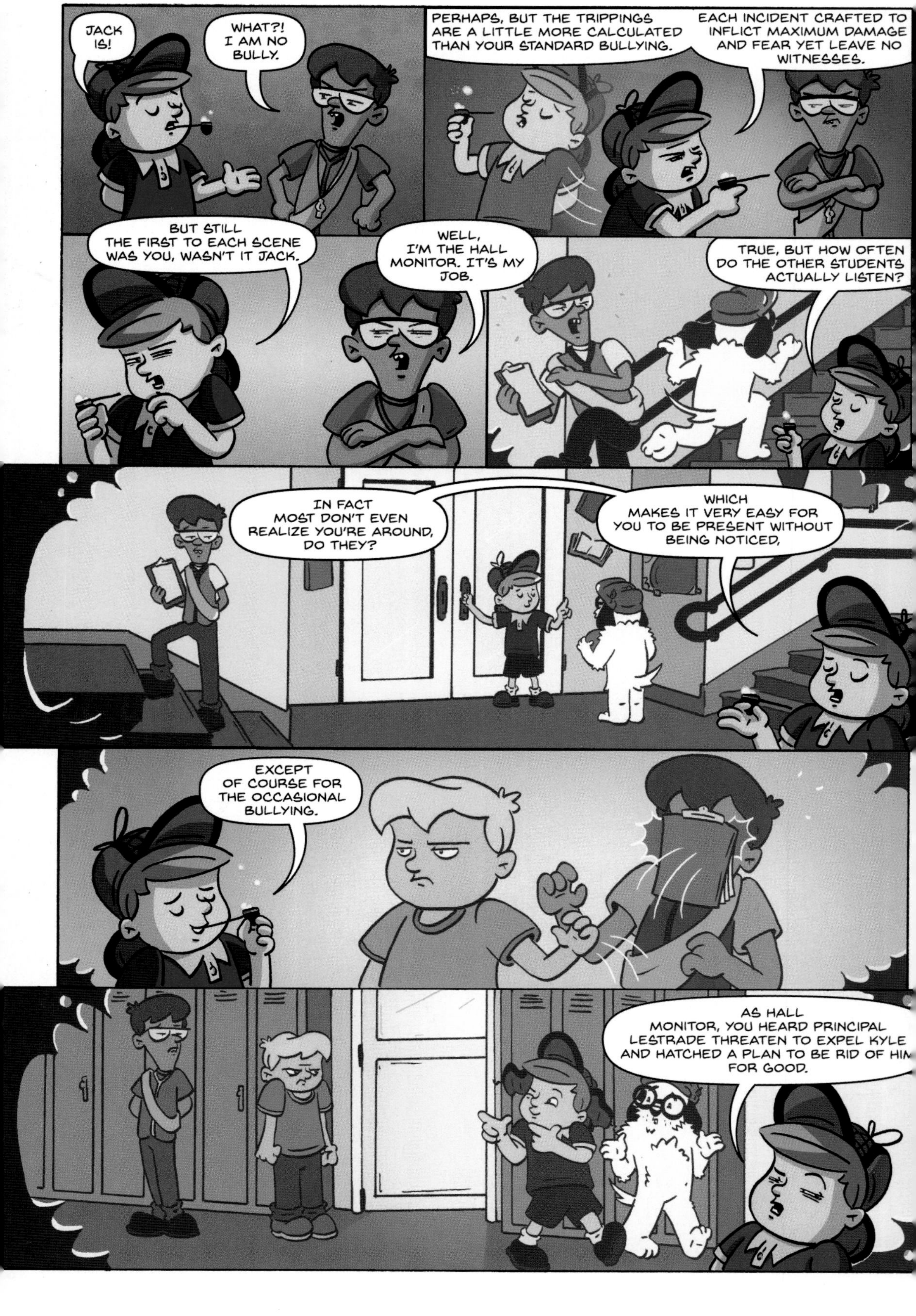
JACK IS!
WHAT?! I AM NO BULLY.
PERHAPS, BUT THE TRIPPINGS ARE A LITTLE MORE CALCULATED THAN YOUR STANDARD BULLYING.
EACH INCIDENT CRAFTED TO INFLICT MAXIMUM DAMAGE AND FEAR YET LEAVE NO WITNESSES.
BUT STILL THE FIRST TO EACH SCENE WAS YOU, WASN'T IT JACK.
WELL, I'M THE HALL MONITOR. IT'S MY JOB.
TRUE, BUT HOW OFTEN DO THE OTHER STUDENTS ACTUALLY LISTEN?
IN FACT MOST DON'T EVEN REALIZE YOU'RE AROUND, DO THEY?
WHICH MAKES IT VERY EASY FOR YOU TO BE PRESENT WITHOUT BEING NOTICED,
EXCEPT OF COURSE FOR THE OCCASIONAL BULLYING.
AS HALL MONITOR, YOU HEARD PRINCIPAL LESTRADE THREATEN TO EXPEL KYLE AND HATCHED A PLAN TO BE RID OF HIM FOR GOOD.

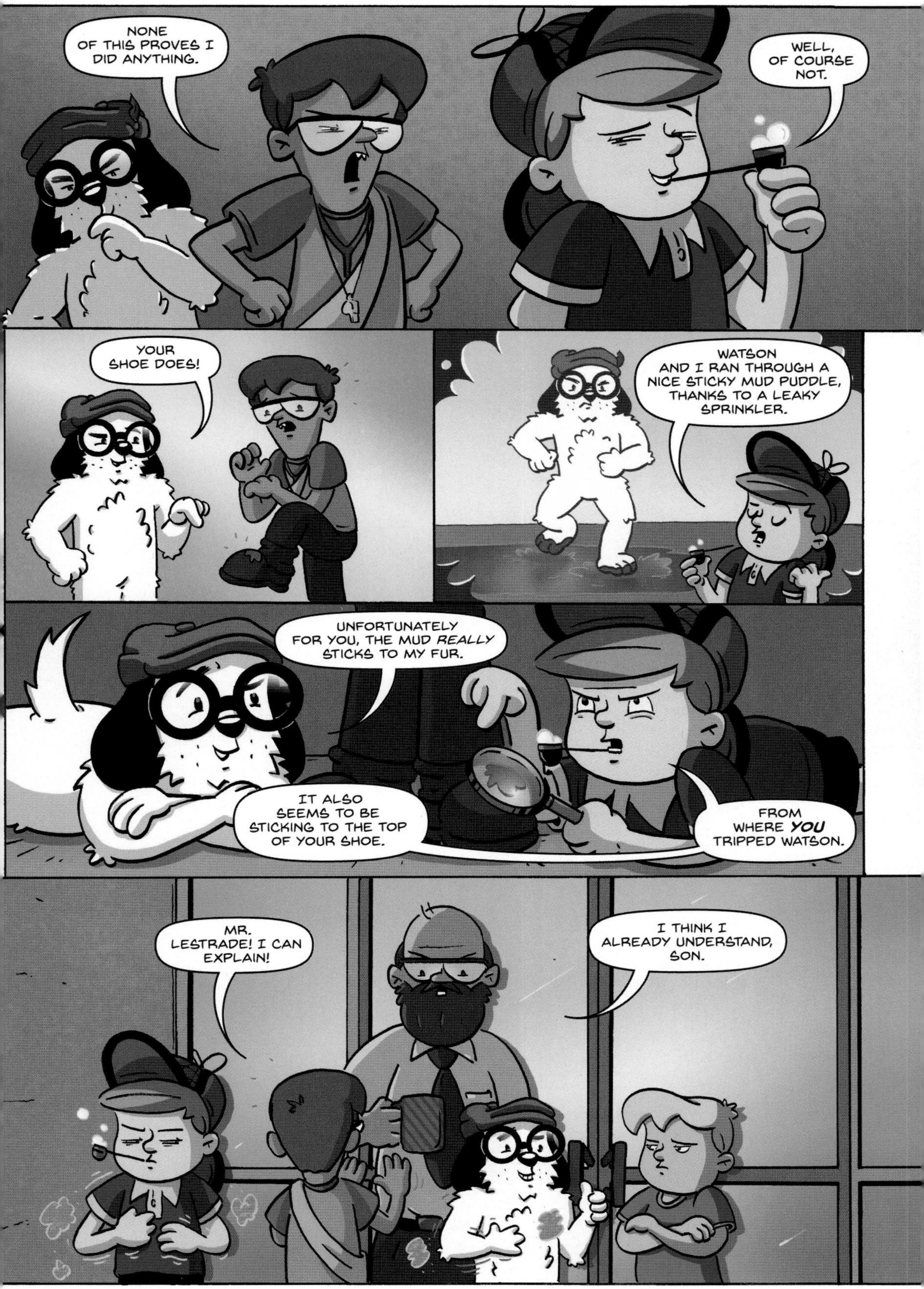
NONE OF THIS PROVES I DID ANYTHING.
WELL, OF COURSE NOT.
YOUR SHOE DOES!
WATSON AND I RAN THROUGH A NICE STICKY MUD PUDDLE, THANKS TO A LEAKY SPRINKLER.
UNFORTUNATELY FOR YOU, THE MUD *REALLY* STICKS TO MY FUR.
IT ALSO SEEMS TO BE STICKING TO THE TOP OF YOUR SHOE.
FROM WHERE ***YOU*** TRIPPED WATSON.
MR. LESTRADE! I CAN EXPLAIN!
I THINK I ALREADY UNDERSTAND, SON.

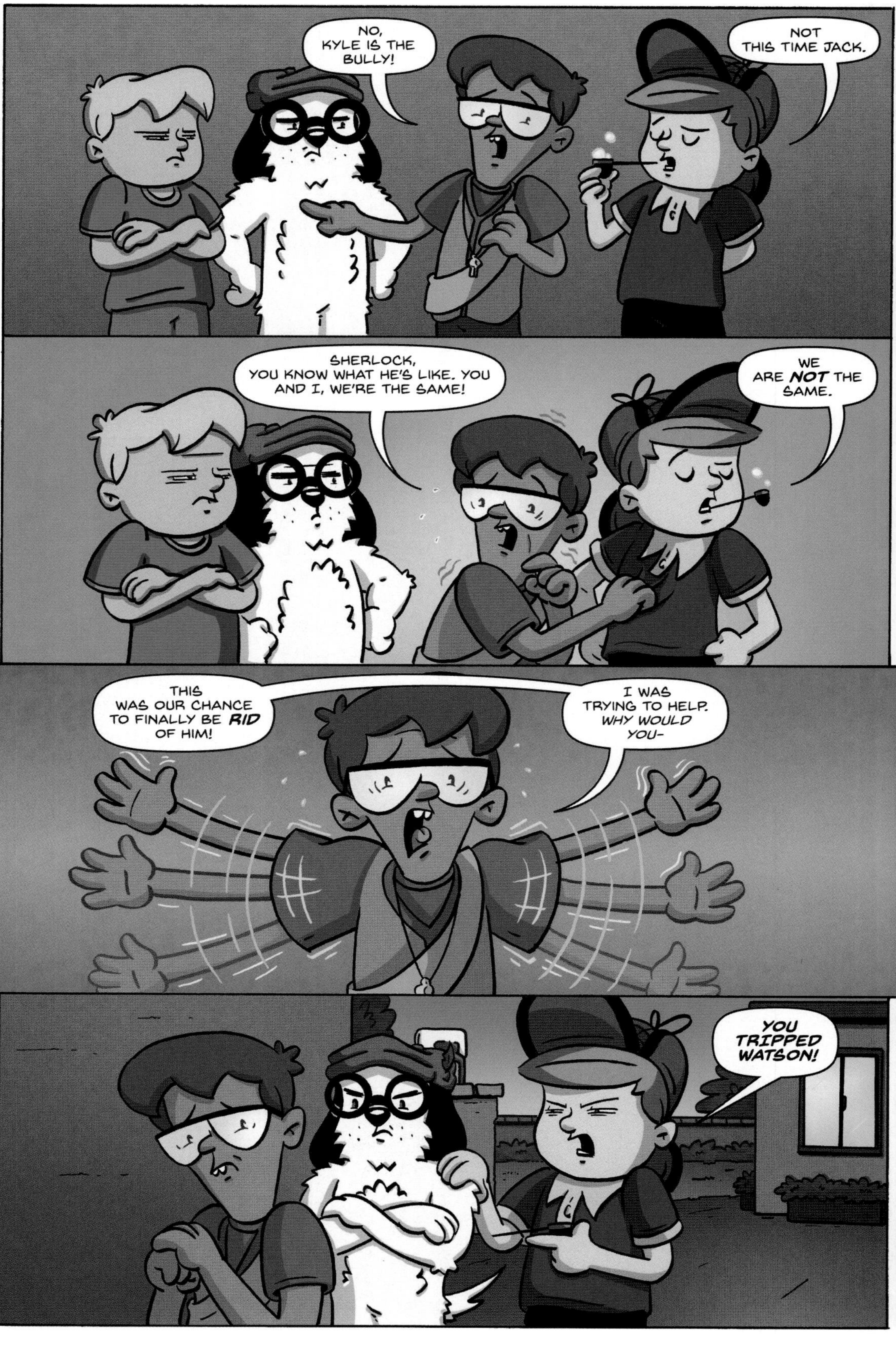

NO, KYLE IS THE BULLY!
NOT THIS TIME JACK.
SHERLOCK, YOU KNOW WHAT HE'S LIKE. YOU AND I, WE'RE THE SAME!
WE ARE **NOT** THE SAME.
THIS WAS OUR CHANCE TO FINALLY BE ***RID*** OF HIM!
I WAS TRYING TO HELP. *WHY WOULD YOU-*
YOU TRIPPED WATSON!

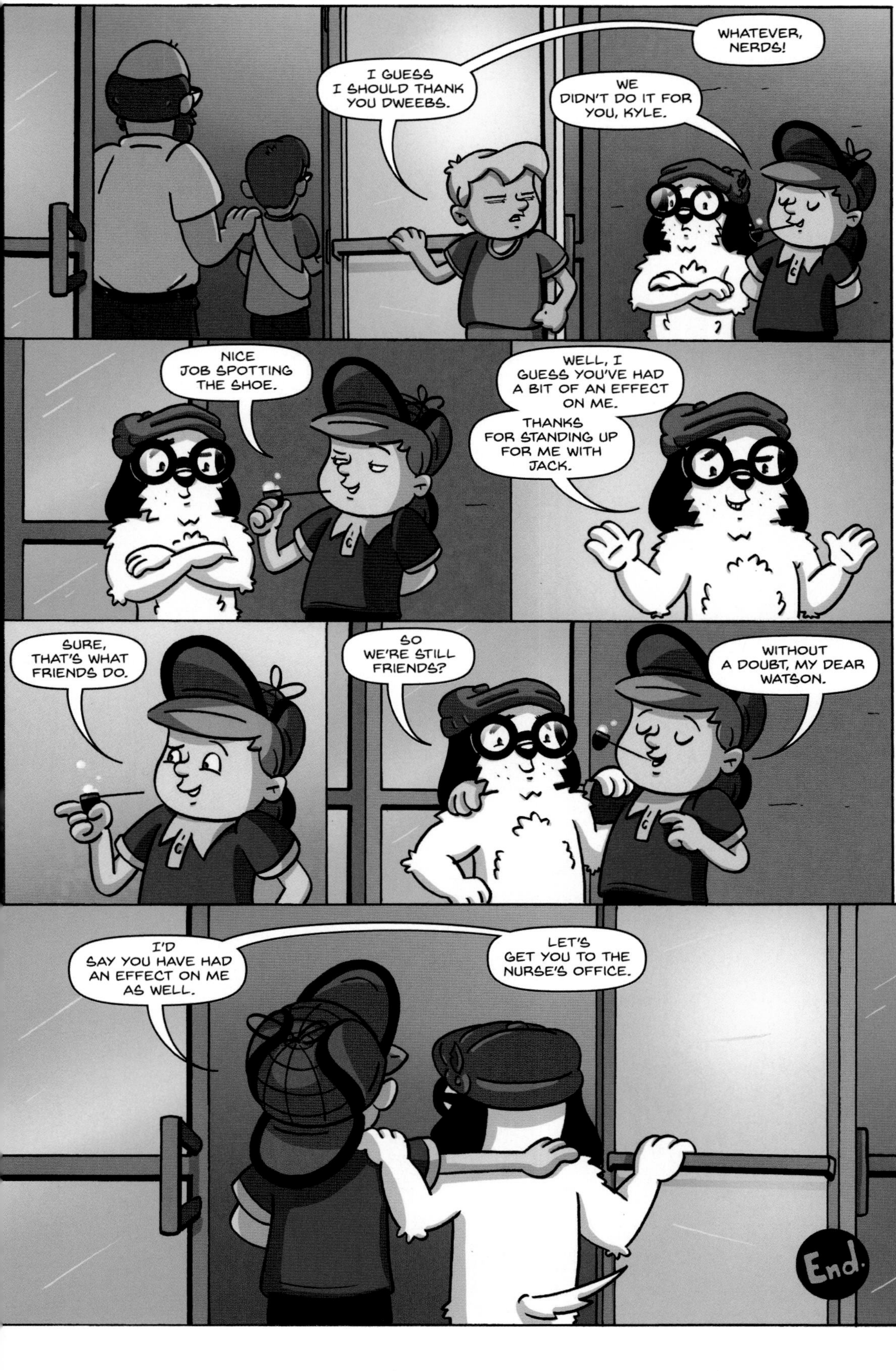
I GUESS I SHOULD THANK YOU DWEEBS.
WE DIDN'T DO IT FOR YOU, KYLE.
WHATEVER, NERDS!
NICE JOB SPOTTING THE SHOE.
WELL, I GUESS YOU'VE HAD A BIT OF AN EFFECT ON ME.
THANKS FOR STANDING UP FOR ME WITH JACK.
SURE, THAT'S WHAT FRIENDS DO.
SO WE'RE STILL FRIENDS?
WITHOUT A DOUBT, MY DEAR WATSON.
I'D SAY YOU HAVE HAD AN EFFECT ON ME AS WELL.
LET'S GET YOU TO THE NURSE'S OFFICE.
End.

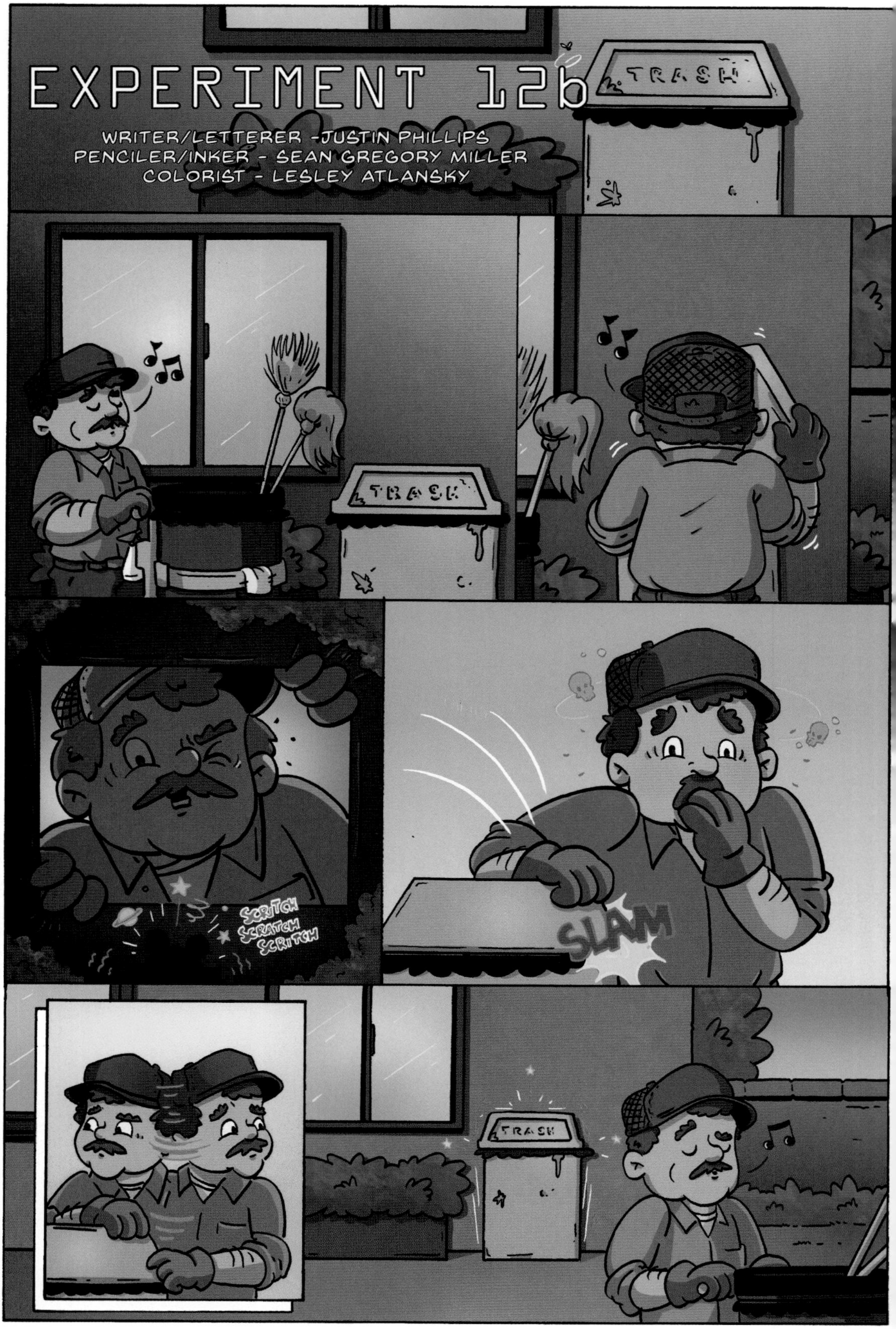
EXPERIMENT 12b
WRITER/LETTERER -JUSTIN PHILLIPS
PENCILER/INKER - SEAN GREGORY MILLER
COLORIST - LESLEY ATLANSKY
TRASH
TRASH
SCRITCH
SCRATCH
SCRITCH
SLAM
TRASH

LEARN TO DRAW!

YOU'VE LEARNED THE BASICS. NOW LET'S TRY SOMETHING MORE CHALLENGING!

BODY LANGUAGE
(EXPRESSIVE ANATOMY)

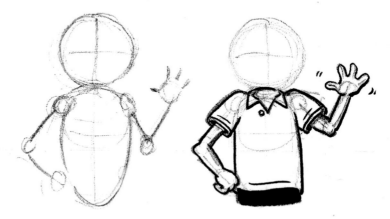

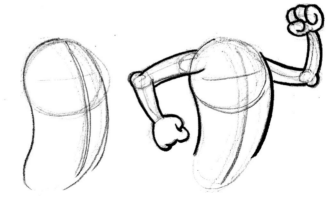

MUCH LIKE THE EXPRESSIONS ON A CHARACTERS FACE, THEIR BODY LANGUAGE CAN CONVEY A LOT ABOUT WHAT THEY ARE THINKING OR FEELING!

FOR EXAMPLE, NOTICE HOW SHERLOCK'S BODY LANGUAGE ENHANCES THE SUSPICIOUS LOOK ON HIS FACE.

JUST THINK HOW BORING A COMIC WOULD BE IF ALL THE CHARACTERS ONLY STOOD IN STRAIGHT, STIFF POSES. JUST LIKE IN REAL LIFE, CHARACTERS ON THE PAGE COMMUNICATE WITH MOVEMENT!

AS WITH THE OTHER LESSONS, A CHARACTERS BODY CAN BE DRAWN WITH JUST A FEW SIMPLE SHAPES, BUT TRY CURVING THE CHARACTERS "SPINE" TO SHOW MOVEMENT OR DIRECTION!

LEARN TO DRAW!

YOU'VE LEARNED THE BASICS. NOW LET'S TRY SOMETHING MORE CHALLENGING!

SCENERY

NOW THAT YOU'RE A PRO AT DRAWING CHARACTERS, YOU NEED TO PLACE THEM IN AN ENVIRONMENT!

BUILDINGS ARE SOME OF THE MOST FUN THINGS TO DRAW TO HELP FILL OUT YOUR BACKGROUNDS.

DON'T WORRY TOO MUCH ABOUT MAKING THEM LOOK SUPER REALISTIC. THIS HELPS GIVE THEM A MORE CARTOONY LOOK AND GIVES YOUR SKYLINES MORE CHARACTER.

TREES AND BUSHES MIGHT BE THE EASIEST AND QUICKEST WAY TO GIVE YOUR ENVIRONMENTS SOME LIFE.

OUTDOOR SCENES WITH LOTS OF FOLIAGE ALSO LOOK MORE INVITING.

GO AHEAD. GIVE IT A TRY!

TRY DRAWING OTHER THINGS LIKE WALLS, FENCES, ROCKS, GATES, AND BRICKS.

THIS HELPS MAKE YOUR ENVIRONMENT LOOK A LITTLE MORE "BELIEVABLE" AND ADDS MORE TEXTURE AS WELL!

IF YOU'D LIKE TO KNOW WHAT KIND OF TOOLS TO USE WHEN DRAWING YOUR FIRST COMIC, HERE'S WHAT SEAN USES TO DRAW KID SHERLOCK:

STRATHMORE 300 SERIES PAPER

PENTEL 0.9 GRAPHGEAR MECHANICAL PENCIL

KURETAKE FUDEGOKOCHI BRUSH PENS

COLORING WITH LESLEY!

EACH ISSUE OF KID SHERLOCK HAS USED A FLASHBACK TO HELP THE READER SEE HOW SHERLOCK HAS SOLVED THE CASE.

A FLASHBACK HAPPENS WHEN THE STORY IS INTERRUPTED SO THAT A SCENE FROM EARLIER IN THE BOOK CAN BE SHOWN AGAIN. THE FLASHBACK USUALLY GIVES THE READER NEW INFORMATION SO THAT THEY CAN LEARN NEW THINGS ABOUT THE PLOT.

LESLEY USED COLOR TO HELP MAKE THE KID SHERLOCK FLASHBACK SCENES LOOK DIFFERENT THAN THE MAIN STORY.

THE FLASHBACKS ARE A LITTLE DIFFERENT IN EACH ISSUE. IN ISSUE ONE, THE SCENES WERE TURNED A GRAY-BLUE COLOR, LEAVING ONLY THE IMPORTANT PIECE OF INFORMATION IN THE NORMAL COLORS.

IN ISSUE TWO, WE SEE SHERLOCK IN THE FOREGROUND EXPLAINING HOW HE SOLVED THE CRIME. BEHIND HIM IS THE PANEL WE ARE FLASHING BACK TO. THIS TIME, LESLEY LEFT THE SHERLOCK IN THE FRONT IN THE NORMAL COLORS. THE PANEL BEHIND HAS BEEN COLORED IN SHADES OF ORANGE INSIDE A SPECIAL BUBBLE.

COLORING WITH LESLEY!

FLASHBACKS ARE A COMMON AND IMPORTANT TOOL IN WRITING.

SHERLOCK IS KNOWN FOR SOLVING MYSTERIES BY SEEING IMPORTANT DETAILS THAT MOST PEOPLE DON'T NOTICE. THE FLASHBACK SCENES IN KID SHERLOCK HELP THE READER GO BACK IN THE STORY AND SEE WHAT ORDINARY DETAIL THEY MAY HAVE OVERLOOKED THAT HELPED SHERLOCK SOLVE THE CASE.

COMICS OFTEN USE FLASHBACKS TO TELL A STORY, AND IT CAN BE UP TO THE COLORIST TO SOLVE THE MYSTERY OF HOW TO MAKE THE SCENES LOOK DIFFERENT. ONE OF A COLORIST'S MOST IMPORTANT JOBS IS TO MAKE THE ART AND STORY CLEAR WITH THEIR COLORS!

NOW YOU SHOULD BE READY TO GET OUT THERE AND START COLORING, RIGHT?!

COLOR, COLOR, COLOR!

NOW IT'S YOUR
TURN TO PRACTICE COLORING
WATSON AS HE LIVES OUT HIS WORST
NIGHTMARE...DODGEBALL!

USE MARKERS OR CRAYONS
TO COLOR THIS PAGE.

YOU CAN EVEN SCAN IT ON YOUR COMPUTER
AND PRINT MULTIPULE COPIES TO
PRACTICE COLORING AGAIN
AND AGAIN!

MAZE!

HELP SHERLOCK FIND THE CLUE AT THE END OF THE MAZE!

HINT:
ACTUALLY, THERE ARE NO HINTS FOR THIS ONE. WHERE'S THE FUN IN THAT?!

FUN FACT:
MANY EARLY VIDEO GAMES FEATURE MAZES!

WORD SEARCH!

SEE IF YOU CAN
FIND ALL THE WORDS
FROM THIS ISSUE
HIDDEN IN THE
WORD SEARCH!

```
V P O B T L V U O S A X
S L F B V K M P S C Y I
S E O F K T S Z L H J K
Q J M Y A R D E R O W X
V F V D O I C N I O S X
J R Q Z W P A M X L J B
J Q Q D G P T U E L A L
Y P F R I E N D P T N Q
G Y S H E R L O C K I F
E I Z S C N P A E P T T
C L U E Y P F G A L O Y
R L R J A C K U D E R A
```

JACK

TRIPPER

SHERLOCK

FRIEND

MUD

JANITOR

SCHOOL

YARD

CLUE

DID YOU FIND THEM ALL?

HINT:
LOOK FOR
WORDS GOING
ACROSS *AND*
UP AND DOWN!

FAN ART!

CHECK OUT
THIS PICTURE FROM
OUR FAN!
(WE HAVE THOSE)

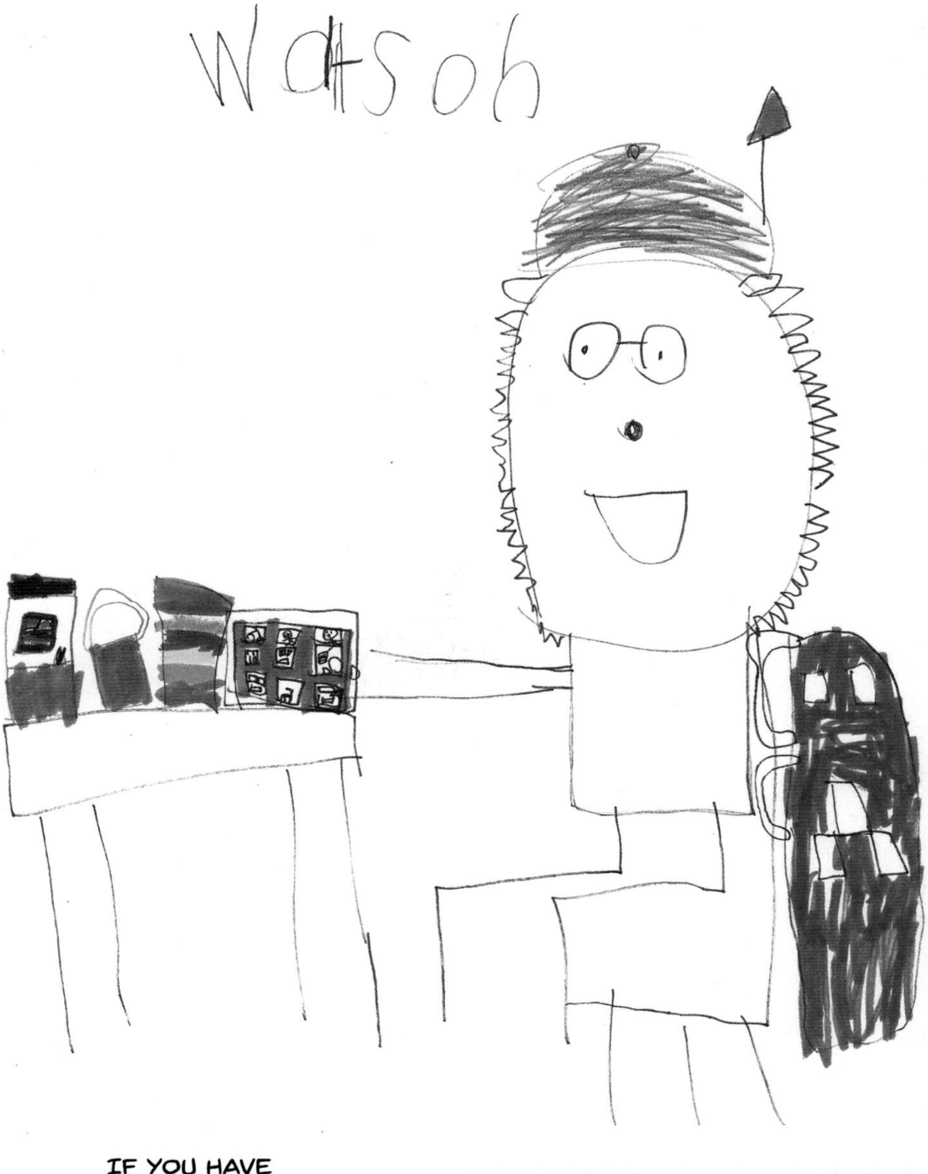
Watson

IF YOU HAVE
ANY ART THAT YOU
WOULD LIKE TO SHARE
OR WOULD LIKE TO
SEND US A LETTER,
YOU CAN!

WE'D LOVE
TO HEAR FROM YOU!

YOU CAN REACH US AT:
KIDSHERLOCKANDWATSON@GMAIL.COM

WATSON BY
AVERY
AGE 7
FROM STOCKTON, CA.